TAYLER MACNEILL

The Darkest Side of the Moon

First edition

ISBN: 978-1-9994882-0-8

Editing by Toni Michelle of Polished Pages Editing

This book was professionally typeset on Reedsy.
Find out more at reedsy.com

I would like to dedicate this book to my mom who always believed in me and to my son who lights my world.

Contents

Acknowledgement

I wrote this book for my family, as they have stood by my side the whole way. Thank you, Mom, for being the wonderful caring soul you are and for guiding me in the right direction. I want to thank my wonderful son for his patience and kindness while I took the time to write this book.

Chapter 1

Dark clouds moved quickly across the sky as the pitter-patter of the rain hit the ground, rolling across the grey sidewalks. Charlie scurried into the doctor's office. She was already late, even though she had never been late a single day in her life.

"I'm here," she whispered anxiously.

Marcy, the secretary, looked up and smiled, "Nice to see you."

Charlie looked around and spotted an empty seat near the window. As she sat down, she gazed out at the city. She moved here at the age of twenty, fresh out of college. The city still looked the same as the first day she stepped into it almost seven years ago. In one direction, there was the vast blue ocean, and in the other, the rugged mountains, and in between, a playground for the children of business professionals. This is the city she learned to love and trust. She didn't have many memories before she moved to the big city of Richmond, BC.

"Charlie, you can go in now," the secretary uttered in a soft but firm voice.

As Charlie entered Dr. Davenport's office, her eyes swung across the room until her eyes met his. "Hi, Jack."

He looked up at her and smiled. "Good morning, Charlie.

How are you today?"

Before responding, Charlie threw herself down in the chair, flopped her head to the side, and then looked at Jack. "Don't you mean, 'How are the voices today?'" Giggling, she quickly added, "I haven't heard them today, so today is a good day. It has been a couple of days since they've spoken. Besides, they never seem to make sense. Well, at least I cannot make sense of it." She chuckled again.

Jack, chewing on his pen, looked over at Charlie. Slowly removing the pen from his mouth, he responded, "It doesn't matter if they make sense or not, we need to figure out why you hear them. This clearly isn't normal, yet I do not sense any mental illness. It would be different if they were speaking to you, but they're talking to each other. I want to be there when you hear them, so I can get a sense of the atmosphere you are in, and maybe we can figure out where they're coming from. What do you think about us meeting up while you're out?"

Charlie nodded, "That's a good idea. I'm going to kickboxing class tomorrow, but Wednesday I'm working at the café. Maybe we can meet there?"

Jack grabbed his pen and wrote it down in his book. "Sounds good. I'll see you then."

As Charlie walked to the door, she glanced back and said, "See ya then, Jack."

The rain fell gently as Charlie slowly headed home. The sidewalks were still wet, but the skies looked forgiving as the sun gently peeked around the clouds. Charlie had a lot on her mind, and with everything going on in the city nowadays, she was always a little leery about walking by herself, especially at night. There were several reports of people missing, many later found dead. Police had been unable to solve the mystery. No one ever seemed to see anything, and the crime scenes lacked evidence, leaving the police clueless, and the public frightened. Charlie refused to feel like a prisoner in the city she loved and continued living each day to the fullest. She lived in a world of her own, oblivious to her surroundings, as if there weren't a threat lumbering around town. The pepper spray she secretly carried in her pocket provided her with the security she needed.

Monday and Tuesday passed quickly. It was already early Wednesday morning. The alarm was buzzing loudly as Charlie forced her eyes open. Bruno jumped up on the bed and onto Charlie, licking her face, letting her know that he was happy to see her. "Bruno, stop! Not my mouth! Eeewww!" Bruno heeded Charlie's commands and lay down next to her. "It's okay, boy. I still love you," she laughed. She jumped out of bed and walked into the kitchen.

Julie was sitting at the table with her coffee, reading the newspaper. She turned to talk to Charlie, "Morning. Breakfast is in the microwave if you're interested."

Stormage ran across the room, meowing as if he were chasing an invisible mouse. Charlie giggled, "When did Stormage get here?"

Julie swallowed her toast. "He came last night. Jesse dropped him off before he left for his camping trip."

Charlie smiled and responded softly, "Nice. It will give Bruno someone to play with for the week."

Gazing at Julie, Charlie inquired, "Are you going to be at the café later?"

Julie quickly nodded. "Yes, there's no school today. Too many kids missing class, I guess. It's crazy, but have you noticed how many people are disappearing lately?"

Charlie shook her head in dismay. "It's not just the kids; every time we turn around, someone is missing. This city has turned into the Bermuda Triangle. There are a lot of crazy things happening everywhere, but I love this city, so I hope they figure out what's going on soon. I heard another plane crashed Monday evening. They think it's terrorism, but they cannot prove it yet."

Julie shook her head softly. "Whatever is going on best stop soon. You can't tell me whoever is doing this is smarter than a whole police force put together," Julie frowned.

"Sure seems so. I'm going to take a shower and then outside with Bruno. We can chat more at the café." Without hesitating, Charlie headed to the shower.

The sun was shining brighter than it had been in days. Charlie and Bruno entered the park where she loved to walk him. Up ahead, she could see beautiful flowers of all colors, planted on mounds of bright green grass. Squirrels were running across the field and up the side of an oak tree. Bruno loved to stop and sniff every bush and flower, checking each out as if it were the social media world of four-legged society. He would lift his leg and leave a message anytime he got a chance. It made Charlie laugh. She loved that little guy. He was a mixture of toy Yorkie and Pug. He wasn't a huge dog, but he had a deep love for life and was very quiet. She never had to worry about taking him anywhere; he always just lay down quietly. They spent a lot of time checking out all the flowers and following the squirrels as Bruno pretended to hunt them. He always thought he could catch them, forgetting about the leash wrapped around his neck. They usually watched them munch down peanuts as Charlie kept some in her pocket to feed them for their walks.

About twenty minutes later, they came to the end of the park. Charlie reached down and scratched Bruno. "Did you enjoy your walk, boy? Let's head down to the café. We'll take a shortcut by the bridge." Charlie walked towards the bridge with

Bruno. The smell of the ocean carried in the breeze. It was so refreshing and relaxed her. She couldn't imagine living anywhere else. Besides, how many places have both the ocean and the mountains within proximity?

Today feels like a perfect day, thought Charlie. It was about a twenty-minute walk, so by the time she arrived at the café, it would be time for a break. Charlie sat on a rock by the bridge. The view was spectacular. She pulled out her sketch book and thought, *I should probably work on this, Bruno, since it's due Monday.* Charlie took an art class on Monday evenings. Most of the time, she sketched whatever came to mind, but sometimes she found herself sketching stuff for no reason at all, like stuff from Julie's dreams. It was a bit freaky when she did that, but cool at the same time. Charlie reached down and scratched Bruno. "Good boy, Bruno. It's a beautiful day. Oh boy, makes you wish it would last forever. Life seems easier when it's just you and I." Charlie leaned back against a pillar and looked at her sketchbook. "We'll stay here for a bit, then go to the café." She picked up her pencil and started sketching.

Later, at the café, Charlie walked in, smiled and waved to Franny. "Hey, Franny, how are you?"

Franny looked at her as she walked over to grab Charlie her coffee. "I was wondering if you would be in today. Julie's already here. She has a table near the window."

Charlie smiled and said, "Thanks," and started walking over

to the table where Julie sat.

Julie looked up from her book and smiled. "Hey, where have you been? I figured you would've been here by the time I got here?"

Charlie reached down and pulled out a chair. Sitting down, she replied, "Bruno and I hit up the park, then we stopped for a while down by the bridge. I had to sketch for a bit. I have an art assignment due for class."

As soon as Charlie put her art book on the table, Julie reached over and picked it up. Opening it to see what her best friend drew today, she gasped. "When did you draw this? This was in my dream last night."

Charlie looked at the picture. "I drew this today by the bridge. I couldn't get the image out of my head."

In the midst of their conversation, Charlie became distracted. Her attention was drawn towards the window. Something outside caught the corner of her eye. This had happened many times before. "Julie, did you see that? It happened again."

Julie looked up. "You mean that weird thing with the face?"

Charlie glared, "Yes, it looks like his face is changing." Charlie sat looking out the window, watching the guy whose face looked human one minute and like a snake the next. Charlie knew this was impossible, so why did she think she saw it? But then again, it was no different than her hearing voices. "Oh my God. I forgot I'm supposed to call Jack. He wanted to come down to the café to see if he could figure out where the voices were coming from."

Julie looked a bit worried and, trying to comfort her friend, quietly replied, "Well, then you better call him now. Maybe he can figure out why you're seeing the faces shift."

Charlie immediately picked up the phone and dialed his number. The phone rang for a quick second, and suddenly she heard, "Hello, this is Jack Davenport."

"Hi. This is Charlie. I was wondering if you would like to come down to the café?"

Jack paused as he looked at his calendar. "I don't have anything happening right now. I'll head down there ASAP."

Charlie hung up the phone and looked at Julie. "I sure hope I'm not crazy."

Julie laid her hand upon Charlie's. "Don't worry about it. If he hasn't found you crazy yet, he won't now."

Just then, Franny came over to see if the girls wanted a refill. "Yes, please," Julie said politely. Charlie nodded in agreement.

Twenty minutes later, Jack walked in the door, his eyes searching the room. Walking towards Charlie, he announced in a firm but polite voice, "Hey, sorry I took so long. Traffic was mad out there." He laughed, pulled out a chair, and sat down next to Charlie. "So, what's up, girls? Are you okay, Charlie?"

Charlie tried to smile, but it looked more like a grimace. "You're going to think I'm crazy. Sometimes when I look out this window, I see people standing around, and when I watch them, their faces change."

Jack looked a bit worried. "What do they look like, Charlie?"

"Well," Charlie paused, "One minute they look totally human and the next minute like snakes. Tell me I'm not crazy, Jack."

Gazing out the window, Jack comforted her. "Charlie, if you were crazy, I would've locked you up long ago. You've been coming to me for years saying that you hear voices that speak to each other. I've told you that wasn't normal, and that I've never seen anything like it, but I've always been supportive of you. So, if you say you see a man's face change, I'm going to sit here and watch this guy with you; if it does, we'll see it together." Charlie smiled approvingly. She knew that Jack believed her, and that was all she needed.

The three of them sat there for quite some time peering out the window to see if they saw what Charlie saw. Jack was just about to give up when a guy who was sitting by the fountain looked up from his newspaper, and as he did, there was a glimmer on his face. He almost looked reptilian. Jack's mouth fell open. "Oh my God, Charlie! I saw it! It's real! But what the hell did I just see?"

Julie looked at Jack and then at Charlie. "What? Am I the only one not getting to see this?" Jack was too frazzled to answer, and so was Charlie.

The two of them sat there for the longest time. Seeing the shimmer of change in a person was like an addiction. They wanted to sit there and see how many more times they could see this happen. Within that time, they noticed there was more than one. Breaking the silence, Charlie exclaimed, "What the heck are we seeing? I mean surely to God, this isn't normal, is it? And we know there's no way everybody at this table is losing their mind."

Jack looked at Charlie. "I have to go back to the office. I need to try to figure this out. I mean what exactly are we seeing?" Charlie nodded. She was happy to find out that she wasn't crazy, but at the same time, she was confused about what they were seeing.

Julie grabbed Jack's hand and said, "Before you go, you need to see this." She picked up Charlie's sketchbook and showed him what Charlie had drawn in the morning.

Jack looked at her. "It's nice. Good job, Charlie."

Before Charlie had a chance to respond, Julie emphatically stated, "No! No! No! That's not the point! The point is this was in my dream last night, and I never told her about it. This seems to be happening more and more, and I know this isn't normal."

Jack looked puzzled, "We'll figure this out." Jack turned towards the door, then glanced back at the girls before he exited the café.

Charlie looked at Julie and uttered, "I'm not even sure what this means. We have no idea if this is something that's been around forever or if this is something new … If it's a threat or if it's safe. Look at all the weird things happening lately—plane crashes, train crashes, people missing, people dying. How do we know it's not linked to this? Do you think anybody else knows about this? I wonder if the police would even believe us?"

Looking back at Charlie, Julie responded, "We need to leave this alone until Jack figures this out."

Back at the office, Jack was sorting through his files. He now had other patients that claimed to see faces change, or what they called shapeshifting. Of course, until now, he didn't really believe them. After some intense searching, Jack gathered two files together. He grabbed a piece of paper and jotted something down for his secretary. He grabbed the paper and the files and brought them to Marcy. "Please cancel all my appointments for tomorrow and get a hold of the patients in these files. Have them all come in tomorrow and the next day. It's really important." Showing her the paper, Jack added, "Here's what you say." He smiled, then turned and walked away, yelling, "Thanks, Marcy."

When he got back to his desk, he picked up the phone to

call Charlie. The phone rang for a few minutes before Charlie picked up. "Hello." Jack took a breath and told her the news. "I was looking through my files and noticed that there a number of people who've seen the same thing we did. I'm setting up appointments for tomorrow and the day after to talk to them. I need to know what they know. I'll give you a call in a couple of days. Will you be okay 'til then?"

Without hesitation, Charlie answered, "Yeah, I'll be okay, but I really wish I knew what we're up against and why strange things are happening in the city right now. I'll talk to you in a few days."

Charlie hung up the phone and then looked at Julie. "I'm going home now." She reached down and grabbed Bruno.

Julie piped up. "I'm coming. Just give me half a second." She swiftly gathered her stuff together. The two girls waved to Franny and went home.

Early the next day, right after finishing their walk, Charlie and Bruno walked into the café. Charlie had to write an article for work. She worked for a magazine company that addressed all aspects of life. Topics included showing people how to get over jet lag, how to move past life hurdles, and how to make the most of the day. This was something she truly enjoyed doing, as writing was always a passion for her. She grabbed a table by the window. She always sat there. Occasionally, it was taken, but more often, it was there waiting for her. Franny hurried over to her as Charlie sat down. "Hi, hon. I'm so happy to see you."

Charlie looked up, "What's up, Franny? You look a bit frazzled."

Franny leaned over as if to whisper to her. "It's Carl. He's gone to his brother's place for the week. Apparently, he isn't feeling well, so Carl wanted to check up on him. That leaves me here alone though, and everything happening in the city makes me a bit nervous."

Charlie gasped, "Oh my God! Staying alone would make me nervous too. I'm blessed to live with Julie. You should stay with us 'til he gets back … Well, as long as you don't mind cats. Stormage is staying with us too—Julie's brother's cat. Mischievous little bugger. He's so loving." She laughed.

Then Franny giggled, "Thank you. I'll give that some thought." She gave her table a quick wipe and said, "I'll be back with your coffee in a flash." Seconds later, she brought Charlie's coffee to her. "Here ya go."

Charlie smiled. "Thank you." Pulling out her laptop, she started to type. She kept peeking out the window in hopes of seeing the strange people whose faces seemed to change. She couldn't help it; the whole thing was confusing. The confusion would probably not be there if she knew what she was seeing and why she was seeing it, but for now, she didn't. She watched for a while but never saw what she was looking for. Quietly sipping her coffee, she got back to work.

As she approached the end of her article, she felt a little more relaxed. Suddenly, she heard a whisper in her ear. *Did you lock them up? Is it complete?* She glanced around to make sure there wasn't anyone speaking to her. By now, she was used to this. These voices in her head rumbled on and on, and it appeared as if she was overhearing a conversation. She slightly shook her head and finished her article, then went home.

It was now Friday afternoon. Bruno and Charlie were just getting back from a walk in the park. The day had started out sunny, but the clouds had shifted in the sky, making it look

11

like it was going to open up and pour down. Charlie yelled up the stairs as she entered the house, "You home, Julie? You're not going to believe this! The one night I choose to go out, it decides to rain, or should I say pour! We practically ran home."

Looking down the stairs, Julie shouted, "I made brownies. Did you want some? Maybe the weather will change before tonight. You never know."

As Charlie was taking off her shoes, her phone rang. "Hello. This is Charlie."

"Hi, Charlie. This is Jack. I just finished the last interview with my patients, and you're not going to believe what I have to tell you! Can we get together?"

Leaning against the wall, Charlie responded, "Yeah, if you want to come over, you can. I'm just getting in. I had taken Bruno down to the park."

Taking a deep breath, Jack replied, "Okay I'm going to head over in about an hour or so."

"Okay, will see you then." Charlie hung up the phone. She sprinted upstairs. "Jack's on his way over. He'll be here in about an hour. Turns out we're not the only ones. There are quite a few people who claim to have seen shifters. I think that's what they call it." Charlie flopped on the couch, then reached over and picked up a brownie. "These look really good. I hope they're as good as they look." Smiling, Charlie took a bite.

Jack hesitantly approached the door. He was feeling a little odd because of the whole situation. It's not every day you uncover something so strange. Gathering himself together, he knocked on the door. "Come in!" yelled Charlie.

Jack stepped in and closed the door. "It's really wet out there.

I was hoping it would slow down, but it hasn't." He hung up his coat and walked up the stairs.

Both girls were slumped on the couch. All the rain had sucked the energy right out of them. Julie picked up the remote and switched off the television. "Hey, Jack," she smiled.

Jack looked at the empty plate, noticing that only brownie crumbs were left. "Did you save me any?" He laughed.

Julie grinned, "Of course, silly. How long have you known me now? Umm, your whole life! They're in the fridge."

He jumped up and grabbed the brownies from the fridge, shoving one in his mouth. He plopped down into the chair. "I've been giving all this a lot of thought. I can't imagine holding this inside and not having anyone to talk to about it. You must've had a hard time not feeling like you were going crazy when you saw the shift before. I mean ... I know we're not, but it feels crazy all of us seeing that together."

Charlie gazed at Jack and said, "It's not like I don't have a bundle of weird things in my life already. Seeing a few faces just added to it. Oh, by the way, I was sitting in the café yesterday working and I heard the voices again. They said, 'Did you lock them up? Is it complete?' Do you think this all can be connected?"

Putting his feet up on the coffee table, Jack laid back in the chair. His eyes had a faraway look in them. "I have no idea," he said. "All I know is that what we saw is real. I have dozens of files of clients who claim to have seem the same thing. I didn't believe them "til you said you saw them. I feel really bad about that too."

Charlie turned over on her side to see Jack better. "You shouldn't feel bad. How were you supposed to know something so incredibly weird was real? You were just doing your job."

"You guys hungry?" Julie asked as she sat up. "Should I order some pizza, and we can chill with some movies tonight?" Both Jack and Charlie nodded.

Jack sat up a bit and looked at Charlie. "I noticed when I was going through the files that these sightings happened all over the city, and there are even some videos on YouTube with evidence of this. Julie, you might get a glimpse of what we're seeing if you look on YouTube. Some of them are pretty clear. None of the patients I spoke to know any more than we do. I was thinking maybe we could do a bit more research ourselves, maybe do a little sight-seeing throughout the city and see if we spot anything. What do you think?"

Now intrigued, Charlie sat up. "I think that's a great idea. I want to know more. We can cover more ground if we split up, but then Julie doesn't see them like we do."

Julie piped up, "Yeah, but I might this time. You never know. I want to be part of this, too."

Jack waved his hand to calm her down. "Chill, we all are a part of this, and we'll all figure this out together."

Just then, the phone rang. Julie leaned over and picked it up. It was Franny. "Julie, can you let Charlie know I appreciate her offer, but I am going to rough it out for the week."

Julie looked at Charlie. "Okay, I'll let her know." She hung up the phone. "Franny says, 'Thank you for the offer, but she's all good.'"

Charlie nodded then looked over at them both, "So, once we figure out if there are more of these shifters, what do we do then? I don't know about you two, but I have no idea what to do next."

Both Jack and Julie had blank stares on their faces, then Jack spoke. "You're right. I have no clue what to do next either. This is way out of my field of expertise. I say we dig deeper first, and if it turns out that there are more, then we'll figure out the next step. Have either one of you considered that this could be a prank? Though I cannot imagine how they could pull it off, what if it is?"

Charlie sighed, "There's no way in hell that this is a prank. To me, this is no different than the voices."

Leaning forward with his elbows on his knees, Jack interrupted, "Then I have no clue what we're up against. So how about Tuesday all three of us take it upon ourselves to figure it out?" The girls nodded.

"I need to cancel my appointments for Tuesday. I'll do that Monday." Jack leaned back and got comfortable again. "Let's order that pizza, watch some movies and take our minds off this for a while. I don't know about you, but I find this whole thing exhausting." He laughed.

Chapter 2

A black streak tore across the room as Bruno barked. Charlie's eyes opened to see what was happening. Bruno's head swung Charlie's way as he scurried up the bed and started licking her face. "Good morning to you too, boy. Are you barking at that cat again?" She laughed, "Is he in here being a brat?" Just then, she realized it was Tuesday morning. Today was the day they were to explore the city to see if they could spot more people like the ones by the café. In some ways, this was exciting, but it also was a bit scary. *Maybe we can find some answers today,* she thought. She grabbed her clothes and threw her hair up in an elastic as she went to the kitchen to see Julie, who was always up early.

Julie was out on the patio with her cup of coffee. Charlie grabbed a coffee and went to join her. "Morning."

Julie looked over and smiled. "Look at this view. You would never know anything was happening in this city. I watched the news this morning, probably shouldn't have, but I did. They found a couple of bodies this morning in the same place. The bodies were all killed in different ways, but all of them had white hair and looks of fear on their faces. Don't you feel there's something weird about the way these bodies are showing up? I mean, one was killed by a chainsaw and had paint all over his body, kind of like clown paint. The other two were drowned and run over by a huge truck. The killer must be sitting there and trying to come up with new ways to kill people. Oh, and get this—a man was found wandering the streets this morning. They have him in custody. He claims to have no memory of who he is or where he is from. They have found four of these cases this month."

Charlie's eyes widened, "Where do you get all your information from? I'm sure they didn't show all this on the news."

Julie shook her head "No. Lorretta called me. She has been examining bodies all morning."

Charlie was shocked. "You mean the city coroner? Isn't that Jack's ex-girlfriend?"

Julie grabbed her coffee cup and walked to the door. "Yup! That's who I'm talking about."

Charlie, now wide-eyed, followed Julie in the house. "Does she have any idea of what's causing the deaths?"

Julie shook her head. "No. She says they all are similar to each other in some ways, and it's definitely by the same killer." Charlie sighed and reached over and grabbed the dog and cat food to feed the pets. Both were doing circles around their bowls, anxious to eat. After making sure they were fed, she went to get ready for her day.

Just as Charlie was finishing blow-drying her hair, the phone starting ringing. Diving onto her bed, she answered it. "Hey Jack."

Charlie flopped on her back, "I was just getting ready for our mission today."

Nearly dropping the phone, Jack murmured, "Okay. I'm driving, so I'm going to get off this phone. I'll be there soon." Jack hung up instantly.

Grabbing an elastic for her hair, Charlie yelled down the hall, "Jack is on his way!!" Charlie grabbed her bag and started to pack it with what she needed for the day. She wondered how many she'd get to see, if any. What if one of those strange people were to sit down next to her? There were so many what-ifs. A little nervous, Charlie headed out to find Julie. She was done getting ready and already at the table reading a newspaper while waiting for Jack. "Julie, how do you feel about today?"

She looked up and whispered, "I'm a little nervous, but excited to see what you guys see. I took a look at the videos Jack told me about. They're so weird. Is this really what you guys see?"

Charlie glared at her. "Yeah, that's what we see. It happens so quickly you almost can't blink."

Laying the newspaper down, Julie looked up and muttered, "Keep your phone on today, Charlie. That way I can text you. We might not want to talk about this in public, especially if it turns out to be something serious." Just then, there was a knock at the door.

Jack stood waiting on the doorstep. The sky was iffy. There was a battle going on between the sun and the clouds. If the clouds won, they could be stuck with a very wet day, but there was always a chance the sun could conquer the clouds, and the day could turn beautiful. Both girls stumbled out the door. "Hey," said Julie.

Jack smiled and walked towards the car. "So, who's covering where today? How about someone take the West Side Mall and someone take the square by the courts, while I cover the mayor's office and the surrounding part of town?"

Charlie smiled and asserted, "I'll cover the mall if you want."

Both Julie and Jack agreed. Everyone piled into the car. Bruno jumped in, claiming the window seat. He loved when they got to ride in the car. He had been to the mall many times. It was nice being so small; people never really seemed to care if he went shopping with Charlie. She always brought the bag with her, so he had a place to sit while she did her thing.

Jack dropped the girls off at their destinations and headed to the mayor's office. He wasn't sure what excuse he had for hanging around there for any length of time, but he was sure he would be able to think of one. Finding a spot to park, he pulled in and turned the car off. Leaning back, he thought to himself, What *Pandora's box have we opened? I never thought I would see people make their faces change. What if there are snake people living among us, and who the hell would believe us?*

Jack jumped out of the car and sauntered towards to the mayor's building, shaking his head. Looking around, he noticed a lot of people sitting on benches drinking coffee and chatting. 'Nothing suspicious about that,' he thought. Walking over to a nearby stand, he looked at the guy. "I'll have a double/double please." The guy quickly got his coffee for him. After paying, Jack searched for a quiet place to sit, somewhere he could observe his surroundings. Luckily, the sky agreed on sunshine, so the day was turning out to be a nice one. Enjoying his coffee, he gazed around, wondering if he could trust his eyes. How many of these people were who they pretended to be? He took a deep breath and continued to people watch.

Meanwhile, Julie was sitting at a small table in the midst of the squares. She had pulled out a book, though not her favorite; she didn't want to get lost in it when she was clearly here for different reasons. The waitress from the café in the square had just served her a nice hot cup of coffee. It smelled like heaven on

this beautiful day. Sitting comfortably and pondering, Julie wasn't sure how this really worked. It's not like there were rules written when it came to watching people. She would peek over the edge of her book, so as to not seem rude and just stare. Many people walked through the square on a daily basis; it was the centerpiece of town. It led to many offices and usually represented a businessman's break room. She wasn't a stranger to the business world. She was a second-grade teacher, but her older brother Hank was a lawyer that ran with the business crowds. Julie recognized some of the faces as they scurried by in a hurry to get back to work. Just then, her phone beeped. It was Jack texting her.

Jack: Hey, Julie, how is it there?

Julie: It's quiet here. And how about there?

Jack: 'Yeah, here too, but it's been only a short time.

Julie: Yup, gonna sit here and absorb the sun. Enjoy your day.

Jack: K. Let me know if you see anything.

Charlie stood looking at some dresses that were hanging by the door of a local store. The tags were marked 50% off and had a cute floral design on them. She reminded herself that she was not there to shop; she was there to people watch. Moving on, she looked around. People were hurrying through the mall in every direction. There were a few times Charlie had to do a double take to see if they looked strange, but it turned out to be a false alarm.

Finding a place to sit, she pulled Bruno onto her lap. "What do you think, boy? See anyone who looks different?" Hugging him, she looked around. There was a woman in a suit. She was tall and leaned against the pillar in the mall and was talking to a gentleman who was even taller than she was. She knew it wasn't nice to stare, but something about them seemed odd. Just then, it happened, and not to just one face, but both their faces changed. Charlie gasped. Not being able to take her eyes off them, she continued to watch. The woman's face hadn't changed back quite yet. Her tongue flickered. Turning her head quickly to the right, her mouth fell open. What the hell! She thought about picking up her phone but decided against it. Instead, she sent both Jack and Julie a text: Guys, I saw what we were looking for, though this time, I see more than one. She laid her phone down, not bothering to check to see if they texted back. She didn't want to lose track of the couple. They were business people, like the man she saw outside the café. Charlie grabbed her phone and held it as if she were looking at it, and quickly snapped a picture of the two. She got up and walked in their direction. She looked at the woman and politely inquired, "Excuse me. Are you Melonie House?"

The woman gazed over at her and replied, "No. Sorry."

Charlie looked her right in the eyes and continued, "Oh, I'm so sorry. I thought you were her. My mistake."

Bruno started to growl—something he never did before. Pulling him closer, Charlie turned and walked away. When she looked the lady in the eyes, her eyes turned a silvery color and her slits changed. It was very freaky, and Charlie felt she had seen enough.

Julie had been sitting long enough, so she got up to stretch her legs. Grabbing her purse and her book, she started to walk towards the river. While she was walking, a young man bumped into her, knocking her book out of her hand. Leaning down at the same time as he did to pick it up, she noticed a

21

tattoo on his neck. She realized it was something she had seen before, but from where? Smiling, she took her book from him. "Thank you," she uttered in a soft tone.

As she walked away, Julie began to feel a little dizzy, so she reached out for a nearby tree. Leaning against it, her mind flashed to a place she didn't recognize. All she could see was someone with a tattoo. The guy in the dream looked different than the one she had bumped into, though. He wore a dark robe, and there was something different about him, but she couldn't put her finger on it. The flash disappeared as fast as it came. Taking a deep breath, she looked around. Picking up her phone, she called Charlie. It didn't take her long to answer. "Hello? Charlie, it's Julie. How are things there?"

Charlie whispered into the phone, "I've had enough. I'm ready to go home. Can you and Jack come get me? If not, I'm taking the bus."

Julie looked around as she whispered back. "I had enough too. I'll get a hold of Jack, and we will grab you. Wait outside by the mall entrance."

After hanging up the phone, Julie texted Jack: Hey! We had enough. Can you get us and take us home? Charlie is by the mall entrance, and I will meet you where you dropped me off.

Jack texted that he would pick them up. He wondered if the girls had had a morning like he did, as some strange stuff had

happened. He definitely knew something was going on in the city but what was it exactly, he was not sure. As he went to get the girls, he thought to himself. *I can't wait to get back to the house. I need to tell them what I saw.* Driving away, he shook his head in dismay.

After returning to the house, all three of them flopped down on the living room furniture. They all sat there in silence, as they did while riding in the car home. None of them truly understood the stuff they saw or what it meant. Jack sat there quietly. He wanted to tell the girls what he saw that day but was enjoying the silence. His world suddenly felt as if it was on a rollercoaster. He remained very still for the moment, and he wanted to enjoy his peace. Julie reached over and grabbed the remote and turned the television on. "We'll talk later. I'm making chicken tonight with a salad to go with it. Do you want to stay, Jack?"

Jack lifted his head, "Yes I'd love to. Sounds yummy!"

The three of them laid back and watched the television for a bit, with not many words spoken. Julie got up and walked to the kitchen when the commercials started to play. News suddenly flashed across the screen. 'Just coming to me live from downtown,' the reporter emphatically stated, 'two more bodies have been found directly in front of the police station. The police are asking witnesses to come forward. If anyone has seen anything, please speak up; they are offering a large reward for any information.' The commercials continued, and both Jack and Charlie looked at each other.

Jack shook his head. "What is this world coming to? It used to be pretty safe, but now it's no different than a game of roulette; who is next?"

Charlie didn't want to agree, but she knew he was right. "I don't know, Jack. All I know is I want to wake up and find out that it was only a dream." Jack nodded in agreement. Moments later, Julie came back to the room. The three of them sat watching the television for the rest of the afternoon.

When dinnertime came, the house smelled like a dream. Julie had been cooking since she was a little girl. It was something she found relaxing. Charlie would always say that

23

Julie could cook a feast with her eyes shut. This would always make Julie laugh. As she set the table, Julie yelled to the others, "Dinner is ready, guys. Hope you're hungry." Both Charlie and Jack jumped up and rushed to the table. They had to deal with the temptation of the aroma of her cooking all afternoon. The three of them sat quietly eating. It was obvious they had a lot on their minds.

Jack looked at both girls and said, "This has been quite a day. I'm not sure about you, but I've been avoiding this conversation. I couldn't wait to tell you when I was out, but the more I thought about it, the crazier it sounded. But we really do need to talk about it. By the way, Julie, this is delicious."

Julie smiled, "Thanks, Jack. You know," she continued, "I've been doing a lot of thinking since earlier, and none of this makes sense to me. Down in the square I sat and sipped coffee for a bit, enjoying the beautiful sunshine. I felt very relaxed and nothing seemed out of sorts. After an hour or two of just sitting around, I got up and went for a walk. I bumped into a man ... well, he bumped into me, but that's not the important thing. He had a tattoo on his neck. It looked like some kind of ancient symbol. A few minutes later, I got really dizzy and some kind of flashback happened. It was really strange; I can't explain it. But the guy I saw during the flashback had a tattoo very similar to the guy I bumped into. He was wearing a dark robe. He was different from the man I bumped into ... not sure how, but the flash left as quickly as it came. It really bothered me though and left negative feelings with me all day. As for seeing someone's face change, that didn't happen. I've had flashes like that before, but none so unsettling."

Just as he was finishing his last bite, Jack laid his fork and knife down. "That sounds strange and very unsettling, but I think I have one on you. I was sitting and having a coffee as usual, and yes, I saw one of the people whose faces change, but that's not what was boggling to me. Moments later … after I saw them, I turned around, and a guy in a suit was walking by. He looked like me! I mean he really looked like me! For a minute or two, it almost seemed like the world around me stopped … like it was frozen. I looked around thinking maybe someone was playing a cruel joke or something, and when I looked back, the guy's face had turned into a woman's face. Talk about unsettling!"

Charlie's mouth was hanging open by now as she spoke and shared what she saw during the day, "I saw two of them at the mall, not as extreme as that, but I was brave and went up to them and spoke to them. I looked the woman right in the eyes and for a second, they flickered and changed to silver. They looked almost lizard like." The three of them all looked at each other. None of them felt at ease. Julie got up and started clearing the table. Charlie decided to get up and help.

Reaching back and rubbing his sore neck, Jack looked over at the girls. "This isn't normal. Something doesn't feel right about the whole situation. For the first time in my entire life, I don't feel in control because I don't know how to deal with this situation." Julie knew Jack his whole life. For him to feel this way, it had to be serious.

"I'll make coffee, Jack. Go sit and relax in the living room. We can discuss it more then." Leaning over to Charlie, Julie added, "Go sit with him. He's trying to understand this whole situation, and it just isn't going to happen … not yet." Charlie nodded and drifted into the living room to sit with Jack. Julie finished tidying the kitchen and put on coffee. She thought about the events of the day. There were so many seemingly impossible things happening, forcing them to open their eyes. How could they turn away knowing that what they saw could be connected to all the trouble happening in the city? She prepared the coffee and brought it into the living room.

Placing the coffee on the table, she sat down and sighed, "Guys, you both need to take a deep breath; all of us do. We all agree that something weird is happening to us. Jack, this has to be hardest on you. As a psychiatrist, you were taught things are a certain way. Well, now you have to look beyond that and go with your gut."

Frowning, Jack sat up and responded, "I know you're right, but there is nothing normal about this. Who are these people and why do they change? I've heard stories about shapeshifters, but up "til now, that's all they have been—stories. We don't even know if they are dangerous or if there is a connection with what is happening in this city, or if this is a coincidence. Charlie, when you hear the voices, is the man in the suit nearby? Have you seen him at all during that time?"

Charlie thought about it. "Maybe. I never really gave it thought before, but it's something I'll pay attention to in the future. I understand the term shapeshifter, being able to change appearances but by changing their looks, does that make them dangerous?"

Jack shook his head, "No, but we only know the rumors about shapeshifters because that's all the stories told us. What if there is more to them, and what if they are behind all these deaths and disappearances in the city? Oh my God, what if!"

"Enough of the what ifs!" yelled Julie. "Get a hold of yourself. You need to let go of the doctor part of you, for now, and just be you. Today, you believe in anything and everything. Okay?"

Jack nodded, "How did you get so wise?"

Julie laughed. Charlie laid her head back on the couch and bit her lip. "So, what do we do now? It's not like we can pretend we didn't see anything and just go on living a normal life. Besides, how long will it be before we show up dead or missing, just like every other victim in this city!" Julie looked at Charlie. She felt a little worried. After all, this was a girl who loved her city as much as she loved life.

Walking over to her, Julie leaned over and hugged Charlie, "We'll be just fine. We're in this together, and we'll deal with this together." Looking at Jack, Julie said assertively, "I don't want you being alone tonight. You can stay in the guest room. I'm not taking 'no' for an answer." Jack nodded. The three of them sat in silence for the longest time, then one by one went to bed.

Morning came. The day was dark and cloudy as the thunder roared through the sky. Charlie opened her eyes and listened to the thunder for a bit before reaching over and petting Bruno. "Hey, boy, think maybe we should stay in bed today? Maybe we might just stay here for the rest of our lives?" Bruno jumped up and started licking her face. Leaning forward, he rubbed his face against hers. "I love you too, boy."

Charlie got up, put on her clothes, and threw her hair up in an elastic. It was chilly in the house this morning, so she put on a sweater, and turned up the heat. She could smell the coffee before she even got to the kitchen. 'Julie must be up,' she thought. Both she and Jack were sitting at the table. Julie was reading the paper and drinking coffee while Jack was on the phone cancelling his appointments for the week. 'This will be a long day,' thought Charlie.

THE DARKEST SIDE OF THE MOON

Grabbing a coffee, Charlie walked over to the window. The sky looked how she felt, rough. She had hoped that when she woke up, the solution would be waiting for her, but she felt hopeless and empty with no answers. She took out her phone and googled shapeshifter. Not a whole lot came up, except 'the ability to change appearance.' *How does this help?* She thought. *I mean, we already know they can do that. What am I missing?* Her thoughts continued, *What if they're connected to the*

murders, and they commit these murders as different people each time? We would never catch them then. Her eyes widened as she drank the rest of her coffee. She asked Julie, "Anything in the paper today?"

Julie looked up, "Nothing you want to know about." Taking a deep breath and exhaling loudly, she sat back. "Things have gotten worse out there. Three planes crashed last night. The security checks are not working, so they have put a ban on flying. It is not just happening here; this is happening everywhere. The mayor is holding a meeting today, and from what I hear, he's thinking about imposing a curfew. So many people are going missing or dying every night. This isn't normal. All these deaths! This is worse than what a serial killer would do. I'm almost to the point of giving up reading the newspaper. Every day is worse than the day before. I don't know how yet, but I think this is all connected."

Charlie leaned down next to Julie's chair, "I think you're right. We need to figure out what's happening and what we need to do. I have some money saved. I'm going to take some time off from work. It's difficult to concentrate with things the way they are."

Julie nodded, "That sounds like a good idea. My job seems

to be on hold anyway. The parents are keeping the children home—what is left of them, that is. They are scared to take their eyes off of them, and I don't blame them."

Jack laid the phone down on the table and joined the conversation, "I took some time off from work myself. This situation is a priority at the moment. So, you both think this is connected to all the murders and missing folks?" Both girls nodded. "Well, then we need to figure out what to do next."

Julie giggled to herself, "Welcome back, Jack."

Sitting on the couch, Charlie pulled out her sketch book. She found it relaxing when she sketched. Looking through it, she noticed that the number of pictures she had in common with Julie were adding up. Maybe she and Julie were connected through their dreams. She wished she knew what she was drawing during these times; instead, she was just going with the flow. Leaning back against the couch, she started to draw. She remained on the couch for over an hour, sketching and taking her mind off all the stressful details of life.

Meanwhile, Julie and Jack headed out to the grocery store. Julie thought that with everything going on, it might be wise to stock up for a bit; after all, who knew what would happen? They had agreed that Jack would stay with them for a bit, because they felt safer staying in a group. Loading up the carts, Jack turned to Julie and said, "I have groceries at my house, too. I'll stop by my house and grab them and some personal stuff after we leave here."

After picking up a large bag of dog food, Julie's eyes scanned the cat food section. "Yeah, that sounds okay. I'm thinking we can go online tonight and see what sightings there have been, and if anyone has any information about any of this. So, make sure you grab your laptop."

Jack grabbed the bag of dog food from her and put it in his cart. "That sounds like a place to start." It took a few hours, but they finally completed their tasks and came back to the house.

The groceries remained on the kitchen floor as Julie stood in the kitchen putting everything in its place. She knew it would be overcrowded, but it was better to have too much than to be without when in need. *There had to be others who have seen this stuff,* she thought to herself. *We can't be the only ones.*

In the living room, Charlie was sitting on the couch. talking on the phone. Franny had called, wondering why she had not seen the girls lately. Their smiling faces lit up the café, especially on gray cloudy days. "The café is quite empty today," said Franny. "I might just close it. Do you want some company?" Charlie loved when she came to visit. She was cheerful and fun, but then thought to herself that with everything going on, it just wasn't a good day.

"Maybe not today," she replied. "I'll give you a call later this week and then we'll get together." She hung up the phone and laid it on the table next to her and headed to the kitchen. "Julie, did you guys grab more coffee while you were out?" Spotting it on the counter, Charlie added, "Oops! Never mind. I see it."

"Where's Jack?" Charlie asked.

Julie turned and looked at Charlie. "He's putting his stuff away. I've asked him to stay with us for a bit. I thought it would be safer for all of us. Oh, and I came up with the idea of doing a search on the internet to see if there's anything out there related to what we've seen. Maybe someone else has some information."

While looking out the window, Charlie noticed that a lot of

neighbors were away. Some have been found dead, but others were just missing. The neighborhood felt empty without them. "Do you think it will ever get back to normal around here?" she asked Julie.

Jack wandered out into the living room carrying his laptop. All he could think about was surfing the internet to see if anyone had more information about the shapeshifters. *There has to be someone who has seen something. We can't be the only ones in the entire world, could we?* he thought to himself. Jack opened his browser; he paused for a moment before typing in shapeshifting. *What would someone think if they saw me googling this?* He laughed as he pressed enter. A large selection of sites appeared in front of him. Some sites advertised mattresses that shift to fit your shape; others were weight loss sites. There were two though that seemed different from the rest. One was a forum with the topic shapeshifters and the other was a book written by RH Henry called *Shifters among Us*. He decided to go to the forum first, thinking maybe he would find others who had seen stuff. The forum had tons of areas to look in, but one particularly stuck out. It read, 'Has anyone else seen them?' Clicking on it, Jack read the contents of the post: *Everywhere I look, they are there. I think they are shapeshifters. Not that I am sure of what that truly is, but whatever they are, they are everywhere.*

Jack yelled for the girls, "You won't believe what I found!" Both of them came running into the living room.

Charlie leaned over to see what Jack was looking at. "What did you find?" she asked curiously.

He turned his laptop so both girls could see what he was looking at. This person had seen them too. There were a few people that had. Clicking on reply, he typed in, *We've seen them too. Do you know anything about them? We are in Richmond, BC. Where are you?'* Pressing enter, he looked back at the girls. "Maybe we can get an answer on what's happening. It might take a bit for an answer."

Jack switched over to the site with the book. It was an eBook about shapeshifters, and what one man had seen. Jack filled out the information needed and downloaded the book. He figured he could sit and read this while waiting for an answer on the forum. He put his feet up on the table and leaned back, eager to find out if this man knew more than they did, and if so, what. Jack spent the rest of the afternoon reading while the girls went about the house doing their own thing.

While sitting at the table with a cup of coffee, the girls sorted through Charlie's sketches. They were trying to figure out which ones had meaning towards what was happening and which ones were connected to Julie. Bruno was lying at their feet, stretched out, with not a care in the world. So far, there were a few she recognized from her dreams, but the one that stood out the most was a symbol. It was small—the shape of the moon and the sun together. It had jewels on both sides, and a feather. This was the same symbol the man in the square had on his neck. It was also in the flashback she had. Julie held the picture in her hand as she looked at it. "It's identical, Charlie. Somehow, you and I are connected to each other. You draw my dreams. Even more, it's connected to whatever I saw in the flashback. Do you think it's connected to the shapeshifters?"

Charlie knew how worried Julie was, but she was always the strong one in all situations. "Our connection is good. Maybe we're psychically linked," she laughed. Julie laughed too. Charlie reached over and took the sketch from Julie.

"Whatever this symbol is, I'm sure we'll figure this out. I have no idea if it's connected to the shapeshifters, but it's kinda odd you had that flashback while all this was happening. So, my guess is yes, it must be connected."

Later that day, Charlie stood on the patio while having a smoke. The patio was part of the reason the girls chose this place. In one direction, they could see the bridge and in the far distance, the ocean. Either way, there was a great view. She knew what was happening was much more than simple face changing. This was something that could not be held between the three; others needed to know. Putting out her cigarette, she went into the house. Jack and Julie were sitting at the table. "We got a response from that site," said Jack. "They said that Texas is overrun by shapeshifters. They're reptilian-like and are somehow connected to all the murders and missing people. People are scared to death and are clueless. Not too many can grasp the idea of shapeshifters being behind all this." Looking up at the girls, he continued, "You know what this means? This is more than a local issue. What is happening in this city may be happening all over the world."

Charlie gasped, "Oh my God! This is crazy! What do we do?"

Julie got up to grab another coffee. "We don't have any choice. It's time to find others who have seen this within our city."

Jack looked at Julie and then at Charlie. "I read that book from the website earlier. It was interesting, but he didn't know much more than we do. He did say he thought they all seem to be linked to the government, as he had never seen one out of a suit."

Taking a deep breath, Charlie pulled out a chair and sat

down. "I was afraid of this, and you're right, Julie, we need to speak up. We can start at the café. I can talk to Franny tomorrow and see what she has to say about all of this. Who knows? Maybe this isn't such a big secret after all. Jack, do me a favor. Find all you can on this. See if you can show proof of the shifters, murders, and missing people happening elsewhere. Oh, and the plane crashes … maybe we can see where they've been happening. My printer is set up in my room. You can use it. I'm going to go turn on the TV and see what's on the news. Then I have a few things to get ready for tomorrow to help it go smoothly. It'll be hard not to feel crazy telling others what stuff we've seen. I'm not staying up late tonight. Tomorrow is going to be a long day." They all agreed and started preparing for the next day.

Chapter 3

Wide awake, Charlie wondered if she would ever get proper sleep again. She could hardly shut her eyes, thinking about everything that was going on. Even Bruno was not the life force he normally was in the morning. He lay curled up in her arms as if he knew how difficult a night's sleep she had. She felt guilty looking at him. He hadn't been out for a walk in two days, and she wondered how much longer it would be safe to walk the streets. She hated the idea of confining him to the back yard but was worried for his safety. As much as she hated to do it, after today, he would have to stay home for a while just 'til she knew it was safe. Today, though, she would take him to the park and pretend it was a normal day. She jumped out of bed, her heart flopping at the thought of going to the café, but she knew it had to be done. Grabbing some clothes and putting her hair up, she went to see what the others were doing.

In the kitchen, both sat at the table. Jack was dressed up as if he were ready for work. "Are you going to work today?" she asked. "I thought you had time off?"

Laying down his coffee mug, Jack looked up. "No, I'm not working, but I have to stop at a few places, including work. I have to take a closer look at both my co-workers and others within my profession. I need to know if these strange events are happening in the business world or government."

Julie grabbed Jack's hand and assured him, "You are a wise man, Mr. Davenport. Charlie and I can handle the café today. We will meet you back here later. Did you get any sleep, Charlie?"

Frowning, Charlie sighed, "Not a drop, but with everything going on, I should just be thankful I am still functioning."

Julie started laughing. "God is testing us and what a test this is!" The three of them chuckled and finished getting ready for the day.

"Bruno! Bruno, come get your leash on, boy. We're going for a walk." With the cat running closely behind him, the dog headed to the door. Stormage flopped down onto the floor when he saw Bruno getting his leash on. Guess it was time for a catnap. Scratching behind his ear, Charlie yelled up the stairs, "Ready to go?"

Julie grabbed her purse. After putting the folder with all the paperwork in her purse, she zipped it up. "Yup. I'm ready. Haven't been to the park in a while. Should be a nice walk. See you later Jack!" she yelled.

The sun took over the sky as the three of them walked up the road towards the park. "You know, Julie. I'm worried that after today, it will never be the same. Up 'til now, it was always safe to walk down the street or walk through the park." Bruno tugged on the leash. He knew exactly where he was going. "Slow down, boy! We'll get there soon," she laughed. "This is my favorite thing to do—take him to the park so he can sniff the flowers and enjoy the fresh air."

Julie reached out and opened the gate to the park. "Well, one can hope today will go smoothly, and that we can find a way to quickly end the terror in the city."

When Charlie let the leash unravel, Bruno ran to the closest bush and lifted his leg like a ballerina. This made her giggle. "He always makes me laugh." Together they walked down the path leading through the park. "So, how do we start to explain all this to Franny?"

Julie looked over at her. "We just tell her what's going on. They either believe us or they don't. It's up to others to decide what they think, but whatever that may be, they cannot change what is happening around us. We have to be the brave ones."

Charlie nodded. "Yeah, you're right."

The two walked for a bit while Bruno did his thing. The breeze was warm and made the walk very relaxing. It was nice living close to the ocean. She used to believe it was impossible to be stressed out living in such a wonderful place, but maybe she had been wrong.

Standing outside the café, Charlie looked around. This was a place she loved. She used to feel secure here, but now, not so much. Julie grabbed her arm. "Come on. Let's go in."

Pulling open the door, the two girls went inside. Franny was busy wiping down the tables, but quickly ran to get the girls coffee when she spotted them. "Oh my God! I'm so glad to see you two! Where have you been? It has been so quiet around here, especially with all those folks going missing."

Julie had known Franny for most of her life, and Charlie had known her for the past seven years. It wasn't hard for the girls to tell she was upset over everything happening. Julie grabbed Franny's arm. "Can you sit with us? We want to talk to you."

The girls chose the window table. Franny took a deep breath and grabbed a seat next to them, then quickly asked. "What's up?"

Without hesitation, Julie began her questioning. "Have you noticed anything outside of the usual besides what's been all over the news lately?"

Franny thought to herself and answered, "Well, I know a lot of people are scared. They think maybe the government is behind all of this. I don't know what to think about all of this. Why, do you know something more … something I should know?"

Pulling the file out of her purse, Julie handed it to her. "You should look at this and know that both of us have seen this firsthand. Jack also has seen this. He is out on business today. Otherwise, he would've been here too."

Franny opened the files, her eyes widening as she scanned the information about shapeshifters among us. There were articles from all over the world about murders and missing people. She gasped. "Is this for real?"

Julie nodded sadly. "Yeah, I think the only reason we haven't heard about all the other places on the news is that everyone is suffering like we are and are focusing on trying to help their own city, forgetting that the rest of the world exists. I know I have."

Shaking her head, Franny placed down the file. "This is scary! And you say you saw this yourself? Where?"

Charlie pointed out the window to the fountain. "Every day a man sits there reading his paper. I've seen it at the mall too."

Julie nodded, "I've seen stuff too. I find it truly strange that this is happening at the exact time all the terror is happening all over the world. Don't you?"

Franny nodded, "It's a bit hard to swallow, but I've known you two for a long time. Besides, you have a lot of proof in this folder." Standing up, Franny turned to the girls and said, "I'll be right back. I need to make a phone call."

Franny grabbed the phone and scurried off to the kitchen. She thought to herself as she dialed the number and waited for someone to pick up. *I hope he's there. Carl, pick up! This should make sense, but it doesn't.* Just as she was about to hang up, she heard a voice. "Hello."

Franny whispered into the phone, "Carl, I'm so glad I got you on the phone. I think you're going to want to hear this. Charlie and Julie are both here with a file. They have proof of what you were talking about … that the government is responsible for everything going on. But, there's more to it." Carl remained silent as Franny continued. "There are things called shapeshifters. They have seen them. One was right outside the café, believe it or not. They can explain a lot better than I can."

Carl took a deep breath and exhaled. "They have proof? Can I see this proof? Do they know anything about the group?"

Franny whispered, not wanting anyone to overhear her, "No. I haven't mentioned it to anyone, as promised."

Carl sighed, "Okay, set up a meeting for me to meet with them sometime tomorrow at the café. Love you, Franny. I have to go."

Just before hanging up the phone, Franny whispered, "I love you too. See you at home."

Coming back out to see the girls, Franny grabbed the coffee pot and a few cups. "This is going to be a long day, girls. I want to know everything you do." Setting the coffee pot down on the table, she locked the door and turned the sign to *Closed*. As she sat down, she said, "This is the first day I've taken off in years. If any of this is going to sink in, I'm going to have to not worry about customers." Putting her feet up and leaning against the wall, she continued, "So, when did you first see this?"

Charlie grabbed a cup and poured herself some coffee. "I noticed it about a week ago. Well, I think I saw it before, but I thought I was seeing things."

Julie piped in, "Not everyone can see them. I can't, but I watched the videos online and saw it on there." Reaching over to grab some coffee, Julie added, "I'm having weird dreams … as if they are memories from a different life. Charlie has been drawing things from my dreams. The funny thing is I've never told her about my dreams or the stuff she drew from them."

Franny looked at Charlie, shock written all over her face. Charlie giggled, as if to ease the blow. "Yeah, I felt that initial shock too. We're still not sure what the stuff I drew meant or what Julie dreamt about it. She was at the square the other day and had some kind of flashback after a strange man bumped into her. Both the man who bumped into her and the guy who was wearing a dark robe in her flashback had some kind of symbolized tattoo. I ended up drawing it."

Drinking her coffee, Julie looked over at Franny. "I've had flashbacks before, but assumed they were some sort of déjà vu. Jack's experience with all this was a bit different than ours. He was outside the mayor's office in the court area. He was sitting and drinking his coffee when he saw a guy who looked exactly like him. You can't imagine how much this freaked him out! He quickly turned away and noticed that everything was in a frozen state. He glanced back just in time to see the man's face change into a woman's face right in front of his eyes. Then, suddenly everything unfroze."

Franny's mouth hit the floor. She exclaimed, "I can't even imagine! None of this sounds real. I mean how can it possibly feel real when none of us have ever encountered anything like this? I hope you don't mind, but I called Carl when I used the phone. I told him what you said to me. You guys are not the only ones with conspiracy theories. He wants to speak with you both but is not available 'til tomorrow. He has been leading a discussion with a lot of other people who have their own thoughts on what is happening. You don't mind meeting with him, do you?"

Charlie took Franny's hand and said, "This isn't a secret. Of course, we will meet with him. We need people to know about this. There's so much more to it than we know. What if this is connected to the murders and the missing people? We have to figure out what to do … how to stop it. I don't know much about shapeshifters, but the last thing I want is them knowing we know. I'm not sure whether their reactions will be good or bad. I'm assuming that they're bad, in light of everything that's happening."

Julie reached in her purse to answer her phone. It was Jack. "Hey. What's up?"

Eagerly, Jack replied, "I have so much to tell you when we get back to the house. What time will you be back?"

Julie looked at both girls. "We can head back any time. Did you find out much?"

Jack took a breath. "Yeah, a lot more than I wanted to know. I'll be at the house in about an hour. I have one more stop to make. Did you talk to Franny?"

Holding the phone tighter to her ear, she responded, "Yes, we told her, and it was hard for her to digest, but she's on board. Do you mind if I invite her to the house to discuss this further?"

Nodding, Jack agreed. "Okay, see you soon."

Hanging up the phone, Julie looked at Franny and asked, "Do you mind if we move this conversation over to the house? Jack will meet us there in an hour."

Franny stood up. "No. Not at all. Let me do a few things, then we can go." Franny went into the kitchen.

About twenty minutes later, Franny came out, coat and purse in hand. "Okay, all ready. Shall we take my car or are we walking?"

Julie thought to herself. She wanted to get some lunch prepared for everyone before Jack got back. "I think we'll take the car," said Julie.

Piling out the door, Franny turned to lock up the café. "Can't be too careful," she said. Jumping into the car, the girls returned to the house. Bruno pressed his face tightly against the window, excited to head home.

Charlie thought to herself as she entered the house and took off her shoes that it was nice that Franny took it all so well. This could have gone badly in so many ways. Tossing her coat onto the floor, she climbed the stairs. Bruno ran ahead, searching for the cat to play with. Charlie passed the living room and went right to the kitchen. Her smokes were still on the table. Smoking was a habit she had not heavily indulged in before, but lately, it seemed she had been smoking a bit more than usual. Grabbing a cigarette, she walked out to the patio, leaving the door cracked so she could still speak to the girls. Charlie moved her neck around, cracking it ever so lightly. It felt good since her neck was a bit stiff from not sleeping well. Looking around, she knew the city wasn't ever going to be the same. Life felt so different right now. She missed going to the café to write or sketch. She also missed going on daily walks with Bruno or taking off to attend an art class. It felt like a few weeks had passed since she was at the club with her friends letting loose.

Shaking her head, she finished her smoke and went back inside. Julie was at the counter making sandwiches while Franny sat at the table looking a little frazzled. "Any of this sink in yet?"

Charlie asked. Franny nodded. Charlie pulled out a chair to join her. "You know, I googled a few things last night. There have been over 2,000 deaths in the last month in our city alone. They all end up in the same place, left in front of our local police stations at 6 a.m., just after the sun rises. There have also been seven cases of people suffering from amnesia wandering aimlessly in the streets. There's been a total of 4,000 missing persons. This is only one city, yet so much has happened … and to think, this is happening everywhere! I cannot even imagine how many worldwide have suffered."

Just then, Jack walked in the door. Quickly entering the kitchen, he blurted out, "If this was a virus, I would have to say it was widespread." Shaking his head, he added, "I never knew how closed-eyed I was; they're everywhere. There's a psychiatrist right in our building that is a shapeshifter. Can you believe it? Right down the hall from me! I dropped by to talk to him about a case I'm working on. Of course, that was just an excuse to speak to him, but it was long enough for me to notice his eyes change color just like you described, Charlie. It was extremely hard to pretend I didn't notice. Oh, and Marcy was telling me a friend of hers has been to three funerals this week just for her family alone yet, doesn't remember anyone dying. She's convinced the grave is empty.

After all, wouldn't you remember someone you love dying? They both are dropping by later. Hope you don't mind." All three women sat at the table looking at him.

Glancing at them, Jack started to blush. "I am so sorry. I forgot to even say hi."

Julie started to chuckle. "It's okay, and no, we don't mind if Marcy and her friend drop by. Have you noticed how empty the roads are? Took us barely any time to get home."

Jack nodded. "Yeah. I was here in a flash. No one wants to be out there with everything going on. A lot of businesses are only open part-time now, except for the government offices and the police. They all want to get stuff done and be in before the sun sets. Have you noticed that every person we saw that shapeshifted was wearing a suit or a government outfit?"

Franny bit her lip as Charlie piped up, "I bet it's all tied in with the government. Maybe the shifters can hide better in a government job. Keeps the little people from asking questions. When they do ask questions, the government has the power to shut them up."

Grabbing the file, Jack implored, "Charlie, help me hang these up." The two of them started pinning up all the proof onto sections of the wall. Standing back and taking a good look at all the evidence they had left them feeling overwhelmed. Talking to himself out loud, Jack looked it all over. "How could I not see all this before? The missing people's list is huge, and this is just from the city of Richmond alone. Yet, this problem is worldwide. The numbers in total are just unimaginable. Bodies have been piling up for months now … every day more and more. At least 8,000 people from this city have been buried recently. There has been an unusual number of patients in the local hospital suffering from amnesia. They were found wandering throughout the town. Planes have crashed. Trains have derailed, and now there are shapeshifters. Julie and Charlie have matching dreams and sketches and Charlie's hearing voices. There seems to be a connection, but how? No memory of loved ones dying, yet there is a memorial for them. Girls, this all has to be connected. There's no way it isn't!"

With eyes as wide as saucers, the three girls stood looking at Jack. Julie walked over to Jack. "There's so much evidence. So, why are we the only ones seeing it? Why haven't the cops figured this out?"

Franny took a deep breath. "You're not the only ones to notice this. There's a group committed to solving this mystery. The difference between you and them is that you uncovered the shapeshifters. That's all I'm going to say about them though. Carl will tell you more when you speak to him tomorrow." All eyes were on Franny.

Wrinkling up her lips, Charlie mumbled to herself, "I hate having to wait 'til tomorrow to find out more."

Walking over to pour himself some coffee, Jack turned and looked at Charlie. "We all hate waiting, but this has gotten serious, and we have to play this safe. I'm sure if Franny was able to tell us more at the moment, she would, but it's probably better we wait for Carl himself to tell us what we need to know."

Julie reached over to answer her phone. The ringer was on low, but she thought she had heard it. It was Loretta. "Hello," said Julie. "How are you?"

Loretta was mumbling something to someone just before she answered. "It has been quite a day. It's a never-ending circus around here. The police need to figure this out soon and catch this psycho, so I can catch my breath. Oh, and just a heads-up, I think the police are setting up a curfew in town. If they can keep everyone off the streets after the sun sets, then maybe they can catch this creep. Personally, I don't think they're doing enough. How can all these cops have no clue about what's happening on the streets they are dedicated to protect?"

Interrupting, Julie whispered, "There's a lot more to it, but we'll have to discuss this later. I'm extremely busy at the moment. Thank you for the heads-up though. I'll call you tomorrow, and we can talk about all of this ... even better, maybe you can drop by the house?"

Letting out a deep sigh, Loretta agreed. "Sounds great! I'll come by in the afternoon."

Hanging up the phone, Julie looked over at Jack. "That was Loretta. She'll be coming by tomorrow."

A bit puzzled, Jack asked, "Does she know anything about what's happening?"

Julie walked over towards Jack. "She has a lot of information about the deaths and other weird stuff. You have to remember, she's with police officers all day long, so she hears things and even sees them. I know you and she have a past, but you need to put it aside. She's a great asset and a good friend of mine, and I need to fill her in on what's happening tomorrow." Agreeing, Jack went back to what he was doing.

Later that day both Marcy and her friend Beth arrived. After letting them in, Charlie took them upstairs where everyone else was. Julie was just coming in from the back yard, where she and Bruno had been playing. "Hey!" she said. "Glad you could join us. There are two fold-out chairs in the closet by the back door if you want them." Trying to be a good host,

Charlie walked over to the closet and got the chairs. She thought it was nice to have people over, though it would have been better if it were under different circumstances.

Julie sat down. She couldn't help but giggle as she spotted Stormage out of the corner of her eye. He was in hunting mode, and Bruno was the prey. She was glad the two of them had each other to play with. Looking at Charlie, Julie said, "Jesse should have been back by now. Hope everything is okay with him."

Charlie closed Google and looked up from her phone. "I'm sure he's fine. Maybe he's having a good time and decided to stay long. I'm sure if there were any problems, he would've given you a call by now. So, Beth, Jack says you have noticed something weird about the funerals you have been attending?"

Seeming a little nervous, she looked at Charlie.

"Yeah. It's been a hard week. I've been to three family funerals, and everyone is crying and falling apart, but I don't remember any of them dying. I've never seen one body to prove it. It was as if we went to bed one night and woke up with knowledge of the death and went to the funeral home the same day. That doesn't feel right to me."

Jack grabbed her hand and consoled her. "That doesn't sound right to me either. With everything going on, trust your gut. I'm thinking the graves of your loved ones may be empty; maybe they're missing like so many others."

"Anyone hungry?" Julie asked as she went to the fridge. "I made these earlier." Grabbing a tray of sandwiches, she brought them over to the table. She was pleased when she saw everyone reaching for one.

"Mmmmm. I'm starved," said Jack. Looking over at Marcy and Beth, he continued, "You can take a look at what we found

47

if you like. We hung it up on the wall earlier. It makes it so much easier to look over."

Marcy walked over to the wall, looking from one end to the other. "I knew that what was happening was serious, but I never imagined it would ever go this far. I knew there was a killer on the loose and that people were missing, but I figured that with some pepper spray and a taser, I'd be safe. Should I be scared?" Sitting back down, she looked at Jack. "So, what next?"

Leaning back in his chair and looking a little glazed, Jack sighed, "Seriously, I have no idea. Looking at all this tells me we're in trouble, but the thought of shifters makes me feel silly. It's really strange that we suddenly start seeing shapeshifters, and so many deaths have occurred, and so many people are missing. There must be a connection, and maybe we're the ones who need to do something about it. Please do not ask me what! This is like reading an unknown language."

Charlie grabbed Marcy's arm gently. "If you don't feel safe at home, you two are welcome to stay here with us. After all, safety is in numbers. I'm sure we can make the room. Couldn't we, Julie?"

Julie was in the kitchen putting dinner on. She knew the sandwiches wouldn't hold anyone for a long time. Pausing for a moment, she looked up at Charlie. "Yes, of course, you both can stay. Safety is in numbers, and Lorretta told me earlier there may be a curfew put into effect, so it might be better knowing

everyone is safe. Jack and I hit up the grocery store a few days ago. We thought we should stock up, so we don't have to go anywhere unless it's necessary."

Marcy stood up and grabbed her purse. "Thank you for the

invite. If you really don't mind, I think it would be a good idea for everyone to stay together while all this is going on. I'm going home to grab some stuff. If that's okay, I'll be back later." Seconds later, she was out the door. Beth quietly got up and followed her.

Charlie laid her hand on Franny's back. "You have been super quiet. Are you okay?"

Franny looked up at Charlie. "Yes, just deep in thought. Everything will be so different tomorrow. I can feel it. This is like a door that once opened doesn't get shut simply by pushing on it. It isn't anything anyone can prepare for either; this is just one of those things that you have no control over."

Rubbing her back, Charlie thought about what Franny had said. "Well, whether we prepare or not, it's happening, but one thing I can be thankful for is that we're not alone. We have each other."

Franny reached over and hugged Charlie. "That's so very true. I'm going to give Carl a call. I'll be right back. I'll get him to come here tomorrow instead of the café. It'll be safer." Franny headed to the living room to use the phone. Meanwhile, Charlie went to the basement, where she had a cot and a blow-up mattress from camping. If she could find them, she could set it up for the girls.

Later that night, the girls returned and settled in. The group had filled their tummies on the delicious dinner Julie prepared and were relaxing in the living room for the evening. Charlie turned the television on, hoping there would be a movie for them to watch, something to break the tension in the room. She knew everyone's mind was preoccupied with what was happening. Flipping through the channels, she noticed the news was on. Turning up the volume, she laid the remote on the table. No one really wanted to watch it, but everyone knew they should. Maybe there would be more information on what had been happening, and they would know what to do. Leaning back against the back of the couch, she started to relax as the police chief came on the screen.

"Good evening, folks. I'm Chief Hillback of District Seventeen. I'm here tonight to inform folks of the curfew I have

instated for the city of Richmond, BC. You all are aware of the murders taking place, and that our missing persons list is skyrocketing. We have no suspects yet, and in order to protect the people of our city, we feel that this curfew must be enforced. I am requesting that folks be off the streets and in their home by 7 p.m. Anyone out after curfew will be arrested immediately. Thank you for understanding. Good night.'

Jack glanced at Charlie. "At least we had a warning, so this is not much of a shock... though I wonder why 7 p.m.? It doesn't get dark 'til later."

Reaching for the remote so she could find a movie, Charlie responded, "Probably because they have no clue what time people actually disappear; this gives them time to clear the area, so they can patrol better." Mesmerized by the flickering channels, Charlie chimed, "Yeah. You're probably right." The five of them sat watching television for the next few hours, then went to bed.

* * *

Lightly opening her eyes, Charlie noticed the sun beaming in the window. This was something she loved waking up to, but today she wished it was dark, so she could go back to sleep. Reaching down, she started giving Bruno a belly rub. She felt him roll over, so she could reach the opposite side. This always made her giggle. "Time to get up, boy, though for what, I'm not sure anymore. Carl is coming today. Guess that's as good a reason as any. Don't you think?" Slowly crawling out of bed, Charlie grabbed her clothes and put her hair up. The house was exceptionally quiet this morning, and the kitchen was empty. As she walked over to make some coffee, she thought, *Julie is always up; she must be so stressed over all of this to still be in bed.* Watching the last of the coffee brew, she poured a cup and sat in a folding chair on the patio. Both Bruno and Stormage followed her. They loved to lie in the sun any chance they got. Leaning back against the house, she lit a smoke. 'I wonder what time Carl is coming' she thought to herself. As she smoked her cigarette, her attention was drawn towards the bridge. She missed sitting down by the water, sketching with the cool breeze hitting her in the face. Putting out her smoke, Charlie went back inside.

Julie was standing in the kitchen. "Morning," she said.

Charlie smiled, "Can you believe it? I'm up before you."

Julie rolled her eyes and went to grab some coffee. "Jack and the girls left early this morning. Both Marcy and Beth had groceries they wanted to grab. Hopefully, we have room in the fridge." Stormage slowly wrapped himself around Julie's leg. "Will you get him some food?"

Charlie went and grabbed both the cat and dog food and filled their bowls. "Come on, guys," she said as she patted her leg.

Pulling out a chair, Charlie sat and laid her head on the table.

"I'm so incredibly off. The other night I tossed and turned to the point that I thought I would never get any sleep again; yet, now all I can think about is sleeping my life away. How messed up is that?"

Julie nodded. "I can relate. So, Franny just texted me. She said they're on their way over. I told her just to come in when they get here." Now laughing, Julie added, "It probably would take you forever to answer the door in your sloth state of mind."

Charlie looked at Julie as she snickered to herself, "Very funny."

Passing Carl her coat, Franny climbed the stairs and walked into the kitchen. She laid her purse on the table and grabbed a chair. "Morning, girls. Did you hear the news last night?"

Julie chuckled and nudged Charlie's lifeless body that was slumped over on the table. "Any one there?"

Shaking her head softly, she pulled out a chair and sat next to Franny. "If you mean about the curfew, yes, we all saw the news."

Charlie lifted her head just as Carl entered the room. "We have a lively crowd here," he chuckled.

Charlie looked up at him, "It's a rough morning. Hopefully, some coffee will help."

Julie jumped up to grab some coffee, while Carl sat down at the table next to his wife. Laying his hand on his wife's, he looked over at Charlie. "So, Franny tells me you and I should talk. She says you have information about what's happening in the city?"

Sitting up straighter, Charlie took the coffee from Julie. "Thanks. You should have a look at the wall behind you, Carl, and after you have had a good look, we can sit and talk about it."

Carl turned and looked at the wall, his eyes widening. Getting up, he took a good look at all the information they had attached to the wall. He stood there for quite a while hemming and hawing to himself, then returned to the table. Looking at his wife then at Charlie, he exclaimed, "I'm absolutely speechless. Maybe not speechless but lost for the right words."

Franny laid her hand on his. "I know it's a lot to take in, but it's happening, and I figured you could work together."

Carl nodded, "That's a good idea, Franny. Charlie, I need to take a little bit to let this absorb, then I need to explain this to the group. I'll get back to you tomorrow."

Charlie looked puzzled. The group? Carl looked at Franny. "Oh, you didn't tell her?" Looking back at Charlie, Carl added, "I'm the leader of a revolutionary group. We have been watching the government for a long while now, trying to figure out how they're connected to everything that's been happening." Standing up, Carl leaned over and kissed his wife. "I'll see you all later."

As Carl left, Julie got up and opened the fridge. "I'm going to make breakfast. If we're going to make it through the day, eating might be a good idea."

Franny shook her head no. "I'm going home. Thank God I brought my own car. This is a day for going back to bed."

Charlie laughed, "Yeah. I think after I eat, that's where I'll be going."

Julie shrugged, "Maybe that's what we all need. A day to just sleep and not have to think about all the stressful things that have been happening. Jack and the girls can

Chapter 4

After lying in bed for what seemed to be hours, Charlie was certain it was time to get up. She had spent all of yesterday napping and lazing around. All the stress from what had been happening had finally caught up to her. But now, it was 4 a.m., and she was no longer tired. Jumping out of bed, she decided she was hungry. Grabbing her clothes, she walked down the hall.

The house was dark, so she turned the lights on as she made her way to the kitchen. She put the coffee on and threw some breakfast burritos in the microwave then stepped out on the patio for a cigarette. Leaning against the patio rail, she lit her smoke. The skies were still dark. She could see half of Main Street from the patio… not that there was a lot to see at 4 a.m. It took her a few minutes to finish her smoke, but as she was putting it out, she noticed a man standing on the corner. He was just standing there looking around. The police who patrolled the streets drove by him and continued as if they never saw him. 'How is that possible?' she thought. Why didn't they arrest him? Charlie ran back into the house and grabbed her cell phone, then back to the patio. She started to record the man. Maybe this was something the others should see. She stood there for almost thirty minutes 'til, once more, the police drove by. Again, they kept going as if the man was not standing there. Turning off the camera, she walked back into the house, very puzzled about why the police didn't seem to see the man standing there during curfew hours. After pouring some coffee and grabbing her burritos from the microwave, she took a seat at the table. The coffee tasted good. It was a little stronger than when Julie had made it. Just as she went to lay her coffee cup down, the words, "It's almost time", echoed in her ears. Looking around, she realized she had heard the voices again. It was different this time since it happened at home and not the café. Taking a deep

breath, she ate her breakfast then sat on the couch to watch a bit of television before the others woke up.

A few hours later, the house became alive. She could hear Julie in the kitchen making breakfast and Jack in the washroom gargling with mouthwash. Marcy and Beth sat at the table talking about how they slept and how it was nice not to be alone during all this. Julie wandered into the living room, "Oh, you are up. I thought you were still asleep."

Charlie paused her show and looked up at her.

"I have been up since 4. That is not something I want to make a habit of," she laughed. "Oh, by the way, there is a video on my phone you're going to want to see. I was out having a smoke this morning, and I couldn't believe it. There was a man standing on the corner, and the police drove by him twice without arresting him for violating the curfew, or even looking at him. With all the murders and missing folks, how can they let him be out there without questioning him?"

Julie sat down in the chair next to her, "Wow! That doesn't seem right or even possible, knowing how serious they are about keeping the streets empty at night." Grabbing the phone,

Julie headed to the kitchen. "I'll have a look at it as soon as I'm finished making breakfast."

Charlie jumped up and followed her into the kitchen. "Are you making bacon?"

Julie giggled, "Yes, I'm making bacon."

Charlie grabbed a seat next to Beth. "I heard a voice again. It said, 'It's almost time', not that I get it or anything. But maybe, just maybe, it's important."

Marcy looked at Charlie. "I've heard you refer to the voices before. Can I ask what all they have said?"

Charlie turned to her, "Well, I've heard them talk about doing something, asking if it's complete. I've heard them say, 'Did you follow instructions? Are they secure for the night? What did you find out?'" Charlie paused for a moment as if trying to remember everything. "Oh yeah! And I heard them speak about a mission. I'm not sure what any of this means, but I wonder if it's linked to anything else that's going on."

Marcy nodded, "Sounds like they are up to something."

Julie grabbed the food and some plates and headed for the table. "I'm pretty sure we'll have to figure out how on our own.

Charlie reached over and grabbed some bacon. "Mmmm, this smells so good."

Jack wandered into the kitchen. "Morning, ladies." Grabbing a coffee, he sat down at the table. "What are you watching?"

Julie looked up at Jack. "This is a video Charlie took this morning." Now turning it so Jack could watch too, she added, "Look. They don't even see that man. How is this possible? Charlie, I think you are really onto something. We're lucky we got this footage on video. Others need to see this though

I'm confused as to why they don't see him."

Charlie grabbed the phone as it started to ring. Hitting speaker phone, she said, "Hello?"

Clearing his throat before speaking, Carl responded, "Charlie, it's Carl. I've given what you've told me a lot of thought, and I've brought it to my group's attention. And we think you are right. Something weird is going on, and there are a lot of strange things happening. This city is unsafe for anyone. Are you there, Charlie?"

Taking a deep breath, Charlie replied, "Yes, I'm here. Sorry. I was just listening to what you had to say. I agree. This city has become unsafe. It's a scary thing to have to walk anywhere today not knowing why so many people are missing and with bodies showing up out of nowhere. That's why we've been gathering here at our house, so no one has to be alone. Safety is in numbers. Well, I'm hoping we are safer. Oh, I have something new for you to see."

Carl switched the phone to the other ear. "Charlie, I don't think any of us are safe, but together, we are stronger. Your house is only so big, and there are quite a few of us, so maybe we should find somewhere bigger and get all of us together. What do you think?"

Charlie looked over at Julie and then at Jack. "So, what do you have in mind?"

Carl let off a sigh. "I'll have to get back to you on that. I'll text you a location in a bit. Got to run, Charlie. See you later."

When Charlie hung up the phone, she had a puzzled look on her face. "This feels so much more real. Up 'til now, it has been just us, but now we are a group. This is how it has to be, guys. We have to go with the flow. We all know something is happening that is out of our control. We see the dangers that are facing us. Maybe as a group we can do something about it. What do you guys think about moving to a bigger place? I know he's right about us all being together, but I feel safer at home."

Jack sat up and looked at Charlie, "I feel safe here too, but this is something that is not going to go away by hiding in the house. I think if we all stand together as a group, we have a bigger chance of figuring out how to end this. This way, we at least know who the good guys are." Everyone nodded.

Charlie leaned back in her chair. "Yeah, okay. That makes sense. So, we agree that when Carl finds a bigger place, we'll lock this place up and go there 'til we figure out how to make this city safe again."

Julie jumped up and joined in, "Well, we have a few things to do before any of this happens. The proof we have needs to be gathered and put together in a folder. We need to pack some food and an overnight bag to take with us. I don't think we need more than that."

Charlie grabbed her cigarettes and headed to the patio. "I'll grab a box and pack some of the groceries as soon as I have a smoke." Shutting the door behind her, she went and leaned against the railing. The day was gray, yet the skies were dry. She was thankful that it wasn't pouring. Sometimes it could rain for weeks in Richmond. Looking around, she realized just how all the violence had taken a toll on the city. How could the police not have any idea as to what was happening? She wondered if any of them could see the shapeshifters. Then she thought, 'What if they are among the police too?' Putting out her smoke, she went returned to the kitchen, grabbing a box on the way. "Jack, so far we know the shifters are involved in business and government, but what if they are part of the

58

police force too? Maybe that's why they haven't gotten a suspect. They wouldn't arrest one of their own. Would they?"

Jack was at the table sorting through the paperwork. She could hear him mumbling under his breath. Finally looking up at her, he uttered, "Yes, Charlie. That is possible, and it would explain why there's no one being questioned."

Charlie sorted through the fridge, looking for stuff that would expire. "We need to speak to Loretta and see what she knows, and if she's noticed anything strange about the police that she works with."

Reaching into her pocket, Charlie pulled out her phone. She had felt it vibrating while she was digging in the fridge, which usually meant she had a text waiting. It was a text from Carl: 'Charlie, we found a place. One of my men runs a hotel down by the bridge called the Georgia Hotel. He says business has gotten slow because of everything happening in the city, so he has shut down the business temporarily 'til the city becomes safe again. It has lots of room for everyone—a board room where we can meet and have discussions and a kitchen where we can prepare food. Meet me there. Okay?'

She replied, 'Okay,' then put the phone back in her pocket and continued packing the groceries.

Charlie packed her overnight bag. She didn't need much—just a change of clothes and anything that would be of help to her. She folded her clothes and put them in the bag, grabbed her laptop and a notebook and a few other items, then put them in with the clothes. Looking around, she thought to herself as she zipped up her bag, *I wonder how long this will take? I really do hate leaving home.* She left her bag by the door with the rest of the stuff. Julie had Stormage waiting in his carrier, and Bruno was by the door ready to get in the car. She was thankful there were two cars. They wouldn't be so crowded driving to the Georgia Hotel. Within minutes, the five of them headed towards their final destination.

As they pulled into the parking lot of the hotel, they paused before exiting the car. Charlie leaned forward to look at the hotel. "Well, it's definitely big enough. I'm really nervous about this even though I'm sure this is the right thing."

Jack opened the door and added, "It's like a leap of faith, Charlie. We're all hoping this is the right move, and that we can somehow put an end to all the dangers we face."

The five of them all headed towards the hotel. Surprisingly, they were greeted at the door by Carl. "Glad you made it here safely. Hurry in. I want to keep this place confidential, if at all possible. That way we can remain safe." Carl locked the door behind them and showed them to their rooms. "When you're settled, meet me down at the board room. Oh, and bring the paperwork, if you don't mind."

There were three rooms next to each other on the sixth floor; all were facing the bridge. Charlie took the first with Julie, Jack took the next one, and the two girls took the third. After they let Stormage out of the kennel and Bruno off his leash, the two restless animals took off and started to play. Charlie threw her bag on the dresser next to Julie's. "This isn't too bad; after all, I just need to remember it isn't a vacation." She giggled.

Looking back at the windows, Julie sighed, "I guess Carl figured that we don't have to live poorly to have everyone together, which is nice considering we may be here a while. We have to remember we're not the only ones leaving our home to be with strangers."

After feeding both pets, Charlie flopped onto the bed. It felt nice, although she wished it was a vacation. "Yeah, it's nice that not all of them are strangers though. Franny is here and maybe Loretta will be. Besides, Carl is Franny's husband, so he is only half a stranger."

Julie giggled, "I like the way you see things." Picking up the file and grabbing the keys, both girls walked to the board room.

The room was set up with chairs lined wall to wall. In the front, a board stretched across the room. The curtains were drawn for privacy, and below it lay a table with a large coffee machine set up for those attending the meeting. Carl looked up as the girls entered the room. "If you two would like to hang up the evidence, I would really appreciate it," he said smiling. "We have had a lot of theories up until now. It's nice to have something more concrete; though you must admit, it is a little hard to swallow, even with the proof. It's there in front of us, and we need to have enough faith as individuals and as a group to try to figure this out and put an end to the fear and harm in this city."

As Charlie started to pin up the paperwork, she read the headlines over and over. "Carl," Charlie asked, "Why do you think the cops have not seen anything or don't have any leads? Do you think they are part of this, maybe?"

Carl grabbed some pins and started to help her hang stuff. "They may be, Charlie, but I'm not sure how we can prove it either way."

Stopping, she turned to Carl, "Loretta works there, and I know she isn't part of it. I really think she should be brought into this. She is the coroner and works with them on a regular basis."

Pinning the last of the papers up, Carl turned to Charlie and answered, "That might be a way. Keep it in mind, will you? By the way, what was the new thing you wanted to show me?"

Handing him the camera, she implored, "Check out the last video. I took it this morning." Carl smiled and sat down in a chair to watch the video. Charlie sat next to Julie. "This didn't feel very real before, but it is starting to now." People piled into the room, filling the chairs quickly. Both girls were amazed about the number of people present. Jack walked in with Marcy and Beth. Smiling, they took a seat a few chairs away from them.

Moments later, the room was full. Carl walked to the front, and with his big voice, spoke to the large crowd. "Hello, everyone. I'm happy we are all here and that all of you are safe. I want to start off by thanking Mark Summers for lending us the hotel during these rough times and for having provided us with safety, as we try to figure out what is happening. Some evidence has come to my attention, and I have spoken to a number of you about it. Today, we have it all here for you to have a look at. It is a true eye opener and without it, we would still be blind to the incidents happening in this city. Remember, when you are looking at it, that it is real and very dangerous. To ignore it, would be ignorance on our behalf. So, if you don't mind, please step up in single form and take a look for yourselves. Thank you." Carl stepped aside and sat down next to the girls as the people of the room walked to the board to have a look.

Looking over at Charlie, he inquired, "Did I say thank you to you?"

Looking puzzled, she gazed at Carl. "For what?"

Now crossing his arms, he sighed, "Because we would still be at square one without this information, and that puts us more in harm's way than we need to be."

Resting her hand on his shoulder, she replied, "No need to thank us. Everyone needs to know what's going on, and they all need to open their eyes to reality, as weird as it may be. Like you said, we may not be safer, but we are stronger as a whole."

Just then, Franny, came running over. "Charlie, I am so glad you guys are here. People are shocked with all the new info and want to know how we can deal with it. I never thought shapeshifters were anything but a story. I've never heard anything about them other than that their looks change. What are the chances they are spotted among us? At the same time, all the murders are happening, and people are going missing in such huge numbers. No one thinks it's a coincidence, and neither do I."

Now sitting next to Carl, she placed her hand on her husband's knee and inquired, "Do we have a next move?"

Grabbing his wife's hand, he replied, "No, but I'm sure we'll come up with one. It's something I have to give a lot of thought to." Standing up, Carl yelled out to the crowd of people, "After you're done reading all of it and watching the video, please give it some time to soak in. I have to do some thinking and need to try to figure out what our next step is. I'm open to ideas. The kitchen is open for those who are hungry. Other than that, please stay in your rooms 'til we can figure out a structure that works for everyone. We all have to find a way to pitch in and help, as this is everyone's problem. Some folks have jobs already. If you happen to think of a way you could be of help, please let me know. I'll see you all later." Carl turned towards his room with Franny not far behind him.

Upon entering their room, the girls were greeted with tiny

limbs wrapped around their ankles. Stormage was feeling frisky, and after grabbing their ankles, took off like a bat out of hell to find Bruno, who was flopped on the bed chewing on the strap of Stormage's carrier. Charlie's eyes felt heavy as she flopped down beside him. "You stop chewing that, silly boy." Rolling him over to rub his belly, she looked at Julie. "What do you think I'm good at?" Before Julie could answer, Charlie's eyes closed as she dozed off to sleep. Julie giggled to herself as she pulled out her book and started to read.

Meanwhile, next door, Jack sat at his desk with his laptop open. He wanted to do some more searching, but instead, he sat there staring in the near distance, deep in thought. He was thinking about what life was like before the murders and disappearances and what it was like now. He would have never imagined life would turn out this way. He just hoped it wouldn't stay like this. Changing his mind, he closed his laptop and knocked loudly on the door that connected the two rooms together. Marcy and Beth were in the next room doing their own thing. He yelled, "Are you two okay in there?"

Marcy, a bit startled, yelled back, "Yes, we are fine. Thanks for checking on us." Jack turned and collapsed onto his bed. Reaching over for a pillow to put under his head, he lay there thinking. If Charlie were able to get that footage on video of that man, maybe there was more out there recorded. If not, maybe the group could set up cameras to catch more and keep an eye on things from the hotel. He rolled over onto his side. Maybe after a nap, he would talk to Carl and see what he thought of his idea. Jack shut his eyes. It felt good to fall asleep.

Charlie later woke to a knock on the door. It was Franny. "Charlie, are you there? I brought you something to eat."

Charlie made her way to the door, nearly tripping over Stormage, "I'm here, Franny." She unlocked the door and beckoned, "Come in."

Franny pushed opened the door. "I brought you some food from the kitchen. Made it myself." Placing the plate of sandwiches on the desk, she continued, "Everyone is talking about this. I heard a few of them say that things are finally making sense. They believe in the supernatural. It was just not anything they would have thought of on their own."

Charlie smiled, "Well, it's not really something I thought of on my own either. I had to see it with my own eyes to believe it. Even after hearing the voices for all those years, I never assumed it was supernatural. I'm glad, though, that they understand it better. Wish I did."

Charlie handed Julie one of the sandwiches. "Thanks for these—they are so good. What room are you and Carl in?"

Franny grabbed the empty plate. "Room 209. I'll drop this off in the kitchen on my way back to my room." Before leaving, she looked back and said, "Oh, I saw the video. I couldn't believe it! Either the cops ignored that man or they didn't see him at all. Either way, something is not right." Charlie turned on the television before plopping onto the bed. It was nice to have the distraction, although they seemed to have the shows on a loop lately. It was probably so they could make it home before the curfew, but she guessed with everything going on they were lucky to have entertainment to distract them. Lying on the bed with the remote in her hand, she flipped through the channels and found a movie to keep her busy for a few hours—'til she had to step back into reality.

Jack, who finally awoke after a long sleep, was brushing his teeth when he heard a knock at the door. Laying his toothbrush down and then rinsing his mouth, he quickly opened the door. "Hey, Carl, come on in." Both men walked over to the table by the window and took a seat. "I would offer you a coffee," said Jack, "but I don't exactly have a machine."

Carl laughed, "Yeah, I'm not used to it either. I wanted to speak to you about your experience down by the mayor's office. You say it had your face at first?"

Jack took a deep breath and leaned back. "Yes, it was the strangest thing I had ever seen. It was like looking in the mirror, and I'm sure he saw me. That's probably why time paused while he changed into a woman. If I hadn't seen it with my own eyes, I probably wouldn't have believed it. In my line of work, this is crazy talk." Jack laughed.

Carl leaned forward and put his elbows on the table. Taking a deep breath and with a giant sigh, he continued, "This is so much to take in. I know you guys are not crazy. Some of my men have seen some weird stuff and have been too fearful to come forward less they be seen as crazy, but, damn! How does one take this all in?"

Jack nodded, "I totally understand you. What do you do for a living?"

Carl looked at Jack. "I do construction for Morrisons."

Jack sat up straight and looked him in the eyes. "What if we set up traps for them? We can set up video cams in different places and set up a video in the board room to follow it. Who knows what we'll see or catch? Maybe that way we can see who is who. I think we can also get one set up in the police station too if we are careful. My ex-girlfriend is the coroner there."

Carl sat up, seeming very interested in what Jack had to say. "That's a great idea. I can grab the cams and video and set up today. Can you contact your ex and see if she wants to be a part of this?"

Jack nodded, "Yes, I'll do it later. We should set up a cam by the wharf, by the mayor's office, downtown on Main Street, and maybe the in the square too."

Getting up from the table, Carl looked over at Jack. "It's a plan. Tomorrow morning, we'll put it to use. Let me know what your ex says." Heading to the door Jack heard him mumble, "See you later, Jack."

Pulling out his phone, Jack looked up Loretta's number. It had been months since they spoke, but they were not on bad terms. Sending her a text, he wrote: Loretta, it's Jack. I need to see you as soon as possible. We need to talk about what's happening in the city. Meet me at the Georgia Hotel. I'll be waiting out front at about 3 p.m. Putting the phone aside, he looked out the window. The city still had so much life in it, but it made him wonder how much of that life was lived by shapeshifters? It was hard to know who was who. If he could see someone look just like him and then like someone else the next minute, how could he ever trust that he knew who he was speaking to.

The phone buzzed. It was a text from Loretta: Hi Jack. Yes, I'll meet you there at 3. I'm glad you messaged me.

Jack quickly sent her a message: Okay. See you then.

Jack sat on the ledge next to the window of the hotel at 3:00. It was nice out. There was a refreshing breeze coming in from the ocean. Loretta pulled into the parking lot. Giving a small wave to Jack, she jumped out of the car walked towards him. "Hey, Jack! Beautiful day, isn't it? Why are we meeting here? How come not your house?"

Jack looked at Loretta as she took a seat next to him. She

was as graceful as ever. "I'm not staying there for now with everything going on. Matter of fact, a lot of people are not staying in their homes. Can I trust you with some information?" Loretta nodded as a serious look spread over her face. Jack took her hand. "We may not be together, but I consider you my friend. Or, at least I hope we are friends. You know all the deaths you deal with on a daily basis and all the missing people? Well, we have information about that." Loretta's body posture changed as she sat up straight, listening to what he had to say. "Not just me, but many others have seen something. It may be a little hard to believe, but it is very true. I have proof, so please believe me when I tell you there are shapeshifters among us."

Loretta's mouth fell open. She was quiet at first, but after a few minutes, she took a deep breath and asked, "You say you have proof? Can I see it?"

Jack stood up and pulled her up. "Yes. I was hoping you would ask."

Both walked into the hotel, past security and to the board room. Carl was sitting at the table pulling out video equipment. Taking a moment to look up, he asked, "Is that the ex?"

Jack nodded, "Yes, this is Lorretta. Lorretta, this is Carl." Loretta smiled at him before turning her head to the board. She stood there for the longest time looking through everything. Jack took the time to talk to Carl while Loretta absorbed the information. "So, these are the cams that we're going to put up around the city?"

Carl nodded, "Yup. Just have to figure how to install them without being seen."

Lorretta looked over at the guys. "Wow! How did I miss all

this?"

Carl looked over at her. "There is more. Look at the video on that camera."

She took the camera and sat at the table where she could watch the video. It took about thirty minutes, but when she finished, her mouth fell open, as if she were in shock. "I'm not sure what to think of this—all of this. I work with them every day. Either they are involved, or they didn't see that guy." Looking up at both Carl and Jack, she asked, "What do we do?"

Jack lay his hand on her shoulder. "It will sink in, but meanwhile, it's better you know so you can keep safe. Maybe you can help us."

Sitting up, she lay the camera onto the table. "How can I help?"

Laying his hand in front of himself, he responded, "We're going to put up cams all over the city, and we would like to put one in the police station. We need to make sure there are none amongst us, and that folks coming in are who they say they are."

Loretta nodded, "I can help you there. Half the time, the force is out on the road, and I'm there all alone. It would have to be small though, one they wouldn't notice."

Carl nodded, "I think we can do that."

After a long discussion, Jack walked Loretta to the door. "Thanks for all your help," he said politely. "You know, you can stay here if you want. It would be safer for you to be in a group."

Loretta sighed, "I have to be there in the middle of it all, and after finding out what I now know, I'm not sure I want to be. I have to be, though, but I think tomorrow after work,

I'll grab my stuff and join you guys here. I'll have to keep an appearance up at work for a bit just to keep an eye on things." Reaching over she hugged Jack, then turned and went to her car. "Later, Jack." He felt that they had made progress, and, for the first time, felt like they had the advantage.

Carl was still sitting at the table. Larzo sat at the table with him. Larzo was his runner, one who helps find what the group needs. Of course, Larzo had his own group who did what he needed, always following the line of command. Carl looked up at Jack, "This is Larzo. He is my main man. He can find anything we need." Jack reached out his hand to shake Larzo's hand, but noticed he looked puzzled.

Larzo looked over at Jack, "I've been all over the city and not once did I ever see anything like what was on that board. How could I miss something like that?" Jack sat down and explained. He tried to ease Larzo's mind, but deep inside, he felt the same way. The three spoke for a while about what needed to be done, then went to their rooms.

After a long night, Charlie and Julie headed down to the board room and found both Carl and Jack working hard to set up the video equipment. Jack had Loretta on the phone trying to get the camera just right. She managed to get it right in the main part of the station in the middle of an old bookcase that they hadn't stopped to notice in years. Loretta walked across the floor and waved. "How about now? Do you have a good visual?"

Jack looked over at the camera. "Yes, that's perfect."

Loretta looked around. "I have to go. I think I heard someone coming."

Jack hung up and put his phone away. Looking up at the girls, he said, "Morning. We'll fill you in after we finish."

Carl looked at Jack. "Another one is complete."

The girls turned towards the kitchen. Charlie shook her head, "It's too early to try to understand any of that. All I know is he's been busy with Carl all night and then again, this morning. They must have figured out something."

Julie smiled, "Good. Maybe we'll get to go home soon. Until then, we need to find something to do around here to pitch in. I can't handle another minute of sitting around waiting."

Franny was at the counter in the kitchen. She was cutting up vegetables for soup. "Morning. I'm making soup tonight."

Julie smiled, "Do you want some help?"

Franny paused, "You know, that would be great! How about you finish dicing while I start cooking the meat?" Julie was pleased that she found a way to keep busy and help the group. Charlie grabbed a coffee and headed back to the room to see Bruno and Stormage. Thank goodness, the room was a decent size. It made it easy for the two to run around and wrestle without harming themselves. Charlie filled their bowls and changed the pee pad she had laid down for the puppy. She wished she could take Bruno out but knew it was not safe. *Maybe soon,* she thought. Flopping down onto the bed, she lay thinking about the first thing she would do when the city was deemed safe again. *Hmmm, maybe I'll go to the café and write. Well, after I walk Bruno, that is.* She laughed to herself.

Chapter 5

Two long days passed by. Charlie was at the point of not knowing what to do with herself. A lot had happened over the past two days. Cameras were set up all over the city. Luckily, some of the group members had shops, which made it easy to put up a camera that would monitor the streets and the areas surrounding them. Areas like the square and the mayor's office and surrounding spots were a bit harder, but they managed to get a few up in those public spaces. Places like the supermarket and the hardware store were easy since the owners were involved. This way they had an idea of how safe it was to do a food run. Julie had found her niche in the kitchen with Franny, and Jack was busy with Carl pulling the plan together. Marcy and Beth helped keep things organized, so that it was easier to keep their heads where they needed to be. Charlie was frazzled and frustrated by now, with nothing to do. She had done nothing but eat, sleep, and laze around the last two days.

Throwing her slippers on, she went down to the board room. This was it. She was going out of her mind with boredom. As she entered the room, she noticed one end was set up for monitoring videos, and as she got closer, she started to recognize all the places she was seeing. "What is this?" she asked, perplexed.

Jack looked up and answered, "Oh, hey there! We now have visuals all over the city."

Carl poked his head out from under the table where he had been securing all the cords. "Oh, hey there, Charlie. Don't go anywhere. I need to have a word with you. I have an important task just for you."

Charlie, feeling a little puzzled but excited at the same time, suddenly felt relieved. Pulling out a chair, she sat down next to Jack. "This is cool. Who knows what we'll see on here?"

Carl sat down next to her. "Do you know how to work all this stuff?"

Looking at him, Charlie grinned, "Isn't this just simple computer stuff?" Both guys started to laugh.

Carl put his hand on her shoulder. "Yes, it sure is. I'm putting you in charge of monitoring it, and while you are doing that, you can train some of my men and women how to spot these shapeshifters. Are you okay with that?"

Charlie took a deep breath. She finally had a job, and this one she was good at. "Yes, I'd love to do that."

Patting her shoulder, Carl got up from the chair. "Okay then, if you don't mind, I'll leave you two in charge of this for a bit".

Carl left the room. Upon bumping into Larzo in the hall, he said, "Great job on getting it all set up. Do me a favor and thank your guys for me. Will you?" He then turned and continued down the hall.

Charlie got comfortable in her chair. There was so much to watch. Quickly glancing over at Jack, she smiled and said, "Thought I was going to go crazy with nothing to do. Was this your idea?"

Jack smiled, "Yup. I came up with it a few nights ago, and it was actually your idea, if I am truthful. You captured that guy on camera, and it was great evidence, so I thought it would be a great idea if we set up cameras everywhere. It would help us see what we would normally miss. I'm sure this will prove beneficial." Jack pointed to the top left screen. "Look. Loretta set one up in the police station, and this one next to it is her personal one. It's a pen in one of her pockets. I thought that was brilliant. Don't you?" Charlie was enthralled. She gave a quick nod and kept trying to find a way to keep her eyes on every single one. "Want a coffee?" Jack asked.

Charlie mumbled, "Yes, please, and a cookie if there is one." Jack giggled and headed to the kitchen. He was a bit tired from all the work they just did, but he felt extremely proud. As he entered the kitchen, he could hear humming. Peeking around the corner, he saw Julie. It was nice to see her so relaxed. She was like the mother bird always trying to take care of everyone, and he knew she carried everyone's stress inside.

Sneaking into the kitchen, he filled two cups with coffee. Julie turned around fast, "Oh, you startled me."

Jack giggled, "I didn't mean to. I was trying not to disturb you."

Julie grabbed one of the cups. "Is this for Charlie? If so, she needs cream and sugar in it. Oh, and I made you guys a sandwich."

Jack smiled, "Thanks. Oh, and she wants cookies with her coffee. Are there any?" Julie reached into the cupboard and pulled out some cookies. Placing a few on the plate, she smiled. Jack went out the door but not without turning around just in time to see Julie humming and dancing once again.

Jack was walking down the hall towards the board room, when he noticed Marcy coming the other way. She waved at him. "Hi. I was just walking by the board room, and I noticed the set-up you guys have. That's going to come in handy, don't you think?"

Jack grinned, "That's what I'm hoping for." Smiling, he continued to the board room, happy that this idea was a success.

Charlie was deep in thought as he laid the food tray down next to her. Startled, she looked up and exclaimed, "Oh! Hi. Glad you're back." Jack sat down next to her and got comfortable. After all, this was their spot for the rest of the day.

"Julie made sure you got lots of cookies. Have you seen her lately? She is relaxed when she's working in the kitchen."

Charlie glanced over at Jack as she grabbed a cookie. "She's always loved the kitchen." Before Charlie could say another word, something caught her eye. It was Loretta's private camera. She was speaking to someone. Charlie watched closely. It was Police Chief Bob Marshall. Or was it? Charlie sat up straight and started hitting Jack's arm to get his attention. Pointing to the screen, she blurted, "Jack, look!" The Chief's eyes were flickering silver ever so slightly but enough that both Charlie and Jack didn't miss it. "Oh, my God! I don't think she sees it, Jack."

Jack refused to look away. "No. She doesn't, and let's keep it that way. She's safer not knowing right now."

Charlie jotted down on paper the track number and the time slot on the video and put it aside for Carl and the others to see. "I wasn't expecting to see that, but it explains a lot."

A few hours had passed since the two had been monitoring

the screens. They saw a few things and recorded them on paper, so they could keep track of their findings, but so far, they had not recognized any other faces. They had screenshots though, so

even if they didn't recognize them personally, they would still have a picture of their faces. As the printer slowly spit out the pictures, Charlie turned around just in time to catch Carl walking by. "Carl!" she yelled. Ducking back to look in the room, Carl's eyes widened. "There's something you've got to see!" said Charlie excitedly.

Carl hurried over to the table. "Did you see something?"

Jack picked up the pieces of paper and handed them to Carl. "Have a look. Oh, and there's something you have to see on video."

When he turned on the video of the police chief, Carl's jaw hit the floor. Pulling out a chair, he sat down. "Can you play it again? This time, pause it when you hit that spot. I need a better look." Leaning back, he put his finger against his lip. It was going to take more than a moment to absorb this one. The police chief was, in fact, a shapeshifter, and this time he saw it with his own eyes. "This is more than serious. The main guy who keeps our city safe is one of them. They run our city and if they want to take us out, no one would ever know. Does Loretta know yet?"

Jack shook his head no. "Not sure it would be wise to tell her. As long as she doesn't know, they won't have any idea that we know. Besides, if she knew, I'm not sure that her poker face would get by without being detected."

Carl nodded. "I agree. Let's keep her safe. We'll just keep our eyes on her in case she needs us. I wish there was a way to find out if there have been any witnesses to any of this. I figure there has to be a list at the police station, but I don't know how we would ever get our hands on it, especially now that we know the chief is in on it."

Jack picked up his phone to text Loretta: 'Hey, I know it would be hard, but is there any chance of finding out if there is a list of witnesses to anything that has been happening in this city?' Jack looked up at Carl. "We'll find out in a moment. I just messaged her to see if it's possible."

Minutes later, the phone started beeping, Jack opened the message. 'Yeah, I can have a look, but I would need someone to distract them, so I didn't get caught. Any ideas?' Jack took a second to think to himself, then messaged her back: I'm not sure who yet, but I will send a distractor your way soon. Laying the phone down, he looked at Carl. "Who do we have that can distract the police at the station while Loretta looks for that list?"

Carl took a second before answering. "How about Julie? She is level headed, smart and a looker. She could distract the men in blue."

Jack hesitated for a second. "I don't know about sending her. I would never forgive myself if anything ever happened while she was there. Although I do understand why you chose her, maybe we can ask her, and if she is comfortable with it, we'll send her."

Carl stood up and headed out in search for Julie. After a lengthy search, he found her in her room. "Julie, I was wondering if we could talk."

Smiling, she let him in. "What's up?"

Carl looked Julie in the eyes. "I need a favor, and you can say no if you're not comfortable with it. Loretta is in need of a distraction at the station. She needs to get into the main computer and copy an important file for us. Do you think you are capable of drawing everyone's attention?"

Julie took a deep breath. "Okay. Maybe. I can have my car break down in front of the station by pulling a few plugs?"

Carl was intrigued. "That sounds like a great idea. We'll have our eyes on you at all times. We need this done as soon as possible. Oh, and please be careful."

Julie pulled up to the station. She wasn't exactly sure what was going on, but she knew she was doing it for a good reason. Jack had planted a mini camera on her before she left, so she knew she was safe. After popping the hood, she peered into the front of the car. She reached down and gave one of the plugs a tug, causing it to separate. *There, that should do it,* she thought to herself. Shutting the hood, she walked in the station door. Jack and the others sat in front of the monitor watching every move Julie made. On the other monitor, they watched Loretta. The room was quiet. No one wanted to miss anything.

Julie walked up to the counter. The officer looked up at her and smiled. "Hi. Can I help you?"

Julie smiled back. "I hope you can. My car died, but lucky for me, it was just outside the station. I have no idea what's wrong with it. Is there any chance you can take a look at it for me?"

The officer looked at her. Then laid down his pen. "Okay. Give me just a second. I'll meet you out there." Julie glanced over at Loretta then turned and walked back to her car.

A few minutes later, two officers came outside and walked towards the car. This gave Loretta a chance to get what she needed off the computer. One officer popped the hood and took a look while the other stood there talking to Julie.

Resting his hand on her shoulder, he asked her. "Where were you going before it broke down?" Julie felt flushed and dizzy. Leaning back against the car, her mind suddenly drifted; she was experiencing a flashback. There was a temple before her and a man with silver eyes. He was wearing the same symbol she saw on the guy in the square. Julie started to shake, and when she came out of it, she looked up at the officer. His eyes flashed silver at her. She knew she was in trouble.

Jack leaned forward. His eyes got big. "I think she's in trouble. Did you see that?" He watched as the officer leaned into Julie's face, grabbing both her shoulders. Then the screen went blank. "Oh my god! Where did she go?" The whole room gasped and started yelling, "Where is she?"

Jack turned and looked at Carl, who stood there covering his mouth. "Carl, who was that officer with her? Do you recognize him? Does anyone have any ideas about what we just saw?"

Jack's phone started to buzz. It was Loretta texting him: Thanks, Jack. I got what you needed.

Jack wrote back: Something happened to Julie. Can you look around and see if you can find her? Within seconds, Loretta replied sure no problem.. Jack laid the phone on the table and turned to talk to Carl. "I shouldn't have let her go. I should have gone."

Carl laid his hand on Jack's arm. "Calm down. Getting upset is not going to help her. We'll figure this out. How long before the curfew?"

Charlie looked at her watch. "It's 5:47. We have an hour and thirteen minutes left."

Carl turned and looked at Larzo. "Go to the station and look for her. Don't go alone. It's not safe." Larzo nodded and headed out the door. Charlie continued to watch Loretta's video feed, knowing that whatever Loretta saw, she would too.

Loretta looked around to see if Julie was anywhere in sight. She walked up to Officer Johnson. "Did I see my friend Julie pop in here earlier?"

He looked up at her and replied, "No, I don't think so. It's been pretty quiet all day."

Loretta bit her lip. "Oh. Okay. My mistake. Well, if you guys are done with me for the night, I'm going home. I would like to get there before the curfew."

Picking up her purse, she went out to the parking lot. As she got in her truck, she looked around, hoping to see Julie's car. Loretta leaned against her truck and thought to herself, *There's more going on than Jack told me.* As she opened her door, she noticed Larzo and a buddy walking through the parking lot. She gave him a little wave to get his attention. He hurried over to her truck, "Did you see her?"

Loretta shook her head no. "I'm not sure what's going on, guys, but I need to know."

Larzo nodded, "Yes, you do, but not here. I don't see any trace that she has even been here. Have you seen her car?"

Loretta took a deep breath and opened the door of her truck. "Nope. I took a look around, and I if I hadn't seen her here with my own eyes, I would say she hasn't ever been here. I'm going back to speak to Jack. Be careful, guys." Shutting the door behind herself, she headed back to the hotel. Larzo and his buddy took one more look around before doing the same.

Meanwhile, back at the hotel, Charlie was freaking out. She had quit watching the video feed and went to her room, but not before giving both Jack and Carl looks of death.

After entering her room, she walked over to the window and reached down and gave Bruno a scratch as she walked by. She leaned against the window sill and began thinking to herself, *My best friend is gone. What am I going to do now? Julie is my lifeline and I am hers. I wasn't with her, and now she is missing.*

Jack stood knocking at the door. He felt guilty enough sending Julie into such a dangerous situation and didn't need Charlie mad at him too. Charlie opened the door then turned and walked away. "Charlie, wait," said Jack. "I had no idea anything like this was going to happen. I mean, how could I? This is all new to me too."

Charlie looked over at Jack. "I know, but she is my best friend, and now she is gone. What am I going to do without her, Jack?"

Jack hugged Charlie. "I feel the same. We will do everything we can to find her. I promise." Jack pulled out a chair. Quietly, he mumbled to himself as he sat down. Looking at Charlie, he mumbled, "This is getting so complicated. One day we were living pretty normally and then all of this happened. I was just getting used to the fact that something weird was going on. It never really got to sink in. Now it's just scary. I never imagined how dangerous this whole situation was. I thought there was a psycho roaming the streets at night, killing a lot of people."

Charlie sat next to Jack. "I don't think anyone could have imagined it. I mean seriously—shapeshifters? They are supernatural creatures and are not even supposed to be real."

Jack let out a nervous laugh. "Yeah, I still have trouble even saying it."

Loretta knocked at the door. "You there, Charlie?" After hearing Charlie yelled for her to come in, Loretta stepped into the room and walked straight to the table where the two sat. "What the hell is going on, guys? I feel like I missed something today." Loretta pulled out a chair and took a seat. "Tell me that Julie is not really gone."

Placing his hand on Loretta's shoulder, Jack looked her in the eyes. "I wish I could tell you that was true, but I can't. We're not exactly sure what happened, although there is a factor or two you should know." Loretta sat up straight, feeling a little worried. Jack took a deep breath. "We saw on the monitor that the chief of police is, in fact, one of them."

Loretta's eyes got big. "Are you kidding me?"

Shaking his head, Jack replied, "No, I wish I was. We have it on tape. His eyes turned silver. This is while he was speaking to you. The others that were on duty are also a part of this. One cop laid his hands on Julie's shoulders and then suddenly, her camera stopped working. Now we can't find her or her car."

Loretta looked over at Charlie, who sat there quietly listening. "You okay? This has to be hard on you, with your best friend missing."

Charlie turned and looked out the window. "I'll be fine. We're going to find her. We're not going to stop 'til she's home."

Loretta got up from the table. "It's good to know someone has faith that there will be a positive outcome. I am with you on this. I won't give up either and, furthermore, I'm not going back to that job as long as there are shapeshifters involved. You guys hungry? I'm thinking of going to the kitchen to get some dinner."

Jack nodded, "Yeah, I think we'll join you." Tugging on Charlie's arm to help her up, the three went down for dinner.

Later that evening, the group gathered in the board room. Carl stood up in the front. "Can I have everyone's attention, please? I want to fill you all in about what has happened. Today we discovered that the police department is involved. The police chief is indeed one of them. Officer Johnson and his partner are also suspected to be a part of this. We know that he had something to do with Julie's disappearance. This information has been captured on video feed, and if you would like, you can view it after the meeting. Also, we now have a list of witnesses to events that have occurred throughout the city. Unfortunately, these witnesses have gone missing. My guess is that they could identify someone, so they had them removed. This is past serious, folks. Something needs to be done about it before it goes any further. So, if you have any ideas, don't hesitate to come forward and let me know. Thank you all for coming. We'll talk more later."

Carl walked over to Charlie as the crowd of people started to chatter about the new known facts. "I want you to know we are not giving up on finding Julie. We just need to figure out what happened. Did you get a chance to read the list Loretta brought us?"

Charlie shook her head no. "Is there anything useful on it?"

Carl laid his hand on her shoulder and leaned forward, just a little. "One lady watched her friend disappear after a guy in a suit grabbed her. She said it was like he never even saw her. There also was a homeless man who watched a dead body appear out of nowhere and land in front of him. One man swears that there are no bodies in the graves—that it is some kind of mind trick. If I didn't know what I know now, I would have never believed it." Shaking his head, Carl turned towards the door. "We will figure it out, Charlie. I promise."

Charlie and Jack went back up to the room. Jack sat at the table while Charlie cleaned up and fed the pets. Bruno was happy to see her but wasn't his normal bouncy self. How could he be, locked up in a hotel room? Stormage was stretched out on the bed, as if he didn't have a care in the world. Charlie reached down and rubbed him behind the ears. It must be nice not to worry about everything. "Jack, do you think life will ever be normal again?"

Jack leaned on his elbow and looked at Charlie. "I really don't know. I definitely hope so, but at this point, I'm not sure that things will ever be normal again."

Charlie sat down next to him. Pulling her legs up on the chair and tucking her knees under her chin, she said, "I feel a little numb. My heart is sad, but my mind won't let go of the idea that Julie is out there waiting for us to find her. I want to go back to when life was normal, when I would walk Bruno every day and go for coffee while I worked. I miss clubbing in the evenings and going to art class. I don't even sketch anymore. I just don't feel it."

Jack gazed over at her, "Don't give up hope, Charlie. I believe that whatever is happening will play out in our favor, or at least I hope it will."

Charlie picked up a smoke. "Do you mind? I really don't want to run downstairs to have this."

Jack pushed the ashtray towards her and opened the window. "You go ahead. I need to make a phone call. I want to check out the hospital, just in case, and see if those people were checked in as mental patients."

"Richmond Psychiatric Department, Cathy speaking."

Jack leaned back in his chair. "Hi, Cathy. This is Jack Davenport. I work at West Sides Mental Health Building.

I was wondering if you could do me a favor. I would like to know if a few people I know are in your department."

Cathy grabbed her keyboard. "Okay, give me their names." After Jack gave her the names, she scrolled down the list. "Yes, Dr. Davenport. They are indeed here. Is there anything else I can do for you?"

Jack bit his lip silently, "No, not at the moment. Thank you, Cathy. I'll get back to you if I need anything else. Have a good day," he said as he hung up the phone. Jack got up from his chair. "Found the missing people. I'm going to let Carl know." Charlie got up as Jack walked to the door. "One more mystery solved."

Flopping down on the bed next to Stormage and Bruno, Charlie said quietly, "I might lie down for a bit, or at least try to get my thoughts together."

After Jack dropped by to give Carl the news, Carl and Franny sat at the table together. Franny took Carl's hand and said, "They look up to you. You're the smartest guy I know. I want you to know I believe in you."

Carl smiled at his wife, "I know you do. You're always there right by my side. Now that we know where these people are, do we actually need them, or should we leave them there where they are somewhat safe? My thoughts are, and this is just my opinion, but what if we took them out and the ones who put them their notice? That could be dangerous for us. The shapeshifters might realize they are not a secret anymore, and they would come after us."

Franny felt worried. "You're right. That could be a huge issue. I think we should keep them there. At least we know where they are for the time being."

Carl took out his phone and sent Jack a quick text: Jack, I

think it would be smart to keep the people who are patients in the hospital. We don't want to alert the shifters that we are onto them. This way they will remain safe, and it gives us time. Carl and put his phone back into his pocket. "That should take care of that. We have to come up with a plan to get rid of them. It really is them or us."

Franny nodded and sat twirling her hair. "I know you're right, and I will support whatever you come up with. Have you heard back from any of the other groups?"

Carl shook his head. "No. Not yet. I put an ad on Craig's list to inform them of what has happened. Maybe it's time for another one." Carl grabbed his phone and opened Craig's list. He started to make a new ad. He always wrote in code so only the right people knew what it said: *Uncle Carl looking for worker ants to help clean up a mess. Contact right away through text, 514-276-3389.* Throwing his phone on the table, Carl added, "Let's hope that gets their attention. I've only used the newspaper method a few times. Some of the groups feel the cell phones are not safe enough. Personally, I don't agree. If it wasn't safe, they would be onto us by now." Carl placed his phone on the table next to his bed. Adjusting his pillow behind his head, he turned the television on, hoping to find something to watch. He checked his watch for the time. It was still early, so he was hoping that there was something other than reruns on. Franny lay next to him. As she snuggled up close, her eyes began to shut. This was a good thing, considering how hard it had been to get any sleep lately due to all the stress.

Jack tossed and turned on the bed. No words could take away or describe what he felt inside. The guilt in his heart over sending Julie out to do what he should have done ate at him even though there was nothing he could do now. He thought about the whole situation—the sketches, the voices, and all the evidence they had pulled together. *This all started with Charlie,* he thought to himself. *She is the reason we are alive and safe.* He lay there and smiled at that thought. Maybe tomorrow he would try to do something nice for her, see if he could brighten her world just a little bit. Pulling the blanket up close to his face, he slowly dozed off.

Chapter 6

Carl woke up to his phone beeping. After opening it, he noticed that quite a few texts had been sent to him. Sitting up, he leaned against the wall. He smiled at Franny, who lay sleeping next to him. Upon opening the texts, he noticed that they all were very similar: They are here. Too many of us have seen them. What do we do? Carl sent a group text, making sure not to exclude anyone: Please wait to hear from me. I'm working on a plan. Hopefully, it won't be long. Carl took a breath and laid the phone on the table next to him. He knew in his heart what needed to be done, but this was a huge move and a lot to ask of his men. Leaving Franny to sleep, he headed to the shower. He would gather the group later and form a plan to end this situation. Then, maybe, they could all go back to living life as they once knew it.

Charlie stood looking out the window. The sun was up, and the sky looked so peaceful. *How deceiving,* she thought as she turned and headed to the door and towards the kitchen. As she entered the kitchen, she noticed Beth was already there. "Good morning, Beth. Any coffee on?"

Beth smiled. "Sure is. We must think alike."

She laughed as she took a drink from her cup. Charlie

poured herself a cup. "Anyone else up?"

Beth shook her head no. "I don't think so, or at least I haven't seen anyone."

Both girls grabbed a chair at the table. Charlie reached up and rubbed her neck. She felt a little stiff from tossing and turning all night. "I heard there's a meeting today. Do you know anything about it?"

Beth laid her cup on the table. "No. I see the head guys whispering though. Franny says they're just trying to figure things out, using each other as sounding boards. I can understand that there's no need to worry anyone any more than they already are. I've been keeping busy with a few others, keeping this place clean. Can't think right in a dirty place. At least that's what my mama used to tell me, and she was usually right.

Charlie laughed, "Aren't they all?"

Carl walked into the kitchen. "Morning, girls." Pouring himself a cup of coffee, he glanced over at Charlie. "I need you to go through and make sure we have IDs on all the photos we have gotten off the video feed. I want to know where each and every shifter is out there and who we need to deal with."

Charlie nodded, "Sure thing. I'll get to that right away. Have we come up with a plan to fix the whole situation?"

Carl smirked. "I sure hope so, but it's like anything else. It requires planning, and, without the pictures, we have nowhere to start. Oh, and let Bruno out of that small room, will you? Others are letting their pups run around the hotel. I don't see any reason for him to be locked up."

Charlie smiled, "I'm glad to hear that. Poor little guy needs to run around and play." Finishing up her cup of coffee, she set the cup on the table. "Okay. Well, I'm going to let Bruno out and head to the monitoring station to get the photos required. I will talk to both of you later." Charlie quickly walked out the door.

Charlie cleaned up the room and fed the pets. "You want to go have some fun today, boy?" Bruno wagged his tail and licked Charlie's face. All of them headed down the hall. Bruno ran ahead, then ran back to her. He jumped and wiggled as they walked to the board room. Stormage sleeked down the hall like a black ninja. Pulling out a chair, she sat and stared at the monitors. Stormage rubbed against her legs before jumping up on the window sill. She thought about all that had happened and then about Julie—where she was and if she was okay. Her eyes teared up. Feeling helpless, she started gathering pictures of the shapeshifters. She had hoped that whatever the plan was, it would be done quickly, and that Julie would be found. But, in the end if she wasn't, she realized that they didn't lose her for nothing. Bruno was running up and down the hall with the other pets left roaming. Charlie giggled. It was nice to hear the playful sounds of those so innocent.

Moments later, Larzo ran up the hall. Poking his head in, he asked, "Have you seen Carl?"

Charlie turned and looked at him. "I last saw him in the kitchen having coffee. Is everything okay?"

Larzo took a breath. "No. Worse than it was. Now that you pointed it out, it's kind of hard to miss those things." Turning to leave, his body shivered as he mumbled, "It gives me the heebie-jeebies." Taking a deep breath, Charlie turned around to finish what she had started. She wondered if this would be over soon. She started daydreaming of walking through the park, with squirrels running up the trees and Bruno barking and having fun on a nice sunny day. She longed for those days again.

Jack entered the board room carrying a cup of coffee. "Brought you a coffee. I even remembered your cream and sugar."

Charlie swung around. "Oh. Wow! Thanks. You must have known I needed one."

Jack sat next to her. "I wanted to do something nice for you. I feel we're safe because of you. We could all be sitting out there clueless and have huge targets painted on our foreheads."

Charlie turned to Jack. "Yeah. But now we're sitting in a hotel doing nothing to stop it. We stopped living. Something needs to happen. I want my life back. What about you? Don't you miss it?"

Jack chuckled to himself. "I feel as if I took life for granted before. I should have taken advantage of the small things like smelling the roses or having that morning coffee somewhere relaxing long before I hit the office. Now our lives have changed, and I miss the little things, along with the obvious." Jack opened the window. "Best let some air in; it's a beautiful day out there." Pushing his chair away from the table, Jack jumped up and headed towards the door. "I need to find Carl. I'll talk to you later." Charlie smiled and turned back to the monitors. She had the pictures all together for Carl, but it was important to still watch and make sure they didn't spot any more shifters out there. Scanning each and every monitor, she thought to herself, *How do we get our lives back?* Taking a deep breath and then releasing it, she went to her room, but first stopped briefly to drop the pictures off to Carl.

Larzo darted throughout the building, letting everyone know about the meeting that Carl set up. People started filling up the board room, wondering aloud what it might be about. Jack scurried over to where Charlie sat. "This is it, Charlie. I think Carl has come up with a plan to take us home." Sitting next to her and smiling, he added, "Maybe by next week, you will be walking through the park with Bruno."

Charlie had a serious look on her face, as if in deep thought. *Or maybe next week, we will all be missing or worse yet, dead,* she thought. Looking up at Jack, she replied, "Sorry, I'm having a brief moment of doubt. One minute I see us home and living a normal life, but the next minute, I start feeling like life will never be the same … that we are missing something. What can we be missing? I've sat there watching them, and I guarantee you, we're not getting all the information we need."

Jack patted her knee. "You may be right, but I'm sure Carl has hatched a plan that will get us all home."

Charlie smiled. "You're so full of faith. Maybe you should direct your faith a little higher." Carl walked into the room. Heads started to rise, and the chatter got silent. Charlie sat up straight, desperate to find out what this meeting was all about.

"Evening, folks. So glad all of you could join me here tonight. We have a lot to discuss. I have come up with a plan that will hopefully not only get each and every one of us home but will make this city safe once again. Everyone here has been a huge help in keeping things in order, and I thank each and every one of you for that. We've been watching the government for a long time, and we knew something was up, but didn't know exactly what. Lately, we've learned a lot more. We now know we cannot trust the government or the police anymore. We have proof that the shapeshifters have been running this city. How long have they been in charge? I cannot tell you that, but we need to put an end to it no matter what. I won't ask anything from you that I'm not asking of myself, but it's time to put an end to this situation. Who agrees with me?" Everyone in the room cheered and clapped.

Carl took a deep breath as he continued sharing his plan. "I've gone over everything that we know and replayed everything that we saw over and over in my head, and the only thing I can come up with is that there has to be an elimination. We need to assassinate these creatures, in hopes that this will put an end to the murders taking place. When they are gone, maybe then we can take control and start searching for the missing people. The only way to get our lives back is to take them back."

Mark raised his hand. "So, what are we going to do, just walk up to them and shoot them?"

Carl raised his eyebrows. "Yeah, but with a bit of skill. Do you have a better idea?"

Mark shook his head no, "Not really," he said. "I just wanted to be clear on the plan."

The room started to buzz with whispers. "Quiet!" Carl shouted. "This is quite serious. If you cannot handle it, please exit the room." The room got quiet. "I don't like it any more than you do, but I will be the first to say I want my life back, and I will commit to this."

A hand popped up in the back of the room. "What about the consequences? "Won't we go to jail?"

Carl took a deep breath. "I am not sure what will happen. All I know is the police haven't been investigating any of the murders that have taken place since there have been mass murders. Maybe if we make it look like it was done the same way, they won't investigate. My concern though is what if we don't do anything, and we continue to let others die or go missing? Isn't it our right to fight for our country? Did Julie go missing for nothing? Shouldn't it be for a reason, at least? If it came down to it, and I had to go to jail for shooting the shifters, I would at least know I tried to save this city and get our lives back to what they were."

Franny yelled, "and I would be damn proud of you, honey!"

Carl shook his head with a little chuckle. "No one can be sure of anything at this point, except that they are among us, and that there are murders happening all around us. No one is safe anymore. Do we know if they are dangerous? No. But, it can't be good if they're hiding among us. Can it?"

Marcy raised her hand. "What about those of us who have never held a gun before?"

Carl crossed his arms. "Well, we have a little over a dozen of them and there are a lot more of us. I think we'll have enough experienced shooters, and those of you who don't have experience won't have to worry for the moment. I can't promise this will all turn out as planned, but it's the only thought I have towards solving this problem."

Charlie leaned over and whispered to Jack, "What if they don't die?"

Jack looked at her and tried to reassure her. "Why wouldn't they?"

She looked away quickly. "I don't know. Just what if? It's just a feeling."

Carl looked over at her. "Charlie, will you and Franny please hang up the pictures?" The two girls got up and headed to the board in the front of the room, and as they put them up, Carl continued his talk. "My fingers are crossed, folks. If this works, we'll get to go home, hopefully. An eliminated shifter is not a threat, at least not in my mind." He let out a loud laugh. "I need to send a text. I'll let this sink in while they finish setting up."

Carl leaned against the window. The breeze from outside hit him directly in the face. His eyes shut as he thought to himself, *If only I was out walking in that, or even better, riding my bike. This is all worth it!* He opened his eyes and started to write a text to all the other group leaders: We are working on an assassination plan. It must be done all at once, so no one gets wind of it. It's our city or our lives. I choose us. Let me know your plan!

He tucked his phone away into his pocket and surveyed the crowd with a stern look upon his face. He knew he couldn't let them down. He walked over to the center of the room, and after checking out the board, he turned to the crowd. "These are the faces of the shifters. I need twenty-five volunteers. The rest of you will be excused and will only be brought back into this if we have a specific job for you. Until then, you will go back to your regular duties. Any volunteers out there?" Hands started popping up throughout the room. Charlie's and Jack's hands were among them. Carl smiled and said, "I am proud of you all and am happy to see we all stand together in this. I need the volunteers to stay, and the rest of you are excused."

After the room quieted down, they all moved towards the front of the room. Carl stood there looking at the pictures. Charlie piped up, "So, what next?"

He turned to look at her.

"Well, we need to figure out the best way to go about this. Do we follow them individually or do we find out where they all meet? I mean, if we do this, it has to be done right the first

95

time. There is no second chance! Who owns a gun here?"

A few hands shot up.

Billy, one of Carl's men, shouted, "I have a few!" The whole room chuckled. Those who knew Billy also knew he loved his collection of guns.

Carl cleared his throat, "Sounds great! Billy, we can definitely use them. Can you get them here as soon as possible?" Billy nodded. "The rest of you, if you have guns, please bring them here too. We'll do a weapon count tomorrow evening. The next thing we need to figure out is how do we get as many as we can into one spot. It would be easier that way, I think. Then it can be done at a certain time all together. Although I'm not sure if they ever get together." Carl glanced over at Charlie. "When you were monitoring them, did you ever see them all together?"

Charlie stood up and walked towards the board. She stood looking at the photos. "Well, they mostly seem to pair up. They have to meet up somewhere, but I'm not exactly sure. Maybe I should monitor them a bit more and see if I notice a pattern. Plus, if we put a tag on them, we are more likely to find out just in case it happens somewhere without a camera."

Carl nodded, "That's a great idea. So, over the next few days, you keep an eye on the monitors. I'll assign a few people to help you out and Larzo, you get a few people together who can tag these creatures. Together, let's find out where they all go. Before we end this meeting today, please team up with someone. We all need someone to watch our back."

Charlie walked over to Jack and laid her hand on Jack's shoulder. "You're with me, right?"

Jack smiled, "Wouldn't have it any other way." Looking up at Carl, Jack said, "I'll start monitoring as soon as I hit up the coffee machine."

Carl laughed. "Okay, group. Dismissed. We'll meet back here in a couple days. Meanwhile, I want to see the guns tomorrow." As the room emptied, Carl tapped Jack on the back and said, "You know, some of them might need you afterwards. Some won't be able to shake it off no matter what."

Jack nodded, "Yeah, I'm sure you're right. Affirmations are important. Remember to use them as you speak to them about all of this. It's for the greater good. We're saving lives and putting an end to the murder of innocent people by doing this. This will help it absorb without damaging them too badly. As for the guilt, I can try to help with that afterwards." Patting Jack on the back, Carl headed out the door and towards his room.

Jack went to the kitchen, figuring he would grab some coffee and help Charlie for a bit. As he entered the kitchen, he noticed a mark on the back of Charlie's neck. "What is that?" he asked as he walked up to her. Lifting the edge of her hair, he saw a faded tattoo. "When did you get a tattoo?"

Charlie looked puzzled.

"I've never had a tattoo. You must be mistaken."

Jack let go of her hair and looked her in the face. "No. I'm not mistaken. There's a faded tattoo on the bottom of your hairline. I've seen you plenty of times with your hair up, and not once did I ever see this."

Rubbing the back of her neck, Charlie asked, "Can you take a picture of it, so I can see it?"

Jack pulled out his phone and took a snapshot. "See. It almost looks like the symbol you drew in your sketch book."

Charlie's puzzled look worsened. "I don't know how that

got there seriously, Jack. Please don't mention this to anyone 'til we figure it out. Okay?"

Jack stood back and looked at her. "You have my word. This is between us." He giggled softly, "More mysteries to solve. I just need a mystery machine."

Charlie shook her head. "Really, Jack? A Scooby Doo reference! You big goof!" She reached over and grabbed the coffee, then accidentally brushed her head on his shoulder as she walked by him.

Jack grabbed a cup and poured some coffee. "I'm coming to help you. Just give me a second."

The two sat monitoring the video set for a bit, sipping their coffee. Both were quiet. It was kind of nice to just sit and enjoy the silence. Charlie leaned over and whispered, "I never shot a gun before."

Jack glanced at Charlie quickly, trying not to take his eyes away from the monitor. "It's easy. Just aim and pull the trigger. Just don't aim my way."

Charlie's eyes widened as she thought to herself, 'Oh my God! What if I shoot someone else by accident?'

Jack saw the look on her face change from concern to fear and quickly replied, "Chill. You have nothing to worry about. I was just kidding with you, trying to make you laugh. On a more serious note, I'm worried about something. We've watched all these shifters for a while now. There's a pattern to most of them, but what about the time I saw the one with my face?"

Charlie gasped, "You're right. What if it is different at the time, and we shoot the wrong person?"

Jack frowned, "I keep telling myself that unless they find out we are onto them, how are they going to know? We have to trust our instincts and have faith that we have the right one. Do you know what I mean?"

Charlie laid her head on his shoulder. "I do know what you mean. This is exhausting. My mind just can't take much more right about now. I keep asking myself what would Julie do. Well, she would tell me to get off my ass and keep going. So, I just keep chugging along, hoping it ends soon."

Glancing up at the window, the two noticed Stormage slinking across the window sill. "Wouldn't it be nice not to have a care in the world?" laughed Jack.

Looking up, she laughed.

"He doesn't care about much, just his dinner and whether or not he has a good place to lie down and nap for a bit. Bruno, on the other hand, needs constant attention. He's upstairs with Marcy. Lately, she's been playing with him while I work. I'm so thankful for that. He doesn't need to be affected by all of this. It's bad enough he doesn't get to go to the park anymore. Have you spoken to Carl about the one shifter and your worries?"

Jack shook his head no. "Not yet, but I will tomorrow. I want to sleep on it tonight and see if I can come up with anything. Maybe with a fresh mind, it will look simpler."

After Charlie and Jack had spent a few hours watching the video feed, Larzo entered the room with a couple of women. "Hey, guys. I have some replacements for you. They've agreed to do overnight and let you get some sleep."

Charlie smiled, "Thanks. I'm in desperate need of some sleep." They both jumped up. Jack grabbed Stormage, and the two headed towards their rooms. Charlie yawned and said, "I'm going to grab Bruno. Can you drop Stormage off to my room?"

Jack nodded, "Yup. I'll see you tomorrow bright and early. Just think, maybe we'll be home soon, and this nightmare will be over." Charlie smiled and headed down the hall towards Marcy's room to get her puppy, then back to her room where they could relax and get some well-deserved sleep.

* * *

The sun beamed into the windows of the hotel. Jack lay in bed. He could feel the breeze blowing from the window. It felt refreshing. His thoughts reflected on yesterday's meeting. 'Larzo would be forming a team to follow the creatures today. What if they had some help when following them? Marcy was good at the computer. Maybe she could download the GPS signals from the cell phones and track them by tapping into their GPS positioning. He crawled out of bed and threw on his clothes and headed to Carl's room, nearly forgetting to close the door

behind himself. It didn't take Carl long to answer the door. "Morning, Jack. What's up?"

Jack leaned against the door frame. "I thought about the whole situation and woke up with an idea this morning. What if we track their GPS signals to make it easier for Larzo and his men to tag them? All they have to do is take a look around and see what there is and maybe scope it out and see the best position for our advantage."

Carl was intrigued. "That might just work. Well done, Jack. Do you know anyone who can do this?"

Jack nodded, "My secretary, Marcy, is a pro on the computer. She has a bit of a shady past when it comes to computers, but she's on our side, so that past benefits us. We can get ahold of the cell numbers and load this up today."

Carl laughed lightly. "We have those buggers now." Jack laughed and started walking towards Marcy's room, then to the board room.

Charlie sat in front of the monitors. She got an early start this morning in hopes that she would find something that would make everything go smoother. Then maybe she could go home. Her night didn't go as well as she had hoped. Not only did she toss and turn, but she had a nightmare. It was about Julie. It almost felt like she was reaching out for her, but how could that be possible? Jack wandered into the room and pulled out a chair next to her. "Morning."

Charlie turned to face Jack. "I have to tell you something."

Jack sat down and looked at her. "Okay."

Charlie leaned back on her chair and started recalling her dream. "I dreamt about Julie last night." Charlie looked over at Jack as she continued, "It felt as if she was reaching out to me. In the dream, she was there with us, but we couldn't see her. It was like she was trapped somewhere. The worst part was that where she was seemed dangerous. She was hiding, and I saw a giant spider in the background. At one point, a clown with a chainsaw ran by her. It may not seem scary to you, but she looked scared, and that place gave me the creeps."

Jack crossed his arms and leaned back. "Hmmm. Well, I don't know of any place like that. Let's hope nothing like that exists. That would not be a world I would like to visit. Do you remember anything else about it?"

Charlie thought about it for a minute. "Yeah, I do. There

was a statue there. It was really strange looking, but there was

talking in the background, sort of like the voices I hear. I couldn't make it out, but they seemed to be in the distance."

Jack's eyes widened, "Are you kidding me? You could hear those voices in your dream? You may be onto something, but the bad part is that Julie might actually be in danger."

Charlie sat up straight. "Oh my god! Could she actually be alive?"

Jack drew a breath. "I'm not sure, but there is a chance she just might be."

Marcy came giggling into the room. Bruno barged in right after her. He was being chased by Stormage, who on occasion would get a burst of energy, and Bruno would be the target. "Sorry it took so long, Jack. I was getting these guys ready to run around. Thanks so much, Charlie, for letting me hang with these guys while you were busy. They keep me busy and take my mind off everything." Marcy grabbed a chair next to Jack. "I'm ready to work though."

Charlie wrinkled her eyes. "Oh, what are you working on?"

Marcy smiled, "Jack and I are going to track their GPS signals and help Larzo and his men find out where they all meet."

Jack smiled. "Yes, and Marcy is the best woman for the job.

Charlie smiled. "That's great. If you guys are going to be here for a bit, do you mind watching the video feed? I have something I need to do."

Jack shook his head. "Sure. Take your time." The two of them got to work on setting up the program as Charlie set off to her room.

Charlie entered her room, quietly shutting the door after herself. She grabbed her sketch book and flopped down on the bed. She thought to herself as she hugged her book tightly, *What do you need me to know, Julie?* She reached up and felt the back of her neck. She had been wearing her hair down ever since Jack spotted the tattoo on her neck. Where could that have possibly come from? She didn't drink that much so she knew it couldn't be the result of a drunken experience, and why was it that symbol? How did it connect to all of this and to Julie? She got frightened for a minute. *What do I have to do with this whole situation? How am I connected?* She sat up and pushed herself up against the wall.

Opening her book slowly, a tear rolled down her face. She must be missing something. The question was what. She started going through her scrapbook, looking at all the sketches, remembering the ones Julie dreamt about. She stopped when she got to the one of the symbols. *What does this mean and why am I wearing it?*

She closed her eyes and said, "Julie, I don't know if we have a connection, or if I'm just being a weirdo, but if there is a chance you can hear me, tell me how I can help you. I feel scared without you. All these weird things are happening to me. That symbol scared you so bad, and now I feel as if I betrayed you somehow by wearing it. I truly don't know how it got there. I miss you, Julie. Come home." She laid her book down and got up and stood near the window. It was bright outside, and the breeze made her feel nice. Suddenly, she had a thought. The statue in her dream was where the fountain in front of the café was. How could that be? She knew the fountain still stood there. She recognized the spot because the wharf was right behind it, and she wrote from there every day for almost seven years. She pulled out her phone and wrote her thoughts about it in a text to Jack. Maybe he could make sense of it. Placing her phone on the table next to her bed, she crawled in under her blanket. Maybe if she took a short nap, she could rest her mind about all this. She tossed and turned a little, but moments later, she started to doze off.

Throughout the day, the volunteers dropped their guns off to Carl. He piled them into a box after checking each one to make sure the chambers were full of ammo. He turned to Franny and said, "We have enough guns to do the job." He walked over and rubbed his wife's neck. "Pretty soon, I'll have you home where you can feel safe again."

Franny looked up at him and smiled. "That's a nice thought, but you need to know, I feel safe no matter what, as long as I'm with you."

Carl leaned down and hugged his wife from behind. "Thanks. Hopefully in a day or two, we will have a full plan to put into action." Standing up, he headed for the door. "I'll be back later. I need to go check on our plan and see how it's progressing."

Moments later, Carl entered the board room. Jack turned and smiled. "We just got it up and running. Marcy is loading the cell numbers now. Have you informed Larzo of what we're doing yet?"

Carl leaned on the chair hovering over Marcy as she put each number into the system. "Yes, I messaged him after we spoke. I actually think you made his day. There was relief in his voice when I told him. You have to imagine it was scary thinking about following those shifters every little step with no knowledge of what could happen. This way we can keep everyone informed."

Marcy shrieked excitingly, "It works! Look! It's showing each of them. If we watch them, we can see where they go and what time frame we are looking at. Being on Jack's laptop makes it easy to watch. He can keep it with him at all times or whomever you guys choose to do the monitoring."

Carl looked at Jack. "We need a record of where they are at all times. Larzo and his men can check it out." Carl stood up and patted both of them on the back. "Good job! We're one step closer to going home."

When Carl left the room, Marcy leaned over and whispered to Jack, "I know this all looks like it's working out, but I don't have a good feeling about it. Not at all, Jack."

Jack pulled the laptop in front of him. "Like I told Charlie, we can hope. Without hope, we're lost." Jack picked up the laptop. "I'll be in my room keeping track. You're more than welcome to join me." Jack then turned and left the room.

Three days passed. The group worked hard at finding the information they needed to pull off their plan. Jack found out after watching them twenty-four-hours straight that there was a bar outside town where they seemed to gather late in the evening. Larzo and his men later checked it out and reported back that it was an old silver barn converted into a bar, something the locals on the outskirts of town used to cool down after a long day at work.

After a few days of planning, Carl reported they had found the spot where they would assassinate the shapeshifters. Carl spent the next hour finding all the volunteers and assigning pictures to them, making sure they knew who their targets were. Just as Carl headed towards the elevator to go to his room, Jack scurried down the hall towards him. "Carl, wait up! I forgot to mention something on my mind. It's quite important. Remember I told you about the one shifter outside the mayor's office?"

Carl nodded, "Yes, I do."

Jack continued, "He changed his face right in front of me and that throws a few what ifs out there for me, like what if we shoot the wrong person."

Carl smirked. "I thought about that too. As a matter of fact, I thought of lots of what ifs, but we have the GPS, so no matter whose face they wear, we know where they are. Besides they have no warning of us, so why wouldn't they be themselves after a long day? We will hit them up tonight. You and Charlie be prepared. I need all of you to be ready. Tomorrow, we hopefully will be shifter free." Carl smiled and got in the elevator. "Smile, Jack, it might be all over tomorrow." Jack smiled, but his smile quickly fell as he reminded himself of the tattoo on the back of Charlie's neck. He quickly headed to her room, wondering if she had figured out how it had gotten there. He wanted to let her know about tonight and how, hopefully, tomorrow they could go home.

Chapter 7

It was hours before the attack, and all the shooters gathered in the board room. Their combined voices were a low roar as they discussed the plan within the group.

Billy groaned, "What's the escape plan again?"

Larzo shook his head in disbelief. "You better let it sink in this time, Billy. You don't want to be asking that question when it's time for all of us to get away. We keep the cars close by. The keys stay in the ignition ready to go. We line up and wait. Your partner will have your back, and, at exactly 12 midnight, you take out your targets. Right after you take out your target, your partner will run ahead to the car, making sure it's ready to go back to the hotel. It's not too hard. It just takes cooperation between all of us. Any questions?"

Charlie raised her hand. "Yeah. Where do I shoot? I mean, do I aim for his head or just anywhere?"

Larzo took a second, then turned to her. "Well, I would aim for the heart or the head ... anywhere else, they may survive. That's what I've seen in the movies. And when my granddad took me hunting when I was younger, the deer was always shot near the heart. I've never actually killed anyone, so I'm not a hundred percent sure."

Jack leaned over and whispered in her ear. "You have six rounds—aim for both.

Charlie glanced back at him and replied, "Good idea."

Carl entered the board room. As he walked towards the front, he looked around at those who stood in front of him. They were dressed in black, standing there waiting for orders. He hoped they would all be standing there with him once the night was complete. "Good to see you all ready to go. I need to make sure you all understand what's happening tonight. There's no backing out last minute. These creatures need to be eliminated." The room cheered, then got silent, waiting for Carl to finish speaking. "I'm proud of each and every one of you. You're all heroes in my eyes. I have a box of ski masks here. It will help us stay hidden better. It's about a forty-minute drive just outside the city, so if we leave here by 10:30, that should be a sufficient amount of time. There's an old drive-in movie theater just north of the silver barn. It's a five-minute walk through the woods. We will meet there. It's a safe place to park the cars and talk without being seen. Does everyone understand?" Larzo nodded to reassure him they were ready. Carl nodded and left the room. He wanted some more time with Franny before this went down, just in case it went bad.

Larzo popped his head over the guy next to him and yelled out to Charlie, "You two ready for tonight?"

Charlie gave him thumbs up while muttering under her breath, "As ready as we possibly can be."

Jack laid his hand on hers.

"It'll be fine. We'll do this, and hopefully life will get back to normal. Then we can concentrate on finding Julie." Charlie smiled as she zipped up the pocket that held the gun.

108

Later that night, the parking lot of the old drive-in theater slowly filled up. Charlie leaned out of the window of the car as they pulled into the lot. "Not everyone is here," she said. "I don't see Larzo's truck yet. I hope they didn't get caught out on the roads."

Jack scanned the parking lot. "No, but I'm sure Carl has heard from him."

Jack and Charlie climbed out of the car and headed over to where the group stood. "Where is Larzo?" Jack asked.

Carl headed over towards the two. "I just got off the phone with him. They will be here shortly; they had to take a detour. So, are you two ready for this?"

Jack nodded. "Yeah. We've discussed it on the way over." Charlie looked around at the group. It was odd to see them all dressed in black. Some of the guys stood talking about the plan, while others seemed restless. Feeling a little impatient herself, Charlie pulled out a cigarette and lit it. It was a habit she wasn't too fond of but wasn't too worried about since she really didn't do it much. Leaning back against the car, she looked over at Jack. He was stretching as if he was getting ready for a run. "Because of what Carl said, I just want to make sure I'm ready. I would hate to get a cramp in my leg while trying to get away."

Charlie finished her smoke as a truck entering the drive-in caught her attention. It was Larzo.

Larzo shook his head as he walked over towards the group. "Just goes to show you that you can never be sure of a plan going a hundred percent your way. We had to get off the highway and wait while other cars that were heading towards the barn were out of sight. I didn't want to take a chance of getting caught out after curfew. So, are we all ready for this?"

Carl nodded.

"Yes. We were just waiting on you." Turning to look towards everyone, Carl added, "Okay, so we all know what our jobs are and who we're after?" Silently, they all nodded. "Okay, then let's go. Larzo, you go ahead and make sure they are all there." Larzo ran ahead while the others slowly made their way through the woods. It was a short walk, maybe five minutes at the most. Charlie's stomach turned. She had this awful feeling in the pit of her stomach all day that there was something they were missing but had no proof of anything being off course. The group stopped at the edge of the woods and then got into position. They waited while Larzo checked to make sure all the targets were present and then for the clock to strike midnight. Larzo returned to the group reporting that all was ready and in place. So far, things were going smoothly.

Charlie leaned against the tree and glanced over to Jack. "My heart is beating so hard right now," she whispered.

Jack leaned over. "That's pretty normal for a situation like this, I would assume."

As midnight hit, Carl looked around at everyone and nodded. It was time. Picking up the firecrackers, he lit them and threw them into the parking lot. The firecrackers went off like a wild fire, making so much noise it could raise the dead. The barn door swung open fiercely and out they came. First out the door was the police chief, then the rest followed. Without hesitation, the group fired at them. Their bodies thrusted as the bullets pierced through their chests. The group was just about to turn and run when suddenly, there was a flash of light that lit up the whole sky. Charlie's eyes widened, and her mouth fell on the ground. Jack grabbed Charlie's hand. "What the hell!" he shouted as he pulled her down.

Both crouched close to the ground as they looked around.

Everything was frozen. Time had stopped but only for a few seconds. The barn had disappeared. It was no longer there.

A temple stood in its place. An ungodly screech surrounded them as everything unfroze, and time started again. The shifters didn't look human anymore. Charlie gasped. She had never seen anything like it before. The bullet wounds were now gone. The shifters had self-healed. Standing six-foot-five, they scanned the area for the group. Their large lizard-like tails swung in the air, hitting trees like a baseball bat, sending vibrations through the air.

Bullets started flying again as the fearful group started shooting at them once more. One of them leaped towards Billy, plunging his razor-like claws deep down into Billy's flesh, knocking him to the ground. As it turned, its tail swung fiercely, colliding with Beth's head, killing her instantly. The group stood confused and stunned until Carl screamed, "Run!" Jack ran and grabbed Billy. He nearly stumbled as they tried to keep up with the rest of the group as they ran to get to their cars. Blood gushed out of Billy's wounds as Jack shoved him into the back seat. Jack ripped off his shirt and gave it to him. "Hold this against it," Jack instructed. Jumping into the driver's seat, he yelled to Charlie, "You drive with Carl and find out what's next!"

The group raced down the road. Anxiety built up, and time seemed to have stopped, but only in their minds. No one understood what had just happened. All they knew is that they had to get back to the hotel. Carl looked into the mirror. "Charlie, is there someone following us?"

Charlie looked back. "No, I don't see anyone."

Carl looked in the mirror again. "What about the big semi-truck? I don't remember anyone driving that?"

Charlie looked back and felt very puzzled. "What semi? I don't see any semi- trucks back there."

Carl stepped on the pedal. "I think it's after us."

Charlie looked at Carl. "No one's there. I promise. I don't see what you're seeing. You need to slow down or you're going to crash."

Carl let off on the pedal, still fearful that the truck was behind them, but he trusted her enough to believe her when she said it wasn't there.

Jack drove home as quickly as he could. He was upset and worried for Billy but couldn't help but notice the reckless driving around him. He thought to himself, 'I'm upset too, but I still remember how to drive. What the hell!' A car sped by Jack

and then directly into a tree, bursting into flames. Jack slowed down and pulled up next to it. Jack felt confused over everything happening. He glanced back to make sure he was safe, then he looked to see if anyone had survived the crash. A man's body was flung over the steering wheel. His face looked as if he had seen a ghost. The man next to him lay dead due to an arrow shot directly between the eyes. Jack had a strange feeling come over him. He stepped on the gas and headed back to the hotel. Billy gasped in pain, "What's going on, Jack? This was supposed to be simple. What the hell?"

Jack glanced back at Billy. "We're almost back to the hotel. Keep holding that shirt on your wound."

One by one, they pulled into the parking lot. Not a word was said as they all ran into the hotel. Franny came running, happy to see Carl but screamed at the sight of blood when she saw Billy. "What happened? Did something go wrong?"

Carl grabbed Franny and pushed her aside. "Bring him in here," he said to Jack. "Someone, get Loretta", Carl continued.

"I'm here!" she yelled as she ran over to Billy to look at his injuries. Loretta took a deep breath as she looked at Billy's wound. "Oh, this is not good. Someone grab me some alcohol and something to stich him up. Hurry, please."

Seconds later, Franny came running back with a sewing kit and a bottle of alcohol. "Got it," she said.

"Out of my way," Loretta said politely but firmly. It took a bit to fix Billy up, but with a bit of work, he lay there resting while the rest of the group leaned against the window watching in fear.

Franny's eyes followed every single one of them.

"What happened? You all are scaring me. What happened to Billy?" For a brief minute, she stopped questioning them and looked around. "Where is Beth?"

Loretta looked up. "Yeah, where is she?"

Carl grabbed a chair and sat down on it. He reached up and wiped the sweat off his forehead. He looked up and shook his head. "Beth is dead. Am I crazy or did all of you see the same thing I saw?" Charlie collapsed to her knees, then leaned against the wall. Jack sat next to her.

As the room started to chatter, Larzo spoke up. "What the hell was that? I may not know what a shifter really looks like, but that looked more like a monster or some kind of lizard. I used all my bullets on it, and it still stood there." Larzo turned pale as he sat down.

Carl piped up, "I am as puzzled as all of you. I really thought we had this. Who would have thought something like this could happen? Did everyone see it heal itself?" The group nodded as Carl took a breath. "That's not human. I don't know what it is, but it's not human."

Loretta felt puzzled and scared. "What happened out there?"

Jack stood up. "You guys missed something. Something happened just after the shooting. Time froze again. Both Charlie and I saw this. Did anyone else witness this?"

Carl stood up and walked over to Jack. "What? You mean time stopped after we shot at them the first time?"

Jack nodded. "Yes, it did. Then there was a flash of bright light, and that's when the barn changed into a temple-like building, and the shifters no longer looked human. Then they made this horrifying screech."

Carl interrupted, "I heard that, but I thought it happened as we shot them."

Charlie stood up. "No. It happened after the change did. I'm not sure what happened, but they were definitely angry, and I'm scared for all of us. There's no chance of going home now; not after this."

Carl sat back down. "Did anyone else see a semi-truck chasing us?"

Jack shook his head. "No. There were no big trucks out there other than Larzo's. Some other bad news—Chuck and Mike crashed their vehicle on the way back. They were driving really crazy, as if they were being chased, but there was nothing chasing them. I stopped by the car crash to see if anyone survived and noticed a few odd things... no survivors though." Charlie's eyes filled with tears. Jack leaned over and hugged her. He looked at Carl. "We need to tighten security on the hotel."

Carl looked at Larzo. "Let's make sure all the doors and windows are locked and put on the alarm. Will you? The lights are to be off. Flashlights and candles will be used 'til we are sure it's safe. There will be guys on either door ready to alert us if anything changes from now on. Everyone get to it. Jack, help me move Billy to his room where he can rest and get better. You can fill me in about what you saw on the way."

Charlie headed to the kitchen to grab a coffee. Both Franny and Lorretta followed her. Marcy had already been in the kitchen when they entered. Charlie poured herself a coffee, then turned and looked at all three girls. "I seriously don't understand what happened tonight. It was supposed to be simple and easy but was neither."

Loretta sat down and pulled out another chair and motioned for Charlie to sit too. "This whole thing is messed up. I understand it may be hard to talk about, but I wasn't there, and I need to know what's going on."

Charlie paused for a moment then looked at Loretta. "You all should know... I just wish I could make more sense out of it myself. They look like lizards with giant tails. That's how Beth died because its tail hit her upside the head. Their claws are long and sharp, and they are huge... nothing I expected, for sure. One minute the barn was there; the next it wasn't. A totally different building was there. The sky lit up so bright as if fireworks were flooding the sky. But, I think the scariest thing was when I looked around, and everyone but Jack and I were frozen in time. Their bodies healed so fast. I thought we were all dead for a moment, then it let out that noise, and I remembered to run." Bruno ran onto the kitchen and jumped up onto Charlie's lap. "Hi, boy." Rubbing behind his ears and scratching his neck, she leaned down and hugged her best friend. "I missed you too and so glad to see some things don't change."

Carl entered the kitchen holding a box of flashlights and

candles. "Here you go, ladies. Help yourself. The lights are going off momentarily, so you need to be prepared."

Charlie looked up at Carl and said, "Thanks."

Carl paused. "I thought you had green eyes, Charlie? I must have been wrong." Carl turned and headed back out the door.

Charlie shook her head, thinking he was joking. "I'm going to head up to my room and get some sleep. I've had it for today. Tonight, a lot of weird things happened, and I'm hoping I'll wake up tomorrow and find that it was all a nightmare." Picking up Bruno, she headed to her room. She spotted Stormage along the way. "Come on, Stormage. Let's go to bed." Stormage chased her up the hall playfully and past the door as it gently shut. She fed both of the pets then cleaned up just before she flopped down onto the bed. Her mind raced as she pulled the covers up. 'How were they to find Julie with all this going on?

Could she even be alive?' Letting out a sigh, she turned over onto her side. It was hard to close her eyes. Every time she closed them, all she saw was the shifters and what they had become. 'Please let this be a dream,' she thought to herself. She pulled Bruno up close to her chest. He made her feel safe, even though there wasn't much he could do if they ever stood in front of those creatures. Closing her eyes, she quietly fell asleep. 'Maybe tomorrow will be better," she thought to herself.

Jack sat up in bed. He wondered what was going to happen now that the shifters knew they were onto them. He remembered the look on the faces of the men in the car crash. 'What was that all about?' he thought. 'Did they see something that made their faces freeze that way? Where did the arrow come from?' Jack slid down and pulled up his covers. He could feel his heart beat fast and his chest tighten with anxiety as he clenched his fists. He shut his eyes and repeated over and over in his head, 'Everything will be okay. Tomorrow is a new day.' After about ten minutes, he fell asleep. Slowly, his fists unclenched. The rest of the people in the building, minus the guards who had taken the night shifts, finally settled down for the night as the full moon shone brightly over the little hotel in Richmond.

The sun peeked in the window as morning came. Charlie lay wide awake. The events of the previous night played over and over in her head, and each time it did, she tried to make sense of it. Bruno was asleep underneath her blanket, while Stormage was flopped across her legs. It gave her a feeling of security, having both pets so close to her. She thought to herself, 'How are we supposed to fix this situation now? I was counting on going home.' Slowly, she pulled herself from her comfortable bed, trying to keep both Bruno and Stormage from being disturbed. As she threw her clothes on, she looked around. 'I'm never getting out of here,' she thought. Grabbing an elastic, she threw her hair up as she headed down the hall to Jack's room. Leaning on his door, she started to knock. "Jack, are you up yet? She waited patiently 'til she heard the soft murmur of his voice say, "Come in."

Charlie barged in and flopped down onto his bed. I figured you would be up. "Did you get any sleep?"

Jack opened his eyes and looked at Charlie. "I am now. And no… I hardly slept."

Charlie lifted her head. "Don't you have blue eyes?"

Jack squinted. "Yeah. So?"

Charlie jumped up from the bed and ran to the mirror. She remembered what Carl had said to her about her eyes. He

117

was right. Her eyes were not green any more. They were a silvery gray. "Oh my God, Jack! My eyes… they are not the same."

Jack sat up. "What do you mean?" Jack got up and headed over to see her eyes. "Hmmm, you are right. They are a different color." Looking into the mirror, he then noticed his too were a silvery gray. "What the hell! Mine are different too! This is freaky."

As Jack turned and started to walk away, Charlie gasped, "Your back."

Jack turned quickly. "What about my back?" Jack went to the mirror and turned so he could get a look at his back. "Where did that come from?" In the center of his back, there was a tattoo. The same symbol that Charlie had on her neck. "What's happening to us?" said Jack.

Charlie laughed, "You're the doctor. Not me. This all has to be some kind of joke. Maybe this whole thing is a joke, and any minute Julie will pop out and say, 'Got you.'"

Jack frowned. "No. I wish it was, but it isn't. I'm not sure what's happening yet, so please don't mention any of this to the others."

She nodded. "But, what if they see the color change in the eyes?" Not sure what to say."

Jack shrugged. "I don't know… maybe just change the subject."

Charlie turned and headed towards the door. "Okay. I'm going to see what's going on. See if anyone has come up with a brilliant plan to get us out of this one."

Charlie entered the board room. Carl sat in front of the monitors. He seemed really frazzled, but then everyone was because of the night before. "Hi, Carl, any action out there today?"

Carl turned and looked at Charlie. "Hi, Charlie." Turning back to the monitors, he let out a huge sigh. "I'm sure there is plenty, but I feel as if we are in a different world. What the hell happened and where did these creatures come from? One minute we're taking out a few shifters, a task that was simple and well-planned. The next minute we're confronted by these creatures, and they're unaffected by our guns. I'm not sure where we all stand anymore. All I know is we're definitely not safe, and I don't know how to fix this."

Charlie grabbed a seat next to him. "You have to pull yourself together. The whole group is counting on you. If they see you falling apart, then they might lose faith that we even have a chance. Yeah, we have no clue what is going on, but now is the time to figure it out. Let's put two and two together right now—you and I."

Carl sat up straighter and pulled his chair closer to the table. "Good idea. So, we know they are unaffected by our weapons, and that they are not human at all."

Charlie bit her lip as she thought about the situation. "They have reptilian bodies. Their skin, tails, and eyes are very lizard-like. What if we are not dealing with shapeshifters, just something that can shape shift? What if these are aliens of some sort, and we intercepted some sort of invasion?"

Carl chuckled and snorted, "What the hell?" Then he paused for a second. "What if you're right? I never thought of that. Oh my God, Charlie! Do you realize what's happening?" Charlie leaned back in her chair. She knew what she said sounded foolish coming out of her mouth, but all the evidence lay in front of them. The monitors stood black. Not a sound nor a picture showed on any of the screens. "I think they found the cameras," said Carl.

Charlie looked at all the screens. "What if this is like when Julie disappeared? Do you remember hers stopped working too? I'm not sure how this relates, but I feel this has something to do with it."

Carl turned his body towards her. "Tell me again what happened last night when we were all frozen. Why do you think you and Jack were not affected by it?"

Charlie took a deep breath. "I'm not sure. I do know that some pretty weird stuff is happening, and not a whole lot can be explained right now. I'm pretty sure about one thing though, we should be thankful that we were not affected by it, or no one would know what is truly going on. So maybe we should focus on the stuff we know about instead of all the other stuff. Have you heard back from the other cities? Did they succeed or was it the same result?"

Carl shook his head. "Not all of them messaged me, but the ones who have didn't get any better results than we did. They were left with wounded too. They were left in shock, wondering what they walked into. I told them it was just as much of a shock for us, and the more I think about it, the more I think we are lucky that we knew. We would all be dead if we remained clueless, although I don't feel very lucky at the moment. We didn't even have time to grab Beth's body to give her a proper burial."

Jack walked into the room. "Hey, you two!"

Charlie looked up at him. "We are just discussing the events of last night. Has anyone checked on Billy today?"

Carl nodded. "Loretta has been monitoring him closely, making sure he heals right." Jack turned. "I'm going to grab some coffee."

Charlie bounced up. "Wait. I need some too." The two headed to the kitchen. Charlie sensed that Jack was upset. "What's wrong, Jack?"

Jack poured himself a cup of coffee, then one for Charlie. "I had a dream last night. Julie was in it. She was speaking to me." The two sat down at the table. Jack took a sip of his coffee then continued. "She told me she was alive, and that life was an illusion… to open my eyes, and that we were in grave danger. Then she disappeared. It has to be my mind trying to comfort me about the guilt I feel. I really miss her." He continued drinking his coffee as he thought to himself, 'I'll find her if it is the last thing I do.'

Charlie wrinkled up her forehead. "What do you mean you'll find her? I thought we were going to search for her together."

Jack laid down his cup. "Did you just answer me?"

Charlie snickered, "Yeah, of course I did. I always answer you."

Jack felt puzzled. "I said that in my head though, so how did you know what I said?"

Before Charlie could answer him, her phone started to ring. Picking up her phone, Charlie said, "Hello."

"Charlie, is that you?"

Charlie, feeling a bit puzzled, answered, "Yeah. Who is this?"

The woman on the other end replied, "It doesn't matter who I am. You need to listen to what I'm about to tell you. You and Jack need to be prepared for what is to come."

Charlie shifted the phone and adjusted it to her ear. "What do you mean? Do I know you and how do you know Jack?" Jack leaned in closer as if to listen.

The woman continued.

"It's not important at the moment. There are things I cannot tell you at this time, but what I can tell you is that you need to be careful. Things are changing, and you are no longer protected. You and Jack will start to notice things happening to the both of you that you cannot explain." Charlie looked at Jack as the woman continued. "Once the tattoo pops out, it is just a matter of time before the rest falls into place. The world is in danger, and there isn't much protection for the humans other than the color red. Cover everything with red, including your heart. It will protect you in their presence—that and fire are hard for them to see. Be safe and know we are watching you."

Charlie put the phone away after the woman hung up. "That was weird," Charlie murmured. After telling Jack all that the woman had told her, both sat silently drinking their coffee, in a situation that felt it could not get any stranger. It most definitely did.

Jack got up and refilled his coffee. "I can't just sit here and do nothing. With the monitors gone, we have no idea what's happening out there." As he headed out the door, he turned to Charlie. "What do you think she meant about red? It's a really bright color. Wouldn't that make it easier for them to see us?"

Charlie got up and followed Jack. "Not if they were color blind. Maybe they can't see red. It could cover things up. Make it so they don't exist. I would love to test the theory, but I think I'm too scared to. Maybe we should run it by Carl, but not the stuff about us, just the color red and the fire. I don't understand what's happening to us, so how can we expect others to—not yet, at least."

The two stood at the front door of the hotel. The world looked different to them, but they couldn't put their finger on what exactly was different. After a while of looking around at everything, Charlie burst out, "I got it! Not only is there no one out there but look over there. The buildings are gone. There used to be two tall buildings there, and now they are gone."

Jack stood there folding his arms. "You know, you are right. When did they disappear? I thought I saw them yesterday, but I suppose I could be wrong."

Charlie looked at him. "No, you're right. I saw them yesterday too." The two were just about to go get Carl to show him what they found when a dark gray vehicle swooped by. Charlie squished her face against the window trying to see it. "Did you see that? What was it?"

Jack stood there with his jaw wide open. "If I'm not mistaken, that looks like a ship. I think they call them hovercrafts, but that's only on television."

Charlie swatted Jack's arm. "Is that only on television too? That was real, Jack. Don't go all psychiatrist on me now." The two of them pressed their faces against the window and checked out everything in sight. In the far distance, they could see more hovercrafts moving through the air.

Charlie gasped. "We need to tell Carl and let everyone know. We better tell him about the phone call right away and what they told us about red." Grabbing his arm, Charlie headed to the board room. "Come on, Jack. I think he's down here."

Charlie peeked into the board room. Carl sat at the table writing something in an old book of his. Charlie whispered, "Carl, are you busy?"

Carl turned and looked at her. "No. Not at all. Come on in."

The two of them sat down next to him. "We need to talk about a few things."

Carl felt worried, "Okay, what about?"

Charlie pulled out her phone and laid it on the table. "I got a call earlier from a lady. I have no idea who it was, although she sounded familiar. The lady wanted to stay anonymous. She warned me about the shifters or aliens, whatever they are. She said they can't see the color red. I'm not sure if it's 'cause they are color blind or what, but apparently, they have a hard time seeing fire too. She said to use red as much as we can and to wear it."

Carl looked a bit puzzled.

"How can we be sure this is true?"

Jack jumped in. "We can't be certain unless we try it. That leads me to the other news. We just looked out the window, and not only did we notice a couple buildings missing, but we now have hovercrafts flying around our city."

Carl jumped up and ran to the window, "Holy crap! It was bad enough knowing there were creatures in our city that we couldn't just shoot and kill, but now we have UFOs too! I don't know about you two, but I think we're dealing with aliens. What else could it possibly be?" Jack and Charlie both joined him at the window.

"I thought it might be too," said Charlie, "but I didn't want to assume so."

Carl looked at her.

"So that woman called to tell you to protect yourself with red? How did she even know about us?"

Charlie shrugged. "I don't know. Maybe it's someone we know, but I can't imagine who." Charlie bit her lip as she thought to herself, *I'm going to have to tell him about the rest soon.* Jack swung his head around, and without moving his lips, she heard him say, *Not yet.*

Both looked at each other for a second before Jack spoke up. "I don't think they're hiding among us anymore. I think we blew their cover, and now they're planning on just taking over."

Carl turned away from the window and looked at both of them. "This is bad. None of us are prepared for anything like this. I feel like we opened Pandora's box and now we are screwed."

A few seconds later, Loretta walked into the room. "There you are, Jack. I was looking for you. Billy has been asking for you. I told him I would try to find you."

Jack turned and headed for the door. "You might want to stay and get updated on what's going on."

Opening the door slowly, Jack entered Billy's room. Jack walked over to where he lay and asked, "How are you feeling?" Billy looked up at him. "I thought we were goners. Loretta told me Beth didn't make it. How's Marcy taking it?"

Jack sat down next to him. "She's doing okay. Everyone is still in shock. I'm sure it hasn't really hit anyone yet." Jack looked down at his stitches and said, "So much for simple."

Billy shook his head, "Yeah, easy in easy out. I saw it too, just like you and Charlie did."

Jack paused. "Saw what?"

Billy looked at him and responded, "The flash of light. The one that happened when everyone else was frozen."

Jack raised an eyebrow. "You saw that too? I thought only Charlie and I saw it. I can't understand why we're the only ones not affected by it. One alien froze everyone in the square the first time I saw them."

Billy tried to sit up. "Ugggg," he moaned, then lay back down. "Alien? What do you mean alien? Did I miss something? I thought we were dealing with shifters?" Billy stopped and took a second to think before he continued. "But now that I think about it, that didn't look like no shifter to me. Nothing about it said human. Oh my god! They are aliens!" He looked up at Jack. "Does Carl know?"

Jack shook his head, "Yes. We were all talking about it in the board room. There are hovercrafts flying around the city now. We're really not quite sure what to do next, but at least we know now."

Billy started to cough. "I have a dry throat. Can you get me some water, please?"

Jack nodded. "Okay but let me ask you something first. Have you noticed anything else weird happening to you?"

Billy thought for a moment. "No, not really. Not unless you count finding an old tattoo I don't remember getting. Must've been some drunk that night." Billy lifted his arm to show it to Jack. It was the same symbol both Jack and Charlie had.

Jack took a deep breath. "We have that too."

Billy wrinkled up his forehead. "The same tattoo?"

Jack turned to show him his back. "Yup. It showed up just after we got back to the hotel. Charlie got hers the other day."

After hearing a knock at the door, Jack turned to see Charlie standing there. "Did Billy need water?"

Jack seemed confused. "You were not here when he asked for it. How did you know he wanted it?"

Charlie smiled, "I don't really know. It was like I heard him ask for it, yet he wasn't really there."

Jack frowned. "This has been happening to us a lot lately, hasn't it?"

Billy took a drink of the water, then looked up. "I hear you guys once in a while. Not all the time though."

Jack looked at Charlie. "He has the tattoo just like us, and he saw the bright light while everyone else was frozen."

Charlie looked at Billy and asked, "Do you understand any of this?" Billy shook his head no.

Charlie stood up. "I'm going to go back to my room for a bit. Maybe I can make sense of this if I give it some thought for a bit."

Jack got up. "I'm coming with you. Get some rest, Billy. I will check in on you later." Both of them went to Charlie's room.

Jack pulled up a chair near the window as Charlie cleaned up and fed the pets. Bruno was happy to see them both. He twirled and bounced all over the room. Stormage lay spread out

across the table where Jack sat. "Someone needs attention," said Jack as he scratched the cat.

Charlie curled up on the bed with Bruno. "I'm just going to lie here for a bit. I need to clear my mind, so I can think."

Jack leaned back in the chair. "Go ahead. I'm going to sit here and see what I can see, just in case we missed anything." Everything was quiet for a bit. Neither had noted that the other had dozed off. With all the stress, that wouldn't have been a hard thing to do.

Charlie lay on the bed dreaming. She sat by the bridge looking out at the water. Beside her, stood Julie. "I'm here," she said. "You need to be careful, Charlie. They are extremely dangerous. We're not dealing with shapeshifters. These are aliens. There are so many of them. Warn everyone." Charlie woke up quickly with tears streaming from her eyes.

Half asleep, Jack cried out, "Julie?"

Charlie looked at him. "You saw her too?"

Jack, now completely awake, looked at Charlie. "Yeah, she was with you down by the bridge. I never got to speak to her, but I called out to her."

Charlie felt shocked, "How did you know what I dreamt?"

Jack sat up straight. "I don't know, but I think she really is alive. How else would she come to us in a dream?"

Charlie looked out the window. It was starting to get dark. "This has been a long day, and I don't want to deal with it anymore."

Jack snickered, "Like we get a choice. I think tomorrow we should fill Carl in about the rest of the phone call and what's happening to the three of us".

Charlie nodded. "You're right, but for now, I'm just going to read a book and pretend I'm somewhere else."

Jack got up and headed towards the door. "Good idea. I'm going to my room. I have a good e-book on my laptop. I'll talk to you tomorrow, Charlie."

Chapter 8

Morning came, but the sun didn't shine into the window like it usually did. The sky was gray and cloudy. You would almost swear the sun never shone. Charlie sighed as she pulled herself out of bed. She pulled the covers up over Bruno and gave him a kiss on the forehead. "You stay here, boy. I'll be back in a bit." She walked over to the window to see what was going on and to see why the sky was so dark. It almost seemed as if morning had never come, but the clock said differently. She threw on her clothes as she searched for the elastic that Stormage had found during the night. Pulling her hair up, she went downstairs, hoping to figure out what was going on.

Carl and Jack both stood at the front door of the hotel. Neither had noticed her right away, as they were so busy trying to figure out what was going on. Jack stood with his arms folded. It looked like a scene from a horror movie. Carl had his finger on his mouth and looked concerned. "This is just great. I don't even want to know what's going to jump out of that." Charlie walked up to where they stood. As she did, she noticed that outside there was a green mist throughout the air. It was like a thick fog. It reminded her of a swamp.

"Morning, guys. At least, I think it's morning." Charlie stood there staring at the green mist with the guys.

"Where do you think it came from?" Jack shook his head.

"I have no clue. I woke up this morning, and there it was. I don't even know if it's safe. If it were white, I would just assume it was fog… but green makes you wonder if there's a monster on the other side of it. Truthfully, with the aliens out there, I'm more likely to believe there's nothing good on the other side."

Jack looked at his watch. "It's almost 9 a.m., and I think the moon is still out. This is really messed up, and I guarantee you, I don't know how to fix this one. Unless maybe my watch is broken. Does anyone else have the time?"

Charlie glanced over at him. "No. I checked the time before coming down. Your watch is right."

Carl looked over at her, then at Jack. "There's something different about you two."

Both Charlie and Jack looked at each other than at Carl. Charlie took a deep breath. "I can't really explain it. Well, but yes, there's something going on. I'll tell you everything, but it has to stay between the three of us, at least 'til I understand it."

Carl nodded, "Okay. Let's get a coffee, and you can fill me in."

The three of them sat at the table with their coffee. Charlie wasn't really sure where she should begin, but decided it be best from the start. "A couple of days ago, before the incident happened with the aliens, this tattoo showed up on the back of my neck." She turned to show Carl the tattoo. "It's the same symbol that Julie saw."

Carl wrinkled his forehead as he leaned forward to have a good look.

"So, it just showed up?"

Charlie nodded. "Yup! Out of the blue. Then you asked me about my eyes. I truly thought you were joking with me. Then, after we got home from the shooting, I noticed Jack's eyes were different and remembered you saying that about mine. He also had a tattoo appear on his back. It's the same symbol I have."

Carl looked at her eyes then at Jack's. "They are the same color. This is really weird, guys. Anything else?" Jack nodded. "The phone call we received not only told us about the color red being beneficial to us, but it warned us that both Charlie and I would notice things happening to both of us, and that we were no longer protected. Whatever that means." Jack stopped for a second, and inside his head he tried to speak to Charlie. *I don't know if this will work, but I don't want to mention that we can talk to each other inside our heads quite yet. Okay? Just nod if you can hear me.*

Charlie nodded in response to Jack, then told Carl, "Jack and I not being affected by the freezing is something too. I don't know what's happening, but as long as it works in our favor, then it's all good."

Carl agreed, "Yes. It's weird though. I'm glad you trusted me enough to tell me. I won't tell anyone. This is going to stay between the three of us."

Jack piped up, "Oh! And Billy too."

Carl's eyes widened. "Billy too? This is happening to him also?"

Jack nodded. "Yup! Found out last night."

Carl shook his head and looked at Charlie. "You'll let me know if my eyes change. Won't you? Seems to be happening a lot. Why stop at me?" Glancing back at the window to see the mist, Carl asked, "Think it's all connected?"

Charlie looked up and out at the mist.

"I have no doubt it is. There are way too many coincidences happening. I really think we need to take this red thing seriously, Maybe surround ourselves in red fully."

Jack looked over at her. "Yes, but we need to test it out today to make sure it isn't a ploy. I mean… yes, I'm pretty sure it will work, but just in case."

Charlie nodded. "Okay, so today we'll go out and test it. But this green mist, we have no idea where it came from, or if it is safe or not. For all we know, it is poisonous and will kill us all. What if it's a trap?"

Carl leaned back. "We don't have answers. Today we need to form a team and see who is willing to take a few risks. We need volunteers to understand that the stuff they do may kill them, but they should be willing to take the chance." Carl stood up. "I hate this. None of this feels right. How do I ask these men and women to volunteer for such a thing?"

Charlie bit her lip. She felt like she probably would regret it but blurted it out anyway. "I'll volunteer for it. I seem to not be affected by the rest of the stuff, so maybe it will be okay for me to go out."

Carl looked at her. "Yeah, but that's just it. What if you are not affected by it? The rest of us might be. What if you went with a team? That way if it doesn't affect you, and something happens, you have a level head?"

Charlie nodded. "That's a good idea."

Jack got up and headed over to the coffee machine. He poured himself a cup, then turned and looked at Carl. "I'm going too. We have a better chance sending two who may not be affected by whatever is going on. That way if anything happens, we can get everyone back here safely."

Just then, Franny entered the kitchen. "Has anybody looked out the window? The fog is green."

Carl pulled out his chair and patted his lap. Franny sat down and wrapped her arms around her husband. He shook his head. "We know as much as you do at the moment. We're going to test it out today and make sure it's safe. As a matter of fact, we should get to that." He motioned for Franny to get up so that he could move.

Franny jumped up. "I'll test it out." Franny headed out towards the front of the hotel, Charlie followed her, along with the rest of them.

Carl scurried down the hall after her. "Franny, wait! We don't know if it's dangerous yet."

"Wait," chimed in Charlie. "I'm going with you." Both women stepped outside the door. Jack ran out after them. Both Franny and Charlie stood among the green fog. There was no odor to it, and they didn't feel any different. 'This is a good thing,' Charlie thought. "You okay, Franny?"

Franny grabbed her by the arm. "It's hard to see anything out here. I can see you though, and I can see Jack." Jack looked around to see what he could see. The view was a bit restricted with the green fog. He could only see a few feet ahead of him, and most definitely not the view of the bridge nor any of the hovercrafts he had seen the previous day. They would never know if any of those aliens were to walk right up to them, 'til the last minute. Franny started to cry. "This doesn't feel right. I feel like we're being watched." Just then, a man dressed in black ran past her. "Did you see that, Charlie?"

Charlie took a deep breath and looked around.

"I didn't see anything, Franny."

Franny started to scream, "He has a knife, and he's coming

my way!"

Charlie still didn't see anyone, but she grabbed Franny's arm and pulled her back into the hotel. Jack continued to look around. He turned and looked at Charlie as she stepped back outside, "There's no one out here." Charlie responded, "It's almost like they're seeing something that we can't see. This happened to Carl on the way back from the barn. He saw a semi-truck trying to run us down, but I didn't."

"Hmmm," said Jack. "Maybe there's something in the air affecting them, but we are not affected, so that's why we can't see it. Hallucinations of some sort." Jack sniffed the air. "It's odorless. There's no smell. Where is the ocean smell or the city smell? It's like it's just gone."

Charlie grabbed Jack's arm. "Come on. Let's go back in. Something doesn't feel right."

After the two of them were back in the hotel, Carl locked the door. "We don't need any more surprises, especially any from those lizard creatures. Franny says there was a man out there, sneaking around in that green fog."

Charlie looked at Franny. "There wasn't anyone out there. Jack and I think there is something in the air causing hallucinations. Carl, do you remember how you felt seeing that semi-truck? It wasn't there either, but it caused you fear. I also believe both Chuck and Mike had something similar happen that caused them to crash into that tree. If this is the case, we need to figure out how to protect you all from this when you are out of the hotel."

The four of them walked into the board room. They could hear the sound of scuffing coming from down the hall. "People are starting to get up," said Carl. "I'm going to have to have some answers for them."

Jack, who stood looking out the window, looked back at Carl. "Let me deal with this. I think someone who's not affected should be in charge of preparing them for the outdoors."

Moments later, Larzo, Marcy, Loretta, and a few others piled into the room. "Have you seen outside?" squealed Marcy.

Jack motioned for them to take a seat. "Yes, we did, and we also did some investigating too. It's a toxic gas-like fog that causes hallucinations. For some reason, Charlie and I are not affected by it. I think it was released last night by the aliens, though I'm not sure of this. It's an assumption. No one is to go outside 'til we figure out how to keep the hallucinations from happening. We'll hopefully have a plan by the end of the day, and if, during this period, you have any ideas, please either let Charlie or me know."

Jack walked over to Carl. Both stood there as the others walked over to the window to look at the green fog. Larzo walked over to Jack. "I have to go on a supply run today, so we need to figure this out. What if we tie bandanas around our faces?"

Jack thought to himself for a second before answering. "That might work temporarily. If you do this, make sure you guys are not exposed very long, even with the bandana on.

These hallucinations are nothing to play with. They're scaring people literally to death. Put the Army surplus store on your list today. Grab as many gas masks as you can. This might be the answer to us being able to walk out there without any issues." Larzo nodded. "I will make that the first stop. What kind of hallucinations are we talking about? I need to warn my men about them, just in case."

Jack leaned over and whispered to Larzo, "Semi-trucks

chasing down Carl while he was driving, dark stranger coming after Franny with a knife, and God knows what Chuck and Mike saw before they crashed."

Larzo took a deep breath. "Okay, so it sounds like some sort of fear-based hallucinations. I'll prepare my men before we leave."

Carl reached over and grabbed Larzo's shoulder before he took off. "Oh, and it might be a good idea if you all wore red."

Larzo looked at Carl like he was crazy. "What are we in? A fashion show?"

Carl shook his head. "We got warning that these creatures can't see the color red, and if there's any truth to it, then we need to pay attention. If this is true, then it's of great benefit to us. Wouldn't you agree?"

Larzo nodded. "Okay, then red it is. Just hopefully we don't stand out to them. I would hate to make myself a target just for a hunch." Larzo took off to find his men. They heard him murmur to himself as he left. "I may as well wrap myself in a ribbon for those bastards."

Carl pulled out his phone to check his messages. As he opened it, he saw messages sent from other cities: 'This is a bloody mess, Carl. These creatures are everywhere we look, and now there's green fog. What are we supposed to do? Do you know what's going on?'

Carl started to text back: 'My friends, this is a horrible mess. Nothing that anyone saw coming. It seems that we are under some kind of alien invasion. They no longer feel the need to hide since they've been discovered. I hate to say it, but we needed to know. The green fog is toxic. It causes hallucinations brought on by fear. We are lucky enough to have some folks who are not affected by it. The rest of us cannot go out in it. We're getting gas masks today from the Army surplus. Maybe you folks should do the same. Yesterday we spotted hovercrafts but are not sure what else since this fog has come. We heard that wearing red keeps them from seeing us. We're testing this today.' Carl pressed send, but before he had a chance to put away his phone, he received a reply.

It said: 'We could see them from the top of our building last night before the fog came. There were so many we couldn't count. One more thing… there are countless buildings missing, and the city looks much different than it did before. I will message you later. I will send a team out to retrieve masks and then do some exploring.' Carl put his phone in his pocket. His stomach felt like it had dropped to the floor.

Carl looked over at Jack. "This is more than just us. It's hard enough when we think it's just within the walls of our city, but this is worldwide. If one fails, we all fail. From now on, we'll work on figuring out who they are and how we can get rid of them. I'm not sure where we start or how we go about it. We don't even know what's safe to do and what isn't anymore. Did Larzo and his men leave yet?"

Jack nodded. "Yeah. They left about twenty minutes ago."

Carl reached over and patted Jack on the back. "Okay. Then I need to find Franny." He headed out the door. "We'll meet later and see what Larzo has come up with today."

Meanwhile, across the city, Larzo and his men pulled into the Army surplus parking lot. "Okay, guys," said Larzo. "Let's make this quick. Grab any kind of mask you can find. We also need flashlights. You never know when we'll lose power." It took about twenty minutes, but the guys managed to find what they needed and fit it into the trunk. After hitting up a few different places to gather supplies, they stopped at the IGA. It was time to stock up on food. A couple of the men went in to get started, while Larzo and Mark stood outside. Larzo leaned against the door and looked around, his bandana tightly wrapped around his face. "I feel ridiculous in this getup. I don't think I've ever worn red before. I'm worried it will make us a target."

Mark shook his head. "Yeah, but they said it will protect us. I want to believe they're right. Don't you?" The two jumped as they heard a sharp screech and the sound of something heavy dragging. Mark took a step back. "What is that? Did you hear it?"

Larzo nodded and motioned for him to be quiet. "Crouch down behind the garbage can and be quiet." Within seconds, two large lizard-like creatures tore around the corner, their dragon-like tails dragging behind them. Larzo's eyes widened. A normal reaction would be to shoot them, but he remembered what happened the last time they met. He closed his eyes tightly and hoped they wouldn't see him. All he could think was, 'Holy shit! We're as good as dead!' The creatures came towards them as the two men crouched silently. Within seconds, they passed them by. Larzo's eyes popped open as he thought to himself, 'What the hell? There's no way that they didn't see us.' He looked at Mark and asked perplexingly, "Did they look this way?"

Mark shook his head. "Yes, they looked right at us, but yet almost right through us. Maybe the red does work. I'm never taking off these clothes again."

Larzo smirked. "Guess we have one more stop to make today."

Mark laughed to himself, "Yeah, somewhere that sells a lot

of red." The men spent the next few hours completing the run and then headed back to the hotel.

Larzo and his men started loading the supplies into the hotel. Carl motioned for some of the guys to help take in the supplies. Jack watched as they carried in boxes of masks and commented, "Excellent. That should protect everyone."

Carl smiled and added, "That's the first step to winning this war."

Jack looked at him. "War? Hmmm. Guess I never thought of it that way but you're right. This is definitely a war. I always imagined a war would consist of bombs dropping and gunshots being heard everywhere. But then again, that's what's showed on television."

Carl nodded and headed towards the board room. "Larzo, when you're finished, meet us in the board room." Jack followed Carl. In his head, he whispered, 'Charlie, the guys are back. If you can hear me, we're heading to the board room.' He giggled to himself. If someone had asked him a few months ago if someone could talk to another person in their mind, he would have told them no, and that they should make an appointment with his secretary.

As they entered the room, he heard Charlie coming down the hall. She smiled as she entered the room. "I was in the kitchen. So, the guys are back? How did it go? Did they see the aliens or the hovercrafts?"

Carl turned to look at her. "Slow down with the questions. I haven't had a chance to ask them yet. When they're done bringing the supplies in, they'll join us here and then we can find out what's happening out there."

Charlie sat down at the table. "I can't help it. I'm just so curious. We can't see anything out the windows anymore. It's like wearing blinders."

Carl took a deep breath. "I can't say that I don't understand. I'm so on edge just thinking about it. How do I keep people safe when I'm not sure what I'm protecting them from?

Moments later, Larzo and Mark entered the room. Larzo blurted out as they headed towards the table, "You guys are not going to believe the day we had. We hit up the supply stores as needed, and in the far distance, we could hear hovercrafts zipping all over the place. They sounded like nothing I've ever heard before. It's like a deep hum." Both guys found a place to sit. "I wish the fog wasn't there. It really does keep us from seeing anything."

Jack leaned back and crossed his arms. "Maybe that's their plan."

Larzo reached down and grabbed at his shirt. "This red shirt saved us. Two of those creatures walked right by us and didn't even see us. I thought for sure we were goners. We grabbed all kinds of red stuff. That's what took us so long. I thought it might help protect us if we put red cellophane up on the windows. What do you think?"

Jack smiled as he unfolded his arms. "Well, look at you this morning. You were all bent out of shape about wearing red. Now, you can't get enough of it."

Larzo blushed. "Hey, it worked, and that's enough for me. Although I still don't understand it, I won't question it again."

Charlie glanced over at Larzo. "I think it's 'cause they are color blind, but I'm not a hundred percent sure on that. I'm sure if you were noisy, they would hear you, but wearing a red shirt helps block the heartbeat, and for some reason that makes a difference. Now, if you're driving a big blue car wearing a red shirt, they may miss you, but they won't miss that blue car. So, you still need to be super careful."

Carl looked at Larzo. "She's right. Caution needs to be taken." Larzo's forehead wrinkled as he looked at Jack. "How did you know about the color red being a weakness? I'm pretty sure we know barely anything about what's happening, yet you have an important fact like that."

Jack glanced over at Charlie then at Larzo. "It's pure fluke that we have that information. We happened to receive a phone call by an anonymous source who told us about it, and I've never been so thankful for it."

Larzo looked down at his shirt. "Who would have thought that such a bright color could be such a blessing? I don't think I've ever had such a hard time on a trip." He looked over at Mark.

Mark nodded. "It was a very hard trip. I know we were wearing the bandanas, but I was paranoid as shit. I didn't have any reason to be either. It's not like those creatures were sitting right there on top of us. It would be different if we had to duck in and out while being surrounded by them, but most of them were out towards the outside of the city. We had to hide every once in a while, due to a hovercraft passing by. We saw maybe five. It's not like we can see very far, but you can definitely hear them coming. The whole city is buzzing. I figure the paranoia was coming from the green fog."

Charlie got up and walked over to the window. "So, do you think there are more of them than what we first thought?"

Larzo jumped up and headed towards her. "From what I can see, yes. There are lots of them, but how many, I cannot tell you. If the fog weren't there, it would be easier, but at least we have a little bit of information to help keep us safe."

Charlie leaned against the window. "I'm going out in it

tomorrow. I need to know what's going on past these walls. I don't want to go alone though." She turned and looked at Carl. "Can you find someone to go with me?"

Larzo tapped her on the shoulder. "I'll go with you."

Carl got up and turned to Jack and said, "You can go with her too. The three of you can explore tomorrow and hopefully get the answers we require."

Charlie felt relief and fear at the same time. "Thanks, Carl. We'll do our best. So, you guys hit up the grocery store, right?"

Larzo glanced over at Charlie. "Yes, we mostly got canned and packaged foods. I don't think anyone has restocked the grocery store for a bit, but we grabbed all we could." She looked back out the window. She thought about what could possibly cause the green fog.

"How long will the supplies last?" Just as Larzo went to answer her, the room went dark. The five of them stood in the dark.

Mark whispered, "Did I forget to pay the power bill?"

Charlie reached into her pocket and grabbed her phone. She flicked on her led light and pointed it towards Mark. As she did, she noticed her service sign was gone. "What the hell? I have no phone service?"

Carl pulled his phone out. "My service is gone too. Shit! How am I supposed to get a hold of the other cities without it?"

Jack leaned back in his chair. "Hmmm. Slowly, they remove anything we depend on."

Charlie slowly made her way over to Jack. "What do you mean?"

Jack folded his arms behind his head and looked up at her. "First they took our view. We now have no way of seeing them coming. They also messed with our air by making us feel insane when we ingest it. Now the power and the phone service are gone. We are sitting ducks in the dark, aren't we?"

Larzo jumped in, interrupting Jack, "I grabbed a bunch of flashlights and candles today in case of emergency. Guess that was a smart move. Something tells me this is not a temporary situation."

Carl sat down at the table and encouraged the others to do so too. "Larzo, grab the flashlights and candles and hand them out to the others, then bring a supply in here." Larzo nodded and grabbed his phone. He turned the led on his phone and headed to the supply room. Carl leaned back in his chair. "Well, ain't this a kick in the nuts?" The three of them snickered.

Charlie glanced up at the window. She silently spoke to Jack within her head. *Something doesn't feel right, Jack. None of them have even noticed the sun hasn't shone since the attack. We've sat in darkness ever since. I mean maybe they haven't noticed due to the fact that the first day there were gray clouds and then suddenly there was green fog. I have been staring at the moon for a couple days, waiting for it to go down.*

Jack looked out the window and up at the moon. 'You are right. I knew something felt really off, but I never noticed that the sun never came back out. Funny, I looked forward to the sun rising every day, and when it stops, I don't notice. I guess my mind has been overly occupied.'

Charlie took a breath, then continued, 'Something else I noticed. All these occurrences happened over a short period of time. Like a wave of huge change. I think it was set in motion somehow. I don't think they know where we are... maybe all of this is to flush us out. Do you think they know

143

we are not immune to their games?'

Jack rubbed his head. 'I'm getting a headache maybe because this is so new to us. We can talk about all of this after we deal with the issue at hand.'

Charlie gave a grimace of a smile, then looked at Carl. "We need to keep all doors locked up tight and keep someone watching them at all times."

Larzo shone the light into the room as he headed back into the room. He laid the box of flashlights and candles on the table. "We have supplied the rooms with what they need. These are for in here. The other folks are not freaking out as bad now that they have light. Mark is with the other guys grabbing the generators out of the basement and putting them in the kitchen."

Carl nodded. "Good job, Larzo. Please let the others know I appreciate their good work, just in case I don't say it enough."

Jack looked down at his watch. It was hard to keep track of time without the sun. He was glad that the watches still worked. "It's getting late, guys. I'm going to head up and get some sleep." Charlie got up when Jack did. The two of them grabbed a flashlight and headed towards the stairs. "Guess we'll be using these now that the power is out."

Charlie looked up the stairs. "Glad we are only on the second floor." The two quickly made up the two flights of stairs and headed into Charlie's room. Bruno went nuts. "I'm so sorry, boy. It's been a super busy day." She cleaned up after both pets, filled their bowls, and then proceeded to rub Bruno's little belly. "I hate leaving him alone so long; it feels so unfair."

Jack flopped down into the chair. "I miss the furniture at your house. It's a lot more comfortable than this." Stormage sleeked across the window sill. It made Jack laugh. "It's nice to know they're not affected by all of this; it must be their innocence. We need to talk about what's happening with us."

"Are you there, Billy?" Charlie asked. Both Charlie and Jack looked at each other as they heard, 'Yeah, I'm here.' Charlie smiled. She wasn't sure how this was happening, but it was kind of cool to have such a connection. 'Billy, when I talk just to Jack, do you hear me?'

Seconds later, Billy answered, 'No, only when you include me in the conversation.' Charlie continued, "Good. Not that I mind, but that means no one else can either. I'm not sure why we all can do this, but I think it's a good thing, and I don't think we should tell anyone about this part just yet." Both Billy and Jack agreed.

Jack spoke up, "Okay, we'll fill you in on stuff. We just wanted to see how you were and make sure you can still hear us. I'll come see you tomorrow and tell you all about what is happening." After saying goodnight to Billy, Jack turned and looked at Charlie. "This is weird. Do you have any ideas about what is going on?"

Charlie pulled herself up and leaned against the wall. "The person on the phone said that you and I will be going through a lot of changes. I'm starting to think they know more about us than you and I do. If I didn't have so many memories inside my head, I would start to wonder if my life was a lie."

Jack shook his head. "I was thinking the same thing. I know it's weird, but I actually remember something from a long time ago, yet I know it didn't happen."

Charlie looked at him. "What is it? Tell me."

Jack leaned towards her. "Okay, but it can't be real. I remember being a teenager around the age of thirteen. I remember you and I down at the beach. You were about ten years old. We were down there having a picnic with our family. That's all I remember. Weird, right?"

Charlie wrinkled up her forehead. "We're not even related. That's a really weird memory, and you've never met my family, so I wonder why you have that memory."

Jack smirked. "I know, right? And it wasn't my family either. I don't remember my family. I was in and out of foster homes most of my life. It feels strange to see me with a family. I imagine it's just something I desired and it's appearing due to all the stress in our lives."

Charlie smiled. "I like that you added me to the memory, making me your sister."

Jack shook his head. "You've been the closest thing to a sister I've ever had. I miss Julie. It's pretty bad when I look forward to her coming to me in my dreams. What do you think she's trying to say in them? Do you think maybe it's for real or just something we want? I would give anything to have her back her with us."

Charlie picked up Bruno and laid him down in front of his food, then turning to Jack, said, "I think it's real. I feel as if she's speaking to us. I don't know if it's from the other side or if she's really alive, but I think she's watching out for us either way."

Jack got up and walked over to Charlie. Leaning over, he hugged her. "Well, then if that's the case, she has said numerous times she's here with us. There's a good chance she's alive and in need of rescuing. I'm heading back to my room to get some sleep and, hopefully, I will hear from her. If you need me, just give me a shout." Jack headed out the door, and as the door shut, she heard *Good night.*

Chapter 9

C harlie woke to Franny barging into her room.
"Get up, girl. We need to put this up on all the
windows." Franny stood at the window stretching
red cellophane across it. "The guys are certain this will make
us safer." Franny glanced over at Charlie. "I'm really scared.
If putting red plastic over the window keeps me busy enough
not to think about our problem, then that's what I'm going
to do. In one breath, I want to be out there seeing what's
happening. The other makes me want to hide under the bed
like a big old chicken." Charlie wanted to answer her, but
Bruno was washing her face with his tongue, and the thought
of opening her mouth to speak and having her tonsils cleaned
did not interest her very much. Bruno jumped down and went
to his food bowl. This gave her a chance to get out of bed and
help Franny. Franny reached up and taped the corners and
asked, "Have you noticed we've had no sun? I don't think this
has come to the attention of the men yet, but I'm sure you
noticed."

Charlie nodded. "Yes, I've noticed, and so has Jack. I'm glad
you realize there's more than green fog going on. I'm not sure
many know how to react to all of this. They may not even
know the extent of danger they're really in. Think about it,

Franny. The sun stopped rising. Something is very different about our world. I need to get out there and see what's going on."

Franny finished putting up the cellophane. "I'm coming with you. My eyes are open. I'm not blinded by any of this, and, unlike some folks, I know the danger we're in. I figure if I come with you, I'll spot stuff the others may not see, so please take me with you."

Charlie thought about it. "You're right. I think you should come with us. Let Carl know. Okay? It'll be you and I, Larzo and Jack. Carl, can get you ready for this mission? Don't forget a gas mask."

Franny took off to speak to Carl while Charlie headed to find Jack. "Come on, boys. You two can run around for a while. I have some stuff to do today, but I'll see you later." Charlie stopped before she got to the top of the stairs. In her head, she searched for Jack. *Where are you?* Seconds later, she heard, *I'm in the kitchen.*

Charlie skipped down the stairs and headed towards the kitchen. She was rather impressed by how easy it was to speak to him. This new gift of hers couldn't be a bad thing, could it? As she entered the kitchen, Jack laid down his cup and reached over to pour her a cup. "Morning, Charlie. There's some coffee whitener. Do you want some?"

Charlie nodded as she took a seat. "Franny wants to come with us today. I told her it was okay. She's pretty good at noticing things. She's the only other person who has noticed that it hasn't been sunny since the shooting. Maybe it's because the moon is so bright it lights up the sky. But the background of the moon is still black and filled with stars. It feels a little surreal to me."

Jack placed the coffee on the table. Grabbing a seat, he turned and looked at her. "She came to me again last night. It was short, but she stood there, and she told me she missed us, that there's so much we don't know. She also said that life is but an illusion, and that we are not safe. She had a look of fear on her face and left. I felt so uneasy about it when I woke up. I need to find her."

Charlie reached over and laid her hand on his, and consoling him, said, "The more answers we get, the better off we are. I think she's alive, and somehow she's guiding us, or at least, I want to believe that." Charlie jumped up and put her cup in the sink. "Let's get ready to go. I need to know what's going on out there. I'm tired of being a sitting duck." The two gathered up the others and the supplies they needed and got ready to head out.

Pulling up behind the grocery store, they parked the car. The four of them jumped out and leaned against the store. Charlie looked at Larzo. "Hopefully, they don't see the car. It should be safe here, right?"

Larzo gave her a thumbs-up and went to the corner of the building to take a look. "Let me make sure we're safe to move." Within seconds, he motioned for them to join him. "We're all clear." They stood in front of the store.

Charlie looked around. She felt her heart drop. There was no way this was home. "Did it look this way yesterday?"

Larzo looked around. They still couldn't see very far, but from what they could see, something had changed. "No. This is not the same. The parking lot is gone. There's no cement; it's all gravel roads. Is that a horse trough?"

Charlie continued to look around. "Sure. Looks like one, and it's filled with water." The four walked through the fog.

On the left, there was an old saloon. Next to it stood a '50s ice-cream parlor. Charlie shook her head. "This is weird. It's a collage of decades. How's this even possible?"

Jack stood there looking up. "I'm not sure, but I don't think any of this was here before. This is where my office was, but this doesn't look like my office."

Charlie looked up. There stood a large statue. Franny leaned her head to the right to have a better look at it. "Nope. That doesn't look like an office building. Is that a dinosaur?"

Just then, Jack realized she hadn't seen the creatures in their true form. He turned to her and said, "You need to be prepared when you see them. They are not human anymore. They're very large and look like giant lizards."

Franny took a deep breath. "Carl tried to fill me in. He warned me not to scream when I see them since that would break my cover. We're wearing red, so we should be safe. If we stay hidden and quiet, they won't notice us."

Jack nodded. "As long as you are aware of that, then you should not have any problems. Don't forget to keep your mask on no matter what."

Charlie yelled for Jack, "Oh my God! You have to see this!"

As they headed towards Charlie and Larzo, they both looked up. It was hard to see through all the green fog, but the Statue of Liberty still stood there. "What the hell? I know we're not in New York. It's like there is a little bit of everything from different places or from different decades. How did this happen?"

Charlie had a few ideas but thought it best to keep it to herself for a little bit. "I'm not sure, but any thoughts can be discussed back at the hotel. Let's keep going forward and see what's going on and try not to trip."

As they looked around, they noticed there were bodies lying around. All of them looked like they experienced a frightful death. Franny stepped over the bodies but not without noticing that and asking, "Have you guys figured out why they all look so scared? It seems they were all killed in different ways. I don't understand this."

Charlie grabbed Franny's sleeve and pulled her along. "It's not time to understand. We need to keep moving."

As they walked through the green fog, little things would catch their eyes from time to time, like the occasional person looking out their window and ducking when they spotted them. Jack stopped for a second and sat on a bench. "Do you think these folks have any idea what's going on? Should we be helping them?"

Charlie stopped and looked back. "It would be nice if we could but think about it, we can't trust to take anyone back to our base. We don't know if they are human or alien anymore. It's not like they can't shape shift."

Jack frowned. "Yeah. I guess so. I just feel bad. Guess it's in my nature to want to help." Jack got up and continued walking. They could hear the hovercrafts getting closer to them. "Those things are loud. It's hard enough to adjust to them when they are farther away … not hard to miss when they are close."

The four took cover behind some garbage cans. Moments later, a craft flew by but not without slowing down and checking out the area. They held their breath, trying to be as quiet as they could. A guy came running out from behind a building. His screams were shattering. Jack wanted to jump out and help him, but the craft hovered above this man as if to watch. He screamed, "Oh my God! He has a chainsaw!

Someone help me! That clown has a chainsaw!" The guy thrashed around, and a look of pure fear hit his face. The group looked around but did not see anyone else there with him.

As they watched, the guy was slowly killed before their eyes. He was sliced into two, as if someone had a chainsaw, but in reality, there was no one there. The body lay there in its own blood, and the craft zoomed off in a new direction. Jack looked around to make sure they were alone, then ran over to check out the body. The guy lay there with the same look on his face as the other bodies had. His death seemed to result from what he was yelling about, yet the group had witnessed no such thing. "Maybe the killer was invisible. I know that sounds stupid but we all saw this guy die," suggested Jack.

Franny leaned against the building behind the garbage cans, her eyes filled with tears. "We're all gonna die, and we won't even see it coming." Her mouth fell to the floor. "The guy I saw with the knife outside the hotel... you couldn't see him, but I did. Could he have really killed me the same way?"

Charlie looked at her. "I don't know, but I suppose so. We really need to be careful from now on. No more taking chances."

The group had been walking for a bit. They noticed a lot more changes that were not there before and more people within their homes. They were getting closer to the outskirts of the city and had noticed the hovercrafts flying around more often. Their deep hum got louder and louder. Larzo ran ahead a bit to see what was up ahead, then quickly returned with answers. "We're getting really close to the action, guys. From this moment on, we must use hand signals only."

The four made their way through the fog 'til they came

to an old corner store. Across from it stood a tall temple-like building. It looked like it was made of stone, sort of like a building the Mayans would have constructed. "Wow!" exclaimed Charlie. "That is beautiful! I definitely don't remember seeing that before." They all ducked behind a large garbage bin in the ally next to the store. Larzo motioned for them to be quiet as he peeked around the corner. They could hear the stomping of the aliens' feet as they walked with the sound of their overly large tails dragging behind them. They definitely were not hard to miss. Charlie glanced over at Franny and said, "I don't know about you, but it's really hard to get the image of that guy out of my head. This has become much more real, but I know I have to hold it together. Nothing good comes from falling apart. I've had this nagging feeling of being watched. I keep looking around, but I don't see anyone."

Franny looked around. "I don't see anyone. Maybe it's because we're out in the middle of nowhere, wearing a bright color. In any other situation, where you feel a need to hide, you would never consider wearing red."

Charlie nodded. "Very true."

From their hiding spot, they could see the creatures. The four watched as the creatures' overly large bodies moved in and out of the green fog. Jack whispered, "They must be able to see through this fog, or they wouldn't have surrounded us with it."

Charlie looked around. Nothing felt familiar at all. The tall stone temples stood where office buildings used to stand. 'What has happened to our city?' she thought. "Are those people over there?"

Larzo and Jack tried to get a better look. "I'm not sure," said

Larzo. "They might be. Looks like people, but we can never be sure anymore. We should get back to the hotel. It will take a bit to make our way back."

Slowly, the group made their way back through the fog. They came upon a building which looked like an old telegraph building. Larzo spotted an unlocked door. "We can rest in there." Inside was dusty and full of cobwebs. It looked as if no one had entered for years.

Charlie ran her finger over the shelves as she walked through. "Why do you think they have all these old buildings here? They look super old... like they're not even from this century."

Franny stood looking around. "I don't know. I find it strange that suddenly our buildings are gone. How did they do it?"

Charlie headed over to the window. She had heard something and was unsure of what it was. Larzo looked up. "Make sure you stay out of sight. We don't want to be spotted."

Charlie crouched as she watched. She saw a man running in their direction. "Someone is coming," she whispered. "He's running from something." She looked closely as he got closer. "He looks human."

Jack scurried over to the window to have a look. "He doesn't look like he's freaking out, so he's not running from illusions." Jack looked around to make sure the man was alone—that there weren't any hovercrafts following him. After being sure it was safe, Jack headed out the door and towards the man. "Hey! Are you okay?" The man looked up, shocked to see Jack. "You're human, and you're not affected by the gas." Jack grabbed him by the arm and pulled him towards the building where the rest waited. "Come on. Let's get out of sight." The two made it in. Jack peered out the window to make sure they hadn't been spotted. "What are you doing out there among them?"

The guy looked at the four of them. "Trying to survive. I assume the four of you are trying to do the same. I'm Nick."

Charlie stepped forward. "Hi, Nick. I'm Charlie. Have you been out there long? Do you know what's going on?"

Nick sat down on the floor. "It's been a few days, I think. I'm losing track fast. One night I'm going for a walk, then suddenly, I'm not there anymore. I tried to go home, but my place isn't there anymore. How's that possible? It just disappeared! I know these creatures are everywhere, so I hid and watched. People are dying by some kind of gas in the air, but it doesn't affect those creatures at all. Do you know they have slaves locked up? I can't get close enough to get a good look, but I saw a few of them."

Charlie wrinkled up her face. "What do they do with those slaves?"

Nick shook his head. "I'm not sure yet."

Larzo looked at Charlie. "We can't take him with us. We don't know if he's trustworthy. What if he's one of them?"

Charlie gave Larzo a funny look. "He can see us in red, silly. He also looks human and isn't affected by this green fog. Why aren't you affected by it, Nick?"

Nick ran his fingers through his hair. "I'm not sure yet, but I'm glad I'm not. Have you seen what happens to the folks who are?"

Larzo shook his head. "Okay, we'll take him with us. But you get to explain to Carl why we brought home a stray, okay?"

The five of them left the safety of the building and headed towards the grocery store. A woman ran past them and kept going, as if she never saw them. A stream of webs dragged behind her as she ran. She was screaming that giant spiders were coming ... that everyone should hide. They looked just to make sure it wasn't true, but then realized she was affected by the gas. One could never be too careful. After making it back to the car, the group stood there for a bit. It was a safe place to stop and catch their breaths. Charlie leaned against the car. Looking up, she noticed how bright the moon was. It was brighter than she had ever seen before. It was as if it was running off the heat of the sun. After about fifteen minutes, they jumped into the car and headed back to the hotel. Nick laid his head back against the seat. Charlie looked over at him and asked, "You okay?"

He glanced over at her. "Yes. It's just nice to be able to rest my head, even if it's just for a few minutes." They drove for about thirty minutes 'til they reached the hotel.

The five stood there while Larzo rang the bell to get in. It took a few minutes, but Carl came running to the door. "Great you're back!" he yelled. Opening the door, he noticed Nick.

Immediately, he asked, "Why would you bring someone back with you?"

Charlie pushed past Carl. "I'll explain later. Don't worry. He's safe. I can feel it."

Locking up the hotel, Carl turned to Nick. "If she says you're safe, then I believe her. Welcome, Buddy. I'm Carl." He reached his hand out.

Nick shook his hand. "I'm Nick, and I'm glad to be here."

Charlie took a deep breath. She was glad to be back too. "He's been out there by himself, Carl. He's seen a lot and can be extremely helpful. Plus, he's not affected by the toxic fog." Carl glanced at Charlie and started to speak, but her voice faded as she heard the voice inside her head *Stupid humans want to interfere with my plan.*

Carl reached up and tapped her on the shoulder. "Did you hear me, Charlie?"

Giving herself a slight shake, she looked up at Carl and replied, "No. Sorry. I was hearing something. That voice I heard at the café. I heard him again." She turned to Jack. "It said, 'Stupid humans want to interfere with my plan.' I think it's them, and they are angry. I could hear it in his voice."

Nick interrupted, "You can hear them?"

Charlie nodded. "Only sometimes."

Carl motioned to Jack. "Find him a room, will you? Nick, you get settled in your room, and I'll come up and speak to you in a bit."

Nick nodded. "So, I can relax here? I haven't been able to get sleep in days. I'm so exhausted."

Jack patted him on the back. "You can definitely get some sleep. Everyone here has everyone's back."

The two headed up to the second floor, to Room 211, next to Jack's room. Nick looked around the room. "This is nice. I never thought I'd get to sleep in a bed again. I never thought I'd see people again not affected by the gas."

Jack grabbed a seat at his table. "Not everyone here is immune to it, but there are a couple of us. How have you not been noticed by them?"

Nick flopped down onto the bed. "Oh, I've been noticed a few times. I booted it and hid. Those buggers are not overly fast, but are extremely strong, and have a real hate for people."

Jack peered over at Nick. "Do you know much about them?"

Nick shook his head. "Not really. Only what I've seen."

Carl knocked and entered the room. "How's everything?"

Nick smiled. "Well, I can finally shut my eyes and not worry about those creatures grabbing me."

Carl walked over and sat next to Jack. "I'm going to brief my people later about what they saw, but I'm sure you being out there, that you have seen quite a lot going on."

Nick leaned up against the wall. "I saw so many people die. That gas makes them see things that don't exist, and they actually die from it. I think they're using the humans that survive as slaves. I can't be sure of that because I couldn't get close enough to see it. Do you know how nice it is to be away from the constant hum of their hovercrafts? They are so loud. You have to keep your eyes open all the time, as you're never sure where they are. Here, at least, you could hear them coming. That alone is something to be thankful for."

Carl leaned forward, and placing his elbows on his knees, asked, "Have you noticed any weaknesses or anything that can benefit the human race?"

Nick thought for a moment. "Other than being faster than them, not really. I think they communicate inside their heads. I've only heard grunts and screeches come out of their mouths." Jack's eyebrow raised as he thought of the conversations he, Charlie, and Billy had inside their heads. Nick continued. "They seem to be quite intelligent, and I see some of them doing stuff like lifting with their minds. I once saw one of them lift a big rock without touching it. It was kind of cool but scary at the same time."

Down the hall, Charlie stood by the window in her room. It had been a long, emotional day. As she looked up at the moon, her eyes filled with tears. "Where are you, Julie?" She thought about the people she saw today influenced by the gas and how one man was murdered right in front of her. Tears fell from her eyes as she turned and flopped down onto the bed. She had held a lot in since all of this started. For the first time, she felt as if things were hopeless. She lay there and cried for the longest time. Nick sat up. A strange look spread over his face. Jack listened. He realized he could hear Charlie crying in his head. He saw Nick's reaction and thought to himself, *Can you hear her too?* Nick looked up at him and nodded. Jack's eyes widened. Nick was like them. "Carl, I'm going to check on Charlie. It's been an extremely hard day, and I need to make sure she's okay." As he headed out the door, he looked back at Nick. He looked as puzzled as Jack felt. "I'll talk to you later, Nick. Have a good sleep."

Carl got up too. "Yes. I'll let you sleep. We'll speak more tomorrow." Outside the room, Carl looked at Jack. "He seems okay. Can you keep an eye on him though?" Jack nodded and headed towards Charlie's room.

He knocked and headed in. "Charlie, are you okay? It's Jack."

Charlie looked up and tears flowed from her eyes as she replied, "Yes." She wiped her eyes. "Why are you here? What's wrong?"

Jack sat on the edge of the bed. "I wanted to check on you. I heard in my head that you were very upset."

Sitting up, she looked at Jack and responded, "It's just been an emotional day. That poor guy who was murdered … he never stood a chance."

Jack shook his head. "Yeah, that was pretty hard to watch. I spoke to Nick. He seems okay. Funny thing, I think he heard you crying too. The look on his face told me so."

Charlie felt puzzled. "Could he be like us? Whatever 'us' means. Maybe he knows why we are how we are."

Jack pushed her over and lay beside her. "I don't know, but he's about to get some sleep. I think he heard me inside my head." Jack glanced at the ceiling. *Can you hear me, Nick?* he thought to himself.

Charlie giggled. "Are you trying to speak to him?"

Jack looked over at her. "Yeah. You try too. See if he answers." Both sat there trying to talk to Nick in their heads. Within seconds, they heard, *I can hear you. I'm not sure why though.*

Charlie gasped and sat straight up. 'So, you are like us? Do you know why we are able to do this?'

Nick rolled over on his side and took a deep breath. *No. When I heard Jack earlier, it was the first time this happened to me. It's never happened before, but there has been lots of weird stuff happening to me lately.* Jack jumped into the conversation. *We should let you sleep. We can talk about this tomorrow. Keep this between us, though. This is no time to freak anyone out about what we can do. They think it's freaky enough that we are not affected by the gas.*

Nick sighed. *Yeah. I could use some sleep and no worries. This is between us. Good night.* Charlie smiled. *Night, Nick.* Jack reached over and rubbed Charlie's shoulder. "Feel better?"

She nodded. "Yeah. I actually do. I just had a lot of emotions trapped inside and so much has happened. I couldn't hold it in any longer. Seeing that man earlier really hit me hard. He had to be so scared. Has anyone filled Carl in on what we saw today?"

Jack sat up. "No. I don't think so. We should go see him now and fill him in."

The two jumped up and headed down to Carl's room. When he opened the door, out popped Bruno. "Bruno, what are you doing here?" Charlie could hear Franny in the background.

"He was visiting me. Come in, you two."

They headed over and sat down with Franny. Carl came out of the bathroom. "Oh, hi. Have you two come to brief me on today?" Carl sat down on the bed. "So, what happened?"

Jack leaned back in his chair. He shook his head then looked at Carl. "It's not good. There are a lot of those creatures out there. They're mostly outside the city limit but the hovercrafts scan the city, looking for humans. The green fog is actually a gas released to help them see better. It's toxic to humans, making them hallucinate. I thought at first that the aliens were doing the killing, but it's fear killing them. Whatever they see is how they die. Today a man died after believing he was being chased by a killer clown with a chainsaw, and a woman was running with spider webs on her clothing, believing she was being chased by giant spiders. We couldn't see anything, but the people who were yelling about it sure did. In our part of the city, it isn't too hard to hide, but the closer you get to the outskirts of the city, it gets quite difficult. We have an advantage being here—those hovercrafts are really loud, so we can hear them coming. When you're closer to all the action, you can't tell where they are 'cause that's all you can hear."

Carl let out a sigh of relief. "Well, at least we have that going for us. So, are you telling me the guy Franny saw in the green fog or gas ... whatever you want to call it, could have actually killed her?"

Jack nodded. "Yes, he very well could have."

Carl looked over at his wife. "Thank God, you're okay. Good thing, Charlie, you were with her and got her back in here safely. I don't know what I would've done if I lost her."

Jack nodded as he looked over at the two girls chatting. "I

know what you mean. Have you seen Billy today?"

Carl nodded. "He's with Loretta at the moment. She's changing the dressing for his wounds. He's healing really well and should be up on his feet within the next day or two."

Jack sat up quickly. "Great! That's such good news. Did you hear that, Charlie?"

Charlie looked over at Jack. "No. What?"

Jack smiled at her. "Billy's healing great."

Charlie's eyes widened. "That's great news."

Franny stretched. "Yeah, he and Loretta have been hanging out together a lot." She smiled. "She may be his doctor, but I think there's more to it."

Charlie grinned. "That's good. He's not so lonely up there in his room." Charlie turned to Jack. "I've had this feeling that someone has been watching me today. I just got that feeling again, and I don't know why." Getting up, she headed to the window. "I think there's someone out there. Or am I now being affected by the gas?"

Franny jumped up and looked out the window and exclaimed, "There is someone out there! As a matter of fact, there are two people out there."

All four of them ran down the hall then down the stairs towards the door. Charlie pressed her face against the glass. "I can barely see them." She opened the door, and looking back at them, took a deep breath. "I'll be right back. There's only one way to find out who it is." She walked out into the green fog. "Who's there?" The two figures stepped forward towards her and out of the fog. It was Julie, and with her stood a child. Charlie's mouth fell open as she ran towards her friend. "Oh my God, girl, where have you been?"

Julie looked tired and hungry. "I've been here, Charlie. The problem is you guys were not here. You were all gone."

Charlie grabbed Julie's arm. "Come. You need to get inside."

When Charlie entered the door, everyone's eyes widened when they saw Julie with her. Jack nearly fell over himself. "Julie, you're okay? I was so worried about you." He reached out and wrapped his arms around her. Her body felt a little limp, like she was weakened from the struggle. "We need to get you upstairs to lie down." He turned to Franny. "Can you get Julie and her young friend something to eat? I'm going to take them upstairs and put them to bed. They're exhausted and are in need of some serious sleep. Come on, girls. You can fill us in tomorrow about what happened."

Chapter 10

The hotel was in a buzz when morning came. Everyone was excited that Julie was now back. Charlie sat up in bed and leaned against the back wall, with Bruno on her lap getting his morning rub. She couldn't help but look over at her best friend sleeping. After all this time, she was back. Who was this little girl she had lying next to her? Whoever she was, she was a cute little girl.

Looking up, she watched the green fog roll across the window. It was a quick reminder that none of this was a dream. The events of the previous days replayed in her mind. The picture of the man lying on the ground after being murdered was stuck in her head. Shaking her head, she thought of Nick. He was much easier on the head. *Who are you, Nick?*

As she turned back to look at Julie, she heard a light moan. *Morning, Charlie.* She leaned forward to take a better look at Julie, but she wasn't awake. Then she heard it again, this time with a slight giggle behind it. *What? No good morning?*

She sat up and inside her mind, she whispered, 'Who is this?' She felt curious. Up until now, it had only been Jack and Billy in her head.

Seconds later, she heard the voice once more. *It's Nick. I felt you thinking about me, so I thought I would say, hi.*

Charlie leaned back. *Could you hear my thoughts?*

No, said Nick. *Just felt you thinking about me.*

Charlie felt relieved. It could be awkward if anyone could listen to her thoughts. *Morning,* she said. *I forgot you can speak this way.* She could hear him as clearly as if she were sitting right next to him.

Thanks for trusting me enough to bring me back here with you. I had a great sleep, and I feel so much better.

Charlie smiled to herself. *Good. I'm glad you feel better. I'll come visit you later. I'm just waiting for Julie to wake up. I'll fill you in then.*

Nick whispered, 'Okay. I'll be here.'

Charlie got out of bed and walked to the window. She missed the days when she could look out the window and see water from the distance and have the sun beaming down on her face. She let out a loud sigh as she turned and went to find an elastic for her hair. Julie opened her eyes, "Morning, Charlie."

Charlie whipped around. "You're awake." She ran over and sat on the edge of the bed. "I've sat here all morning making sure this is real, and that you don't just disappear again."

Julie sat up. "I won't. I promise. I'm so glad to be back. You have no idea what I've been through."

Charlie looked at Julie. "What have you been through? Where did you disappear to?"

Julie looked over at the little girl then back at Charlie. "It was all very confusing. One minute I was down at the police station waiting to have them look at the car. The next minute Officer Johnson grabbed me by my shoulders, blew something into my face, and then I landed on the ground. I looked around, but the cops were gone, and so was the station. I got up and looked for my car; it was nowhere to be found. It was extremely confusing. My phone stopped working, and the sun was gone. I had no idea what to do. I tried to get back to the hotel, but nothing was the same. And do you know how far that hotel is without a car? When I finally made it to the hotel, there was no one there. It was as if none of you were ever there. So, I wandered through the city, without a clue about what was happening."

Charlie's eyes teared up. "You must've been so scared out there all by yourself. I was so worried about you, and poor Jack blamed himself for what happened. If it weren't for the dreams, he would've driven himself nuts."

Julie looked at her. "What do you mean dreams?"

Charlie continued, "Dreams telling us to be careful and warning us of danger."

Julie's forehead wrinkled up. "Those were real? I thought I was daydreaming when I saw you guys. I would warn you in my dreams about the danger you were in. That's crazy that you were really in the dreams. I found it hard to get sleep since that day. There was nowhere safe to really close my eyes. I found a few places though. If I lay back against the buildings, I could close my eyes and meditate just a little. You and Jack were always there with me. It made me feel safe." Julie got up and sat next to

Charlie. She leaned over and laid her head on her shoulders. "I'm so glad to be back. I was really scared out there."

A few seconds later, there was a knock at the door. Both girls turned towards it. So as not to wake the little girl, Charlie whispered, "Come in."

Jack and Carl both glared into the room. "Shhh," said Julie. "Don't wake Christie." Both guys peered over at the little girl and continued towards the girls quietly. Jack grabbed Julie and hugged her. He didn't say anything, but she could sense that he felt guilty about her disappearance by the way he held her. "I'm okay," she whispered to him. "I'm really here, and I'm okay."

Jack loosened up and looked at her. "I should've never let you go that day."

Julie laid her hand on his cheek. "Stop it. I'm fine. I'm here with you guys now, unharmed. You need to stop blaming yourself."

Carl stood there with a confused look on his face. "Who's the little girl?"

Julie got up and stood next to him. She glanced over at the sleeping child. "It's a long story, but that's my daughter, Christie." Julie smiled. "She's the only good thing that came out of this whole experience." The three stood there puzzled.

Charlie gazed over at the little girl. "So, you had a child during the time you were missing? I bet it hurt giving birth to her—all fifty pounds!"

Julie started to laugh. "Smart ass. No. I told you it's a long story and a weird one at that. I was out there, not sure what I was dealing with. She sensed me, and without letting the aliens know, she found me. We found a good place to hide and we talked. Somehow, she showed me the missing memories from nine years ago. They took me and put me in the breeding camp, and after I gave birth, they wiped my memory clean and sent me back here. This is not our home. We're in theirs."

Charlie sat down on the bed. "Wow!" she said. "This is so unexpected and good at the same time. She looks like you; that's for sure. So, she knows you're her mom?"

Julie nodded. "Yes. She helped me remember. I remember

everything now. This is something that has been going on for a very long time. They have both a breeding camp and a slave camp for people who survive the gas. There are half-aliens everywhere, and they probably don't even know that they are. Christie has been with them for eight years. She knows everything we need to know, including their history. When she's up to it, I'll have her fill you in on it. I don't want everyone looking at her like she's different though, so please don't tell anyone about her being half-alien."

Carl stood there looking at the little girl. "She looks so sweet. We won't tell anyone that doesn't need to know. I promise."

Jack sat down next to Julie and wrapped his arm around her. "She'll be fine—half-alien or not. If she's a part of you, then she's a VIP to me."

Julie looked up at him and smiled. "Thanks, Jack. Finding her explained a lot. All those nightmares I had and that symbol I kept seeing." Charlie reached up and put her hand on the back of her neck, then looked over at Jack. Inside her head, she heard, *This is not the time.*

Both Jack and Carl headed towards the door. "We have some stuff to do." Jack smiled at Julie. "I'll be back later."

As the door shut, Christie's eyes opened. She looked around. "Is everything okay, Mommy?" Julie reached over and moved her daughter's hair out of her face. "We're fine. I'm just talking to Aunt Charlie."

Christie sat up and looked at Charlie. She leaned her head a little to the right. "Mommy, you didn't tell me that Aunt Charlie was like me."

Julie looked confused. "What do you mean like you?"

The little girl looked up at her mom and smiled as she

continued, "You know half-human and half-alien."

Julie looked at Charlie. "How is that even possible?"

Charlie took a deep breath and sat down on her bed. "I don't know if what she said is true or not, but since you disappeared, a lot of weird things have happened to me." She turned to show Julie her tattoo. "This showed up first."

Julie moved over to where Charlie sat. Running her fingers over the tattoo, she looked over at Christie. "Do you have one of these?"

Christie nodded. "Yes, mine is on my neck too." She lifted her hair to show her mother. "See? All half-aliens have it. It's so they can recognize each other. Not everyone can recognize others like I do. It's a gift I have."

Julie bit her lips and took a deep breath. "What else has been happening?"

Charlie thought for a second. "Well, I'm not affected by the green fog, and I can speak to others inside my head. Well, just some people, like Jack, Billy and Nick."

Julie stood up and looked at Charlie surprisingly. "Jack? He has this too?"

Charlie stood up and waved her hand in the air. "I don't know what this is or what's going on. This is new to me, but yes, he also the same symptoms, but only Carl knows, and now you. Well, actually Carl doesn't know about us talking in our heads. We wanted to figure out what was going on first." Charlie turned and looked at Christie. "Are you sure I'm the same?"

Christie shook her head. "Yes, it's not a bad thing though, so you don't need to be concerned. We're just different. Mommy says we need to keep it to ourselves though because it may scare other people, and she doesn't want me to get hurt."

Charlie smiled. "Your mommy is very wise." She gazed over at Julie. "I would love it if you would help me figure all this out."

Julie's eyes teared up. "I'm not going anywhere. This half-alien thing is now part of my life. She stopped and paused for a moment. "Everyone in my life is half-alien." Her eyes widened as she gave a sarcastic giggle. She reached over and hugged Charlie. "Who's Nick?"

Charlie smiled. "It's the new guy we found yesterday. He's a really nice guy, and he's also going through what I am. Are you going to talk to Jack about all of this?"

Julie shook her head. "Yeah, as soon as I feed this little one. He needs to know I'm okay with this. I'm so sorry I haven't been here for you both."

Charlie hugged her. "I'm heading over to Nick's room. I need to speak to him. Will you tell me more about what you saw later?" Julie nodded as she gathered her daughter together.

"Let's go get some breakfast."

Charlie headed towards Nick's room. She knocked on the door before opening it. "Hey! Are you up? It's Charlie."

Nick stood by the window pulling his shirt over his head. She noticed as the shirt slid down over his back, that he had the same symbol. Turning his head towards her, he answered, "Hey! I was just about to go find you."

Charlie wandered over to his table and sat down. "I was just talking to Julie. Up 'til now, did you know anything about the stuff happening to you?"

Nick sat down next to her. "Not really. All I know is I wasn't affected by the gas, and that I was able to speak to both you and Jack."

Charlie reached down and lifted the back of his shirt. "What about the tattoo on your back?"

Nick tried to look at his back to see what she was doing. "What tattoo? I don't have one."

Charlie pulled him over to the mirror and lifted the back of his shirt. "Look in the mirror."

Nick's jaw fell. "What the hell! Where did that come from?"

Charlie ran her fingers over it. "I saw it when I walked in." She reached up and lifted her hair to show him hers. "Mine showed up not too long ago. I found out this morning why we're different from the rest. If I tell you, it has to stay between you and me. I'll fill in Billy and Jack later, but for now, just us."

Nick grabbed Charlie's hand and pulled her over to the edge of the bed where they both sat down. "Tell me. I want to understand what's happening."

Charlie hoped it wouldn't freak him out. "We're part alien."

He started laughing. Charlie just looked at him as he asked, "Oh, you're serious? How is that even possible?"

Charlie took a deep breath and threw her hands in the air. "I have no clue how it's possible, but it is. I would've never thought it was possible before, but then who would've ever thought the world would be taken over by aliens."

Nick took a second and thought about it. "You're right. It's still a lot to swallow though." He reached over and wrapped his arms around her. "At least I'm not alone anymore."

Charlie's eyes widened as she felt his arms around her. Not only did it feel nice, but he smelled really good. Pulling away, she looked at Nick and stated, "I have a few things I need to do." She smiled at him as she got up. "There's coffee and food in the kitchen, if you want."

Nick smiled back. "Thanks." She nodded as she headed out

the door. As she walked down the hall, she thought to herself, 'Remember, everyone is dealing with a crisis, Charlie. You don't want to get distracted by the new guy.'

Jack knocked on Billy's door. "Come in!" Billy yelled. Jack opened the door and wandered in. Billy laid down his magazine as he asked, "If you see Larzo today, can you get him to drop off more candles? This one is starting to get low."

Jack sat down next to him. "Will do. How are you feeling?"

Billy pulled himself up and leaned against the wall. "Much better. Loretta says tomorrow I can get out of bed. She's a great girl. Didn't you two used to date?"

Jack smiled. "Yeah. For almost five years. We both just wanted different things out of life though, so we went our separate ways. She's a very nice girl though and a great person."

Billy grinned. "So, what's been going on out there? Have I missed anything? She won't tell me anything. She says I need to have stress-free rest."

Jack leaned forward and placed his elbows on his knees. "A lot has happened since that night. As you notice, we lost power, and there are no phones that work anymore. The creatures we saw are out there, and they're not hiding anymore. There are hovercrafts flying around our city, which is covered in a green fog and is toxic to humans. There are a few that are immune to it, but it causes hallucinations that literally kill you if you see them. They have some sort of camps out there, filled with human slaves. It's not a good situation out there, but we did manage to get Julie back and find a new guy named Nick."

Billy's face filled with shock. "Holy shit! And I slept through this? How did this go from a simple assassination to this?"

Jack shook his head. "I'm not sure. I've asked myself the same question. Nick is like us. He's immune to the green fog and can talk to others inside his head."

Billy nodded. "Yeah, but is he trustworthy?"

Jack got up and got ready to leave. "Yeah. I believe so. Charlie trusts him, so why shouldn't I?"

As Jack opened the door, Loretta walked in. "Oh, hi, Jack. I'm just coming to check on my favorite patient. He's doing great … should be back on his feet tomorrow as long as there's no heavy lifting."

Jack smiled. "That's great. Talk to you both later."

Jack headed back to his room. He thought about the events that had led to this day. 'Why has this happened to us? I wish I could understand what led to this. Then maybe I could figure out how to end this.' He opened his door and walked over towards the window. He noticed his candle was starting to get low too. *I*

better remember to ask for more candles, or we'll all be sitting in the dark, he thought. As he stood and watched the fog crawl across the window, there suddenly was as a knock at the door. It was Julie. She walked in and sat down at the table. "Charlie and I spoke earlier. She told me about all the changes you both have been going through." Jack pulled out a chair and sat down with her. She continued, "My daughter Christie is half -alien. She has another name for it, but I can't remember at this moment. She told both Charlie and me that she was like Aunt Charlie. Chances are if she's half-alien, then so are you, since you are having similar experiences. I don't know how this is even possible and maybe that's because this is as new to me as it is to you, but I don't care if you are fully human or not. I love you guys, and I will help you learn more as time goes on. But for your safety and my daughter's safety, I truly believe we need to keep this a secret for now—from anyone who doesn't need to know." Jack was taken aback for a second about being half-alien.

"How is your daughter half-alien?"

Julie sighed. "Well, apparently, nine years ago, I was taken and put in the breeding camp. After I had her, I was sent back to the human world without her." Jack gasped.

"What do you mean back to the human world? I know it's different out there, but are we not in the human world anymore?"

Julie reached over and tried to calm him. "No. We're not. The two worlds were somehow connected, but I'm not sure how. Tomorrow, I'll get a few of us together and Christie will tell us everything she knows. She has been taught the alien history and what they are capable of. She's a good girl, Jack, and I don't want her thrown under the bus because she's half-alien." He shook his head to assure her.

"I won't tell anyone. Whoever you trust is as far as it will go." Jack let out a light moan. "Has anyone told you about Billy and Beth?" Julie shook her head no. He continued, "Billy has been in bed dealing with huge gashes in his side due to these creatures. Beth never stood a chance. She died the night we went to assassinate them. One of the creature's large tails crashed into her head."

Julie shut her eyes and bit her lip. "Oh my God! I can't even imagine how awful that was. I have to get back to my daughter. Don't panic over this, Jack. Our world, their world … either way, we are all together and we'll deal with it." Julie got up and headed back to her room. Jack sat there. He never even imagined they were anywhere but in the human world.

'How the hell were they going to fix this now?' he thought.

Later that day, Charlie stood knocking at Jack's door. "Are you there, Jack?" After hearing him say come in, she headed into his room. "I have some candles for you. I just finished dropping some off to Billy." Placing them on the table, she turned and looked at him. "So, did you and Julie get to talk?" Jack placed his crossword book on the table and took a seat.

"Yeah. We talked earlier. She told me that her daughter says we are half-alien. That sounds a little weird. Don't you think? Well, at least she's not too freaked out by it ... a lot less than I am."

Charlie gave him a half smile. "I was going to come talk to you, but I knew she wanted to, so I went and talked to Nick about it. Did you know he has the same tattoo as we do? It's on his back, right in the same spot as yours."

Jack grinned. "Oh, yeah. How do you know?"

Charlie swatted his arm. "Oh, stop! He was putting his shirt on when I got there. Yes, I find him attractive, but it's not like I need a distraction with everything going on. God, I wish I had some apple pie right about now—with a big gob of ice cream on the side. Nothing better than pie to help you think. I've been thinking about the lady who called us. How does she know us? Does she know we are half aliens?" Jack cleared his throat to get her attention and motioned her to the table. There sat a plate with apple pie on it, and on the side, was a serving of ice cream. Charlie felt confused. "Where did this come from?"

Jack looked as confused as she did. "I'm not sure. It just kind of showed up after you wished for it."

Charlie reached over and pushed it away. "I have no idea where that came from." She stood up and looked out the window. "Do you think it's a trick from those aliens?"

Jack raised an eyebrow. "Yeah, they must be sitting out there saying, 'we will trick her... give her some ice cream and pie. That will teach her.' We are half-aliens. Maybe you get what you really want by wishing for it."

Charlie shook her head. "No matter how it happened... back to the topic on hand. Do you think that lady knows who we are for real? She knew too much to be a stranger—stuff we didn't even know. How can we not know who she is? I can think

back." Charlie paused. "Wait. My memories are different." Charlie sat back down. "Jack, why are my memories different?"

Jack took a second to answer. His mind was sorting through his own memories. "Mine are not the same either. I don't know why they're different or how it's possible. I think I've been living a lie."

Charlie got up. "I need to go think for a bit. This has gotten to a whole different level of crazy, and I'm not sure how to handle it." After opening the door, she turned to ask Jack, "What if these are our real memories? That means someone didn't want us to know."

Charlie headed down the hall and into her room. She shut the door to her room, flopped down onto the bed and rolled over to pet Bruno, who patiently lay there waiting for his belly to be rubbed. "At least your life is real, my little friend. I don't even know who I am anymore. I wish life was simple again and you and I were on our way to the park." She thought about the pie that appeared in front of her. Could she really have done that? There was no one else there so it must have been her, or maybe it was Jack. The lady who called—could she be the woman in her new memories? Charlie felt frustrated. She thought about her family out east. Her stomach felt sick as she realized they were not even real. Jack was now in her memories. *Holy shit! We're related,* she thought. There was so much going on in her head. She was glad to be alone to have time to sort through it all.

Meanwhile, Julie and her daughter sat at the table in the kitchen. Christie was on her second sandwich as Carl entered the room. "Oh, there you are. How are the sandwiches, Christie?"

Christie smiled. "Good."

Julie looked up. "I'm so glad to be back here and safe once again."

Carl pulled out a chair and took a seat. "It had to have been hard out there. What happened while you were out there?"

Julie looked over at the little girl and said, "Take your sandwich up to the room. I'll be up in a few minutes." She whispered to Carl, "I saw a lot of people die for no reason at all. There were women screaming while being raped by the aliens. They were put into a breeding camp where they would be impregnated by them and then sent back to the human world with wiped memories. Some women have been there for a very long time and have become permanent residents of that camp. The other camp is for the slaves—the men who build their city and do all the grunt work for those bastards. I don't think those men ever get to go home. They work them and then shove them back into their cages 'til they need them again. Those creatures let off such a gruesome screech. I don't think I'll ever forget it. Every time I shut my eyes, it's all I hear and all I see. We are in serious trouble, and I don't think anyone truly understands that this will completely eliminate humans if we don't reverse this fast." Julie got up. "I need to go be with my daughter. We need to find a way to get rid of them, and fast." Carl nodded as Julie headed up to her room.

Charlie was leaving as Christie got there. "Hi, Aunt Charlie."

Charlie looked down. "Hey, you. Is that a good sandwich?"

The little girl nodded. "I really like it. Daddy never let me have stuff like this. He always said it was stupid human food. He really hurt my feelings and didn't seem to care that I was half-human. Mommy says he was an insensitive jerk, and that I'm perfect just like I am." Christie smiled as she entered the room. "Now, I can eat these all the time."

Charlie smiled as she exited the room. "Your mommy is a wise woman."

Franny was coming up the stairs as Charlie was coming down. "I'm off to bring our little princess some cookies." She smiled as she walked towards the room. Franny knocked as she entered the room. "Look what I have for you. Fresh out of the oven! They may be a little warm, so be careful."

Christie smiled. "Cookies! Yay!!!"

Franny stood back and looked at the little girl. "I used to dream of having a daughter. Every night as I fell asleep, there she was. Some nights I still dream of her. Silly, really, as I can't have kids. Now I have you to spoil, and it makes me so happy."

Christie looked up at her. "You never know. Maybe you'll have a daughter after all." Christie smiled as she grabbed a cookie and started eating it.

Julie smiled as she entered the room and saw Franny, "I'm so glad to see you. With everything going on, I never really had a chance to tell you how happy I am to be back with you and the rest."

Franny hugged her. "I missed you like crazy. You have a beautiful little girl, and I'm going to spoil her." She laughed as she left the room. "Talk to you later."

Charlie stood by the front door of the hotel. She watched the green fog roll around and across the windows. She knew the lady was out there, and her suspicions were that she might be her mother. A hand touched her shoulder. "What are you looking at?" asked Nick.

Charlie gazed over at him. "Just thinking. All my memories are messed up. None of them feel real anymore. What I thought was the truth is a lie. I have to figure out who I am all over again."

Nick took a deep breath. "I've had some weird memories myself. My parents in my head don't exist anymore. How weird is that?"

Charlie nodded. "Yeah, mine either. I have to find my mother. I think she's out there. I remember a house I grew up in, so maybe I'll start there."

Nick reached over and grabbed her hand. "Well, you're not doing it alone. I'll help you find all the answers you need."

Charlie smiled as she laid her head on his shoulder. "Not only do I need answers, but we need to figure out how to get rid of those aliens. Any ideas?"

Nick turned and looked her in the eyes. "None at the moment, but if there's a way, I'm sure we'll find it. I want life back again, where the sun actually shines, and the moon actually represents the end of the day. I want to go to restaurants and walk through a park filled with flowers. There's so much I want to do again. I'm not about to give up without a fight."

Charlie smiled. "Good … 'cause I feel the same way." The

two stood there for a while before they went their separate ways. The night dissipated slowly, as the people in the group had a lot on their minds.

Chapter 11

Charlie was up early. She fed and cleaned up after her furry crew. "I have a lot to do today, guys. You'll have to entertain yourselves. I can't take any chance, Bruno, on taking you out there. I don't know how you will react to the green fog." As she headed out of the room, she left the door open a smidge so that both Bruno and Stormage could get out if they wanted to. She wasn't sure where she wanted to start, but she had it in her mind today that she was going to find her mother and get some answers. She stood at Nick's door. The thought of him made her smile. *The world may be ending, but at least I got to smile again,* she thought. Before she lifted her hand to knock, the door opened. "I'm all ready," said Nick. "I knew what you were up to before you even said it. Let's go find your mom."

Charlie smiled as she turned and headed for the stairs. "We have to walk. I don't drive. It isn't far from here though. As long as we're careful not to be seen by the aliens, we're fine. I have a flashlight in my purse just in case we need it." The two set off into the green fog. "I don't know if I can ever get used to this," said Charlie.

Nick glanced over at Charlie. "Stay close so we don't get separated. There's nothing about this world that I could ever get used to." They walked down Main Street and towards the park. Nothing looked at all like it used too.

"I used to walk my puppy through this park; only, it was pretty then, and it didn't contain any alien statues. Bunnies and squirrels used to run through the park. I loved to feed them all. I wonder if it will ever look the same again." Just as she was about to continue, the loud hum of a hovercraft got closer and closer. The two ran and took cover behind some bushes. "Damn! We should've worn red. I never thought they would be in this area. I wonder why they're here."

Nick looked at her. "What? Why red?"

She whispered, "They can't see through it. It blocks them from viewing stuff. It's why there's red all over our windows." They watched as the hovercraft passed them by.

"I'm glad those things are loud," said Nick. "It makes it easier to be out here. Imagine if they made no noise. We wouldn't have a chance. How much further to the house?" Charlie stopped and thought about it. Since she couldn't see very far ahead, she had to try to remember.

"It's probably about 40-feet from the park, then we'll take a left and go to the end of the street. The last time I was there, I was seven years younger, or at least I think I was. I don't know what's real anymore. Hopefully, this woman will have some answers for me, especially if she is my mother." They walked and talked for a bit 'til they came to the street the house was on. "It should be just down there," said Charlie.

Nick grabbed her hand. "Are you ready for this?"

She took a deep breath. "I don't know, but it isn't like we had a chance to be ready for any of it. This is going to get worse before it gets better, if it gets better."

He stopped her for a second. "You need to remember, we

are all in this together; you're not alone." They arrived at the house. Both stood there for a few minutes before moving towards the door.

As Charlie knocked on the door, she imagined what she would say when the woman who might be her mother opened it. After standing there for a few minutes, Charlie said, "I don't think anyone is going to answer. Should we just go in?"

Nick pushed open the door and looked around. "It doesn't look like anyone is here."

The two wandered in further. Charlie stopped and looked around. The house was charming and lovely, not at all how she imagined it. On the walls, there were pictures. She walked along each and every one of them taking a good look. There were pictures of her when she was a little girl and next to her was Jack. "Oh my god! Jack really is my brother." She pulled the picture off the wall, took it out of the frame and put it in her purse. "I need to show him this later. He'll want to see this." She kept looking at all the pictures. "I look like her, so she must be my mother." She turned to Nick. "This is where I grew up. All the memories are just now coming back to me. I don't understand why I didn't have them all along. Why the fake memories?"

Nick shook his head. "I really don't know. I have screwed up memories too, but not like yours." He stood at a desk going through paperwork. He came across an old letter for Sarah from Charlie. "There's a letter to your mom from you. Here, put this in your purse. It might help you get answers." Charlie took it, gave it a quick glance, and put it in her purse. "I don't think we're going to get any answers here other than what we already have. We should go." The two turned and as they started towards the door, a voice yelled out, "Charlie, wait!

Don't go."

A woman stood in the doorway that led to the basement. "I was in the basement. Your father had it built to keep me safe in case of a war. I never really have to go anywhere. I had hoped you would come. I figured your memories would start to come back to you after the worlds switched." She walked over and sat down in the living room, then motioned for the two of them to join her.

Charlie sat down and looked at her. "So, you're really my mother?"

The woman smiled. "Yes, I am."

Charlie leaned back in the chair. "I don't get it. Why all the lies?"

A look of guilt covered her mother's face. "Your father and I thought you would be safer if we cloaked your mind, out there with all the others and not having any worries about what's happening. Does your brother remember yet?"

Charlie laid her face in her hands. "Yes, he knows a bit, but this all feels so weird. It's been seven years. How could you keep me away from family for so long, living under the illusion that my family and I don't get along, and even worse, Jack believes he was in foster care."

Her mother, Sarah, took a deep breath. "Your father had a hard enough time keeping me hidden when dealing with his own kind. The thought of having you both in danger is not something I wanted to risk. You and your brother are only out there in the human world because of me. If he would've had his own way, you would be working with the aliens. His love for me is strong, but his alien traits are still there."

Nick took Charlie's hand and whispered, "It's okay."

Charlie looked at her mother. "Are you safe in this house?

With you being fully human, how will you make it through all of this?"

Her mother got up and walked over to the drawer next to the television. "I'll be okay. I promise. I have something for both of you. I wrote down some things you need to know about the aliens. This doesn't apply to half-aliens, as you are built differently than they are. You are half-human, meaning you have humanity and choices." She handed Charlie an envelope. "This contains anything I ever heard your father say about his kind. Maybe it will help our kind put an end to all of this."

Charlie put it in her purse and reached over and pulled her mother towards her. "No more cloaking me. I need to remember everything." She hugged her mother before heading towards the door and said, "You keep safe and make sure he doesn't know we were here."

The two headed down the road towards the park. With so much on their minds, the two walked quietly, hand in hand. Meanwhile, back at the hotel, Julie was frantically searching for Charlie. "Has anyone seen her? Jack, have you seen her?"

Jack looked around. "Nick is missing too. They're probably together. I wouldn't worry too much. He seems like he cares about her and would protect her."

Julie looked over at Carl. "Okay, Jack, can you get Carl and Franny? Christie is going to fill the three of you in on the aliens. Meet us in my room." Julie left to be with her daughter as Jack gathered the others.

Before he got the others, Jack said, "You two head up there while I get Billy. He needs to be part of this too. The more answers we get, the better off we are."

Julie sat on the bed with her daughter. "Make sure you tell them everything you know. This will help us. Hopefully, it will get us home. Just think, when we're home, you'll have your own room, and we can have a wonderful life together."

Franny and Carl showed up seconds later and sat at the table. "We're just waiting on Jack and Billy."

Julie looked up and asked, "Billy's coming?" They waited about five minutes. Then, finally, both Jack and Billy both joined them in the room. Julie looked at them all sternly. "Christie is going to tell you everything she knows about the aliens. Please let her talk, and remember, she is a child. No questions. The answers to any questions are for us to find out, not a child." She looked back at Christie. "Okay. Go ahead. We're all listening."

Christie looked around, then leaned against her mother as she spoke. "We're not aliens, at least not in our eyes. We are Zafarians, and we come from the planet Zafar. There's no water left there, and the air is polluted. I was with my mommy 'til they made her leave." She looked up at her mother and smiled, then continued, "We call the main guy *the mighty one.* He is the one who created the Zafarian world, keeping it away from the human world. They taught us a lot in school. They also taught us that they don't like humans very much. We're not supposed to speak English outside our heads, but someone had to speak to the human children. I'm half-human, so I wanted to know about them. A lot of them were scared. I wanted to tell them they would be okay. We learned a lot about them in history class, like they first came two hundred years after the Mayans first did. They were our friends then, before they started to hate humans. That's where the two worlds separate. The mighty one created a portal there to separate them. They learned to live like the humans, and the people taught our people how to grow their food and build temples. After the Mayans didn't live anymore, the others got mean and told us we were not allowed to live with them. We were not allowed to work, and we couldn't go to school with their children."

Julie smiled at her daughter. "Good job. Keep going."

Christie added, "The Zafarians were forced to cloak themselves and live among you in secret. Daddy says it was unjust and degrading. I don't know what that means, though." She looked up at her mother.

Julie smiled. "It means it wasn't fair, and it made them feel not wanted.

Christie continued, "They used the cloak so they could do all the stuff they used to be able to do and to take care of their families. They left everything from their lives on Zafar in the main ship; it is buried in the ruins. I always wanted to see it, but we were never allowed. That's all we learned in class, but I know more than that. I heard them talking all the time. The gas they use on our world is to sort out the strong from the weak. Only the strong can survive the breeding or are able to put in long hours building temples. It's green, so they can see better. The sun makes it hard for them to see red and orange. We're not allowed those colors. It doesn't affect half Zafarians. They are taking your world because they say it is supposed to be their world. You took it from them. They told us there are lots of us out there in the human world; that pretty soon the humans won't stand a chance. They make me mad. They don't care that I am half-human, plus I don't want my mommy or Aunt Charlie hurt."

Julie hugged her little girl. "That's enough for today. Franny, are there any cookies in the kitchen?"

Franny got up. "Yes, and I can take her to get some." The

two of them headed to the kitchen for a treat as the rest sat and spoke.

"At least we know who we are dealing with now, and why this is all happening." Jack said as he crossed his arms and leaned forward. "I think that if we want more answers, they are buried in the Mayan ruins. Maybe we should take a trip and look for answers about how to get rid of them."

Carl rubbed his hand across his knee. "This is all good stuff to know. We have plenty to think about to figure out our next steps. Thanks, Julie, for letting us listen to Christie. She's a good little girl." Carl walked to the door. Jack and Billy were moments behind him.

"I'll drop by later," said Jack.

Just as the meeting with Christie ended, Charlie and Nick returned, en route to the kitchen. Franny stood at the counter with Christie, putting cookies on a plate. She looked up and smiled, "Nice to see you two are back and safe."

Charlie grabbed a seat at the table. Nick went to his room. Christie ran over to her and said, "I told the others all about the Zafarians. That's us, Aunt Charlie. We're not really aliens; we're just different."

Charlie ran her fingers through the little one's hair. "You are so right. I'm glad I finally got to meet you."

Christie looked up at her aunt and asked, "Where were you? How come you were not here?"

Charlie leaned over, "I was out finding my mother and trying to get some answers. I managed to get a few."

Before heading back to Franny and going back to her room, Christie asked, "Is your mommy a Zafarian?"

Charlie shook her head. "No. She's human. My father is the Zafarian." Charlie laid her purse on the table, then leaned back in her chair and thought about her morning. She was a little relieved knowing she wasn't losing her mind, but at the same time was upset. She was part of what she feared the most. Somehow, she had to tell Jack all about it, and she definitely wanted to wait to open the envelope in her purse 'til he was there. After all, he was part of this too. He was her brother—her real brother. She leaned forward against the table. How could she not have known? They had always had a great connection, but she thought that was because they just got along. She smiled when she thought of Nick. He was really good about all of this. She liked how supportive he was when she spoke to her mother. She wondered if they would have ever met if things were different. She was surprised that any good had come out of this whole mess, but he was definitely one of the good things. Charlie left to check on Julie. The two talked for a while about their respective days. The hotel remained pretty quiet for a good portion of the day.

Later, Carl marched down the hall towards the board room. He was looking for Larzo or Mark—whomever he could find first. Larzo sat by the window drinking a cup of coffee. "Good. I'm glad I found you. Form a team to go out. We need to stay on top of what the aliens are doing. I want to know every step they make. Make sure you're all taking safety precautions and only take those who know what they're doing." Larzo nodded, grabbed his cup and took off to prepare the others.

Carl walked to the window, and as he looked out at the green fog rolling across it, he took a deep breath. He thought to himself, *How do we get rid of these bastards? There has to be a way. Maybe we're just missing it.*

Charlie walked into the room. "Sorry I missed the meeting, Carl. I found out some interesting information today. I kept having all these new memories and none of them were anything I remembered before." She pulled out a seat next to him. "Turns out, my mother lives right here in this city. You know how these bastards were cloaking themselves, right? Well, Jack and I were being cloaked by our father. We didn't know about it, of course. It was for our own protection, I guess. She gave me an envelope which has everything that she wrote down …. anything she can remember my father saying. I don't know if any of it is useful or not, but I'm going to go through it tonight with Jack, and then I will hand it over to you. Jack has no idea about what's happening with us, so I want to fill him in as soon as possible."

Carl nodded. "Wow! How did that feel to find out your whole life was a lie?"

She paused, "But it wasn't … I mean, at first, I thought it was too, but I was still with Jack. I met my best friend Julie, and I found passion in life. I met you and Franny. I have totally enjoyed life for the past seven years. So, no, I don't think it was a lie. I just now have two lives that somehow combine as one."

Carl frowned. "You have a good way of looking at it, but still it has to be a lot to take in. This whole mess is hard to take in. We have groups all over, and I've lost contact with them all. They have hardly any information about what's going on. What's going to happen to everyone, even if we win? The other cities won't stand a chance without the knowledge that we have."

Charlie frowned. "But how can we help them? Is there a way without cell phones?"

Carl threw his hands up in the air. "I don't know. They used handheld radios in the past, and they seemed to work, but then who's to say anyone has one. Besides, where the hell would we ever find one nowadays?"

Charlie bit her lip. "Would it really help us, though?"

Carl nodded. "I think so. It would be the only chance we really have to warn anyone." Charlie remembered the apple pie, and thought to herself, 'I wonder how I did that?' She closed her eyes and thought to herself, 'I really want a handheld radio. We need one to save lives and warn others.'

Carl started spazzing out. "What the hell, Charlie! Where did this come from?"

Charlie opened her eyes and looked at Carl, who was holding a handheld radio. "Oh my God! It worked!" She yelled.

Carl's eyes widened as he asked, "You did this?" She nodded. "Yes. I told you things were getting weird for me. I wasn't sure I could, but I'm so glad I did."

Carl started to set it up. "Well, I'm not sure how you did it, but thank you. You're a life saver."

Carl sat in front of the radio studying it carefully. Then he glanced at Charlie. "I've never used one of these. It might take a few times to get it right. Let's hope we can get a hold of the people we need to." Pressing the button, he spoke sternly. "Is there anyone out there?" He let go of the button and listened.

After doing this for almost an hour, he finally got an answer. "Hello. I'm here."

He pushed the button. "Who's this, and are you with a group?"

The voice answered quickly, "I am Rick, and I am with the Mexican rebels."

Carl took a deep breath. "Oh, wow! Am I ever glad I reached you!" Within seconds, another voice jumped into the conversation. "This is Colonel Beck. I'm with the US Army. I'm sorry to interrupt your private conversation, but in a situation like this, I have no choice. We are facing a pretty serious situation here and without any phone service or power, we have not been able to reach anyone. I couldn't help but to hear the word rebel. Are you an underground group?"

Carl pushed the button. "Yes, sir. We are. We've been following this situation for a bit and have learned a few things. Rick, you need to listen to this too, as it's important for everyone. These aliens have been here since the Mayan civilization. They feel this is their world, and they have a serious hatred for humans. They're unable to see the color red and can't see through it. Orange and yellow are harder for them to see and also confuse them. They are fast on their feet, and their tails are deadly and can kill on contact. Bullets cannot kill them; they are self-healers. We are trying to figure out how to kill them and will fill you in as soon as we figure it out. The green fog is toxic. It causes a person's greatest fears to come true, and it will literally kill them. Gas masks are important when going out. We haven't lost anyone who was wearing one. Oh, one more thing you need to know. This is no longer the human world. We're in the world they created." He let go of the button and looked at Charlie. "I hope they got all that and take it seriously."

The colonel replied, "Well, that explains a lot. If this wasn't happening right in front of my eyes, I would think you were crazies. So, we wear red, and they can't see us? Okay. I've written all of this down."

Carl answered quickly, "Yes, but if you move around them, they have good hearing and can hear you. We have experts with us dealing with this." He looked at Charlie and smiled. "We also have a team going out daily watching their every move. They have camps built for breeding and slavery. Have you seen these yet?"

Rick jumped back into the conversation. "Carl, I just spoke to Mike. He says he's glad you got through. He's been waiting for your call. He found a radio and hoped you would get one. We wrote all this down. We're forming a team to do the same. Colonel, I don't know what luck you guys have had down there, but you found the one guy who can help you through this. He's the head of all this, and he has an amazing team on hand."

The colonel came back on and said, "Keep us informed. We're following your instructions. I'll form a team today and put them on duty—watching the aliens. Your information just might save lives; I've lost so many already, when trying to go against them. I'll check back with you soon. I need to go update my men."

Carl pressed the button. "Rick, something else. I'm thinking about sending a group down that way, but I don't know much about it yet. So, I'll fill you in when I know more."

Rick replied within seconds. "Sure thing. Just let us know, and we'll give them a warm greeting."

Carl hung up the handset and turned to Charlie. "None of this would've been possible without you."

Charlie got up. "I'll see you later. I'm getting hungry." She set off to the kitchen. She hadn't eaten anything all day and knew she needed to, before it made her sick. Marcy and Loretta stood at the counter making sandwiches. Both looked up as Charlie entered the kitchen. "Hey, girls. Oh my God, you're making sandwiches. Can I have one? I'm so hungry."

Marcy handed her a sandwich. "We're making them for the team that's going out on duty. They're going to be watching the aliens and reporting everything they're doing. We're making sure they eat during their shift."

Charlie pulled a chair over to the counter. "That's a great idea. How have you two been?"

Loretta glanced over at her. "I've been good. Been spending a lot of time with Billy, making sure he heals right. He's a really nice guy. I can't say I hated it. I just want to stay busy through all of this and not worry."

Marcy finished packing the sandwiches. "I'm doing better too. Beth died trying to protect us, and I have to remember that. I'm keeping busy too. There's so much going on, and there's a lot to do to keep things organized."

Charlie nodded, "Yeah, there's definitely a lot going on. You two are doing a great job. It may not be said enough, but it takes everyone to keep things going smoothly."

Marcy grabbed the bags of food they prepared and as she passed by Charlie, she whispered, "This is your calling. You were meant to save us." Marcy continued out of the room.

About ten minutes later, Franny came into the kitchen. "Oh, hi there, Charlie. I'm going to get some cookies for the little one. Do you want some?"

Charlie looked up and smiled. "Sure. Why not? Have you seen Jack anywhere?"

Franny grabbed the box and put it on the counter as she looked over at Charlie. "Yes, I have. He's talking to Carl about the conversation he had with the others on the hand radio, then he'll be heading here." Franny put some cookies on a plate and brought it to Charlie. "You okay? You look like you have a lot on your mind."

Charlie glanced up. "Yeah, I'm good. Just have an overload of information in my head. I met my real mother today. It sounds crazy just saying it out loud."

Franny sighed. "Life throws us many curves. Yours are odd curves, but hey, who am I to judge?" She reached down and gave Charlie a hug. "You're okay. Just remember to breathe." Franny grabbed the other plate she had on the counter and went to find Christie. Charlie sat there.

About ten minutes later, Jack wandered into the kitchen and grabbed a coffee before sitting next to her. "Hey, I've hardly had any time to stop and say hi. You okay?"

Charlie smiled. "Yes. I'm okay, but we need to talk."

Jack frowned. "Umm … okay."

Charlie pulled the papers out of her purse and handed him the photo. Jack took it and looked at it for the longest time. "Where did you get this?"

Charlie shrugged. "I got it from Mom today."

He looked at her. "Did you assume I wouldn't want to go? This involves me too."

Charlie gulped. "I'm sorry. I did it at the spur of the moment. Anyway, she gave me this envelope. She said she wrote anything our father has ever said down onto paper. She knew I would come find her. Our father wasn't there, and apparently, that's a good thing. He's not human at all, and he doesn't like them either. Mom says she's the exception, but only because he fell in love with her. She had him cloak us to protect us. He did it for her. If we weren't cloaked, he would've expected us to go against the humans."

Charlie tore open the envelope. In it was a handful of paper. Her eyes scanned over it. Most of it contained words showing hatred towards humans, but something caught her eyes. She held the paper in front of Jack. "Look at this." On the paper, it noted that a high frequency disables the Zafarians, and that they will remain that way as long as the frequency is heard. It has to be very high. Humans cannot hear it. "We cannot hear dog whistles. I wonder if that would work?"

Jack grabbed the paper. "Look at this." Further down the page, it read: There are at least a million half-aliens living among the humans and don't even know they're not fully human. Some are good, and some are bad. The bad ones will help us wipe out the rest of the human race, including the half-aliens on the wrong side. Jack looked at her. "Wow! This is crazy. We need to show Carl this. I'm glad you went. I probably would've been too upset with her. Even more, I'm glad you're my sister." Jack got up to find Carl. He smiled as he left the room. Charlie sighed. She planned to take I warm bath, read the letter again, and then go to bed for the night. Maybe tomorrow would be the day they got to go home. She pushed in her chair and headed towards her room.

Chapter 12

Christie jumped up onto the bed. "Aunt Charlie, are you awake?"

Charlie opened her eyes. Christie was on one side, and Bruno was on the other. "You two need to let me wake up. Maybe you both can wake each other up." She sat up grinning, then pulled Bruno over and started to rub his belly. "See, this is what he likes. If you rub his belly, you can be one of his best friends."

Christie giggled. "He's so cute." The cat jumped on the bed and rubbed against the little girl. "Oh, Stormage, you're so cute too."

Charlie smiled. "If you want, you can be their babysitter. All you have to do is feed and play with them while we deal with the situation on hand."

Julie rolled over. "That would be a great idea. Christie, it will give you someone to play with all day."

Christie nodded. "Okay."

Charlie and picked up the letter she wrote to her mother many years ago. "I wrote this just before I left home."

Julie sat up. "What does it say?"

Charlie read aloud. "Mom, as much as I can appreciate what you're doing, you need to understand. Cloaked or not, I will not tolerate them hurting the human race. I will find a way back, and I will put an end to all of this."

"Even before my memory was erased, I swore I would stop them. I don't understand how my mother could know all of this for seven years and not say anything. I may love her, but this is partially on her. We would've been able to secretly work on this for the past seven years and it could've made a difference."

Julie frowned. "I can understand why you would be upset. She was probably in a pretty bad situation. Maybe she couldn't tell you … it would've interfered with the cloaking. There's always a chance he would detect a change in the cloaking if she told you. Is there a chance he knew you were against them?"

Charlie shook her head. "I don't know. Maybe he did. She says he was still very much an alien even though he loved her."

Julie sighed. "It has to be hard having your life change overnight."

Charlie sat up and started to put her socks on. "Yeah, it is. I feel like two different people. I still remember one life, and now I remember another. Yet I now know the one I thought I had is fake." She got up and headed towards the door. "I'll be back later. I need to figure out what's going on."

Charlie could hear the guys in the board room before she even got there. 'Must be serious,' she thought as she entered the room. "I can hear you guys down the hall. Is something wrong?"

Carl looked over at her. "No, we're fine. Just trying to agree on what to do about this. We may know more about them, but it still doesn't tell us how to get rid of them. I think we need to go to where they buried the ship and investigate it …

see what we can come up with."

Charlie grabbed a seat next to them. "I agree they buried it for a reason … must be something good on it."

Larzo shook his head fiercely. "It doesn't feel right."

Carl leaned forward. "So, don't go then. Meanwhile, we need information. Some of us need answers, so we can put an end to this. Why are you suddenly paranoid about doing stuff?"

Larzo looked over at the window then back at him. "It's one thing to walk into a situation minutes away from the home base, but this is two days away. I guess I can feel the lack of security in this mission."

Jack reached over and patted him on the back. "Everyone has their moments. You're used to playing spy close to home. This situation is different. This is a life-threatening situation, and if we want to survive, then this is a mission that needs to be completed." Jack looked over at Carl. "Let's figure out the best person to go to Mexico. I think someone who's immune to stuff should be present, just in case something happens."

Carl nodded. "Yes, I agree. I'll let you figure out which group will go. When you guys get there, I'll have the Mexican team meet with you and give you a safe place to stay, and a team to back you up just in case of trouble. The ship is buried under a temple. I'm not sure how to find it, but we have to try."

Charlie stretched. "So, besides an overly large ship, what exactly are we looking for?"

He gazed at Charlie. "I'm not sure. Maybe there's something in the ship they don't want anyone to find. We won't know 'til we see it."

She nodded. "Okay. Well, I'm going. I want to see this ship

firsthand. Send Nick too. We're a good team together. Jack, you and Billy should come too. This way we won't have to worry about anyone being affected. Does anyone actually know where these temples are in Mexico? It's not exactly a small place."

Carl moaned softly, "I know it'll take a little research. Maybe I can reach Rick on the handheld. If so, he might have some information. His team would be the ones to meet with you. I'll have Franny and Marcy get the stuff you need together for the trip. Give me a few hours to get some more information, then we'll figure out the rest."

Charlie got up and headed towards the door. "Let me know if you come up with anything. I'm going to go find Nick."

As Charlie stepped out of the room, she whispered inside her head, *Where are you, Nick?* Seconds later, he told her he was in the kitchen. She headed towards the kitchen. Nick was sitting at the table. "Morning, Charlie. Do you know how much I missed my morning coffee?"

She grabbed a coffee and sat down next to him. "We're planning a trip to Mexico. I imagine we'll be leaving today or tomorrow. We just have to get the details. Carl is going to let me know in a few hours if he reached a contact in Mexico. You up for the trip?"

Nick laid his cup down. "If you're going, I'll be right there with you. What do we need to do to prepare for this trip?"

Charlie finished her coffee then put the cup down. "Well, I think Franny will make us some food, and Carl will figure out where we'll stay. We have to look for evidence there, so we'll probably need to search in the dark. Flashlights are a definite. Maybe we should take shovels too. We're going to have to dig. Christie said they buried it. If we take the red van, we should be able to stop at a gas station and pump gas without being noticed. That's if they're not standing right there. I really don't want to encounter them."

Nick got up. "Well, if we're doing a road trip, I'm going to grab a shower first." As he walked by her, he reached down and ran his fingers through her hair. "Let me know if anything changes."

Charlie grinned to herself. "Okay. See you soon."

Later that day, the group gathered in the board room. Charlie looked around at the small group and asked, "So, have we come up with a plan?"

Carl continued to write, then quietly laid down his pen. "I've spoken to Rick in Mexico. His guys are going to keep an eye out for you. They'll assist you in your search and provide a place for you to stay while there. Franny and Marcy have prepared food for your trip, and Larzo went out and got the supplies you need, including flashlights and shovels. I assume you're taking the red van?"

Charlie nodded. "Yes. I think that would be the smartest thing to do, don't you?"

Carl agreed, "Yup. Keep out of sight as much as possible. Okay, so, Charlie, Jack, Nick and Billy, it's going to be a very long drive. Make sure you stay on course. It's the safest route that I know of. Keep track of everything you see out there, and when you get to Mexico, be sure to fill in the rebel leader about what's happening so he can stay on top of the issue there. You'll be passing through White Rock, San Francisco, and L.A. Try to be very careful. They may not be able to see red, but I'm sure they have their own strengths. That puts them at an advantage. The fact that the four of you are immune is something they would not be expecting. With all that said, it's time to hit the road, guys. I'll expect to hear from you two days from now, around dinnertime."

Jack took the first turn at driving. Charlie sat up front next to him. She looked around frantically. "I want to remember everything around me. The more I see, the better off we are. Then maybe we can end this."

Jack pointed to his head. "I have it all up here—every detail, as if I were a PC. I used to have a bad memory, but not anymore. When we get back, I'll help you write it all down. I want to try going around them. I know we're driving a red car, but their hearing isn't gone. They can still hear the engine running, and I don't want to take a chance. We're only ten minutes away from White Rock, our first city. We have no idea what to expect driving through there, so keep your eyes open."

Charlie let out a giant sigh. "Okay. Then let's do this."

When they finally arrived at White Rock, they barely recognized it. It was nothing but farms. Zafarians stood all around the crops guarding them. There were dozens of humans tending to the crops. Jack slowed down, leaning forward to get a good look. After that, they continued down the road. Nick yelled up from the back, "They must be the lucky ones who survived the gas." They kept going 'til they reached the border.

"Looks like the borders are empty because of everything going on. Never thought I would see that. We have about fourteen hours before we reach San Francisco. I'll drive for another six hours. Then, someone else can take over for a bit."

As they drove, they noticed hovercrafts racing through the air. "They must be going almost two hundred miles per hour." Charlie leaned forward as she watched them. "Damn! Have you had a good look at those things? You can only see it half a second, but they don't look like anything I've ever seen. They go so fast you would think the fog would slow them down. I could barely see ten feet ahead. I have to wonder if they make the fog green because they see better in it. If that's the case, it benefits them. I wonder if there's a way to change that."

Billy leaned forward. "I don't think there's a way to do that, but I think you're right about it helping them. Too bad we couldn't turn it red. Imagine how pissed they would be." He laughed. They drove for many more hours, telling stories to make the time pass by quickly. It felt easier driving past the hovercrafts after doing it for a few hundred miles, but the four still stood on guard every time they zoomed past.

Six hours passed. They were halfway to San Francisco. Jack pulled over on the side of the highway and asked, "Who's driving next?"

Nick jumped out and waited for Jack to crawl into the back, then jumped in and took over the driving. After driving for about forty minutes, Charlie glanced over at Nick and said, "I'll never be unprepared for anything after this, if this ever ends, that is. I have no idea how this is going to turn out. What if we win? How are we going to know that we got them all? What if we think we win, and all of a sudden, down the road, this starts again?"

Nick looked over at her. "Slow down, girl. That's one too many ifs. This whole situation is overwhelming, but how about one at a time? What if we never see our world again?"

Charlie looked around as they drove down the highway. "I don't know if I could get used to it here. Maybe it's that I don't want to get used to it. I want to take Bruno out to the park and go to my favorite spots whenever I want."

Billy groaned. "I want to ride my bike again. My house

doesn't exist in this world and that's where it is, though my bike isn't very quiet, so I'm sure they would hear me coming."

Nick grinned and added, "Or maybe your Harley would sound like a hovercraft."

Charlie looked frazzled. "I think what I'm worried about is when we figure out how to get rid of them, how do we know if we got them all? They're all over the world. It's not like we can communicate with everyone to ask."

Nick took a deep breath. "That's a hard one. We'll never know if we got them all. The trick is to get our lives back and then to keep an eye on the world around us to make sure this never happens again. We don't even know if these are the only aliens out there, or even among us. We really don't know anything anymore. Just think—we are half-aliens, and there is no way we are the only ones. Who says they are all good people?"

Charlie frowned. "You're right. We don't know what to expect. I guess the answer is that if we survive this and get our world back, we need to be prepared for anything to come." She leaned her head against the window as she watched the world pass them by. She couldn't imagine not seeing her world again.

Nick pulled over to the side of the road. "There it is, guys." In front of them stood the city of San Francisco. "We have no idea what's ahead of us once we cross that line." The four of them sat looking past the city line for a while, then they slowly drove into the city.

Charlie looked around fiercely. "It looks the same. I think it does at least." Gazing up in the air, she watched as hovercrafts flew by. "Other than them," she continued, "but I'm kind of getting used to them. As long as they don't notice us, do you think there are others around here trying to survive like us?"

Nick drove slowly through the streets. "I wish there were a way to leave messages for people." Nick pulled up to a grocery store. "Wait here." He jumped out and ran over to the side where he wrote in large letters with a marker: 'Handheld radios save lives!' He ran back to the van and got in. "There! It's simple, but hopefully someone is smart enough to read past that. I didn't want to write anything direct. We don't know what those bastards understand."

They continued down the road for about ten minutes 'til they came to a part of the city where there was construction going on. The Zafarians were building a new temple. In actuality, the humans were building the temple because the Zafarians were forcing them to. Charlie leaned forward, trying to get a good look. "They don't look like they're being forced. They kinda look clueless, even a little zombie-like. Maybe they're in some kind of trance or under mind control. I don't like this. I'm glad we're immune, but what about all the people we love? There's no protection for them," She said as her eyes filled with tears.

Nick continued driving. "We're doing something," he said as he glanced at Charlie. "We're going to the ruins to see what we can find to help us get rid of them. We don't know enough about them to get rid of them yet. We know they self-heal and are strong enough to kill us. Let's see what we find first before we let our emotions loose. I think if we get angry instead of scared, it'll give us a mightier force." After driving through the city for about forty minutes, Nick pulled off to the side. "Who's driving next?"

Billy switched places with Nick and smiled at Charlie. "How many hours 'til L.A.?"

Charlie looked at the map. "About five and a half hours." Charlie leaned against the window. "I've been up for hours. I'm going to take a little nap. Do you mind?"

Billy grinned. "No. Of course not."

Jack leaned forward. "Charlie, wake up. Trade places with me, will you?" Charlie opened her eyes softly and then crawled into the back of the van. Jack fastened his seatbelt then looked at Billy. "There we go. How long have I been out?"

Billy slightly glanced over at Jack. "You were out for quite a while. We have about three hours 'til we hit L.A. I had to stop and find gas a while back. We're good though. Luckily, the gas station doors were not locked up and I could get in to release the gas pumps. This world is so crazy. I missed so much being bedridden."

Suddenly, a man ran across the highway like he was being chased, and then he burst into flames. One of the hovercrafts wasn't far behind him. "I knew it had to be them," said Jack. He sighed as he looked around. "It's always them. I can't help but think every time I look around that we are the lucky ones. We have the information about the color red, and we know the gas is toxic. I think that because we are immune, we sometimes forget how dangerous this whole situation is. Our group has a comfortable hotel that, luckily, one of our group members owned. Not everyone is so lucky. Nick's house doesn't exist in this world. So how many people are out running around trying to save themselves, or worse, dead because they had no shelter? I want to run out there and save them all, but I know I can't. I wouldn't survive it."

Billy shook his head. "I understand. This is all a shock to me after being confined to the bed for so long. If I hadn't faced those bastards the first night, I may not believe it myself. Do you think there are many humans left?"

Jack frowned. "Yes, I do. There are an awful lot under their control, but I also think there are a lot hiding in their homes and abandoned places just trying to survive. We have the rebel groups too. There are lots of them all over the world. My biggest worry is if we ever figure out how to win this war, we won't get them all, and it will start all over again." Jack looked at Billy. "The fact that this could happen once is proof. We were never alone, so how many more are out there in the universe and how naive are we to think that if we win, it'll never happen again?" The two guys drove for the next two and a half hours with that piercing thought on their minds—how would they ever get through this?

Just before they reached L.A., they pulled over onto the side of the road. "This city is huge," said Billy. "I bet there are lots of people left. It's too bad we couldn't get a message to them to contact Carl by hand radio, so we could all be on the same page. What you said earlier really stuck in my head. I want to make sure we get them all. If we have any chance at ending this, we all have to be on the same page."

Jack leaned forward. The city was covered in hovercrafts. "Our city is big, yet all the hovercrafts are in the outer part of the city. This place looks like it's covered with hovercrafts. I wonder what the difference is?"

Billy leaned in to look. "Probably has something to do with what they use the city for. Maybe they haven't finished collecting in this city. Ours turned into camps. This city, being so large, may not be as easy to take down. We'll know more when we drive through it." Billy started to drive slowly. "I don't know why, but I'm really nervous about driving through here. Something keeps telling me to be careful. Not sure why. So, just to change the subject, with this half-alien thing, are we more human than alien or the other way around?"

Jack laughed. "I don't know. I'm thinking more alien since we are immune to almost everything they throw our way. That seems to play in our favor, don't you think?"

Billy laughed. "So far, let's hope it remains that way." He looked down at the gas gauge. "We need to find more gas; we're getting low."

A few minutes in, they spotted a Shell station. "Up on the right-hand side," whispered Jack.

Billy pulled into the station. He looked around before jumping out. "I have to go see if I can switch on the pumps. Keep an eye out."

Jack stepped out of the car and looked around. This city was definitely busier than Richmond, he thought. He watched as a hovercraft passed over the station. He looked to make sure Billy remained inside. The hum of its engine was so loud he could barely think. He stood still tightly against the van until the hovercraft sped off towards the center of the city. Jack motioned for Billy to hurry up. "I'm so glad they can't see red."

As Billy stood pumping the gas, something caught Jack's eyes. He walked over to the side of the station. "Hello. Is there anyone here?" he whispered.

A woman peeked over the edge of the garbage bin, her face wrapped in a thick red scarf. "Why aren't you affected by the green fog?" she asked.

Jack smiled at the woman, "I'm not sure, but there are a few of us that are not affected by it. You are smart to wear the scarf. The green fog causes violent hallucinations that actually kill people. Are you by yourself or with a group?"

The woman looked around. "I'm with a small group of people."

Jack nodded. "We have a large group. This situation is one that can't be solved without everyone coming together. Tell every human you can to find a handheld radio. It's the only way for cities to connect and to keep on top of what is happening."

The woman nodded. "Okay. I'll tell everyone. We know of other groups in the city. I'll try to find them and spread the word."

Jack turned and headed back to the van. Billy was just finishing up at the pumps. "Let's get going. This is getting creepy." They got in the van and drove away.

Jack looked over at Billy. "I saw a woman next to the gas station. I told her to find a handheld radio, or to at least to spread the word around to the other humans. She said she would. Let's hope she keeps her word. It'll help let everyone know what's going on."

Billy let out a sigh. "Well, let's hope she does. We really need everyone on the same page. I want to get out of this city as quickly as I can. I keep having to remind myself slow and steady, though. It's just that it's so creepy being around all these hovercrafts. I feel as if they can see us, even though I know red blocks their view. I just know I would feel better out on the highway away from the main action. How far is it to where we need to go?"

Jack picked up the map. After examining it for a bit, he laid his head back against the seat. "We still have another forty-nine hours 'til we arrive in Cancun."

Billy gasped. "I sure hope we find what we need to after going this far. We'll just keep switching drivers and sleeping in between 'til we get there, only stop when we need gas or a bathroom break. Pass me a sandwich, will you? I still have a few hours before it's my turn to drive."

Finally, they pulled into Cancun. They were exhausted and couldn't wait to stretch after being in the van for so long. Charlie leaned forward to read the sign. "I'm so glad we're here. I don't even want to think about the trip back."

Nick pulled the car off to the side of the road. "Does anyone actually know where we're meeting up with them?"

Charlie pulled out a piece of paper from her pocket. "It's called Macchiato Café. It's supposed to be on the main street. We're supposed to park in front of it and wait for them."

Nick looked around. "Okay. We're on the main street. It looks like it would be a main street, at least. They all seem to have a distinct look." After driving around for about ten minutes, they came across the café. Nick pulled in next to it and turned off the van. He looked over at Charlie. "I hope we don't have to wait too long. I'm tired of being in the van." He turned sideways and leaned against the door. "So, we need to dig up the ruins? You know they're located in different places throughout Mexico and El Salvador. How do you know this is the right spot?"

Charlie glanced over at him. "I asked Christie. This is where she told me to come. It's buried under the temple."

Nick turned and looked out the window as a guy wearing a red shirt approached the van. He rolled down the window. The guy smiled. "I'm glad to see you guys made it here safely. Thanks for the red shirt tip. We've been able to move around the city with a lot more ease. That's my red truck over there. If you want to follow me, I'll take you to the warehouse."

They followed him throughout the city. It was about fifteen

minutes before they came upon a warehouse. They pulled up and parked. "Doesn't look as comfortable as our hotel," said Charlie as she pushed her face up against the window to get a good look.

Billy jumped out, and the rest followed. "We lucked out—having someone who owned a hotel. Not everyone is as lucky as we were. We have to remember this could be us." The guy motioned for them to follow him into the warehouse.

Charlie pulled on Jack's arm. "Let's go, guys." They entered the warehouse. It definitely wasn't like the hotel they had been blessed to be in. The place was dark except for a large table near the center that held nearly a hundred candles. People sat on mattresses spread throughout the warehouse. Each had their own flashlight. Charlie whispered to Nick, "I don't know where to sit or to even stand. I don't want to get in anyone's way."

A man with a very large mustache walked over to them. "Hello. You must be the Canadians we've been waiting on. My name's Mike."

Jack smiled and stepped forward. "Hi, Mike. I'm Jack. This is Charlie, Nick and Billy. It was a very long trip here. We're glad to be off the road."

Mike nodded. "I imagine you are. I have a section set up for you all. If you follow me, I'll take you to it." The group followed the man. He took them to a corner of the warehouse where they had four mattresses set up for them and a small table with a couple of candles waiting to be lit. "I'll let you rest. Tomorrow, we'll talk about what's going on. Then we'll go to the ruins and do what you came all this way for. I'll contact Carl and let him know you all arrived. This way there's no worry on his end." He smiled and set off into the dark.

Charlie flopped onto the mattress. It wasn't as comfortable as her own mattress, but she didn't care. "Jack," she whispered. "Do you think we're safe to shut our eyes here?"

Jack pushed his mattress next to hers. "Yes. It's fine to sleep here. Nick is on one side of you, and I'm on the other side. Nothing can happen without all of us knowing." She smiled. "I'm glad you're my brother." She turned over and faced Nick. He smiled as he reached over and took her hand. The four stayed close for the night. They were not used to such an open sleeping arrangement. It took a little while for their minds to shut down, but after a while the group slowly fell asleep.

Chapter 13

Charlie opened her eyes. It was different waking up without Bruno there. She looked around. Nick was asleep on one side, and Jack was on the other. She felt safe lying next to them both but missed waking up to her puppy. Charlie sat up and pulled her knees up against her chest. She hadn't realized how nice they had it back in Richmond. Nick reached up and put his hand on her arm. "You okay?"

She looked at him and answered, "Yeah. I just hadn't realized how lucky we were 'til I looked around."

Nick looked around. "What do you say we get up and see if we can get this done so we can go back to Richmond?"

Charlie nodded. "Good idea."

As they started waking up the others, a woman approached them. She held a bowl of fruit. *"Quieres algo de comida?"* She asked, as she handed them the bowl.

Charlie smiled as she took the bowl from the woman. "Thank you." She looked over at Nick. "Oh my God. I never gave it much thought that we don't even speak their language."

Jack put the fruit into the backpack. "We might need this for later." The four got up and started to walk through the warehouse. As they searched for the man in charge, they looked around at all the people.

Billy whispered to the rest, "How do you say coffee in Spanish?"

Jack glanced over. "Yeah. I don't think we're getting one. They look like they're struggling. Just try not to kill anyone with your coffee withdrawal," he said with a slight giggle. Charlie shut her eyes and wished really hard they all had coffee. She wasn't sure it would work, but it was definitely worth a try. She knew it had worked when she heard the others groan, and the aroma hit her nose. Jack whispered, "Oh my God. I forgot you could do that."

Billy smiled. "It tastes like a cup of heaven. What about breakfast?"

Charlie smirked. "On the road, guys!"

Rick scurried over to them, his eyes on the coffee. "Where in the world did you get that? I'm dying without it."

Charlie looked over at Jack, then back at Rick. "If you don't ask any questions, I can get you some."

Rick nodded. "Not a single question." Charlie shut her eyes. She thought about how much she wanted to share coffee with her new friend. Rick put his hand on her shoulder as she opened her eyes. "I don't know how you did it, but you're my new best friend."

She smiled. "I'd explain, but we just don't have the time for it right now."

Rick turned away. "Come on. Let's find Mike, then we can get out there and find what we need. When you guys head back, do you think I can go with you?"

Jack patted Rick on the back. "As long as the rest are okay with it, I don't mind."

Along the way, Charlie made a coffee appear for Mike. As

she approached him, she handed him the coffee. Rick looked at him. "Don't ask, just enjoy."

The group chuckled, Mike sighed as he took a sip. "I've missed this." They sat down at the table with Mike.

Charlie smiled. "I'm glad to have helped. So how far away are the ruins?"

Mike pulled out a map. "We're here, and the ruins are right there. It's about a ten-minute drive from here to get to the ruins."

Billy pulled the map towards him. "That's not too bad. How heavily do they guard it?"

Mike shook his head. "They don't guard it. As far as they are concerned, no one knows anything."

Charlie laid down her cup. "There isn't anyone that knows about the ruins and their connection with the aliens. This was private information we received. There's a lot you don't know about this whole situation. The aliens have been around for a very long time. They've been breeding with humans, creating half-aliens." Mike's eyes widened, but Charlie continued, "Remember though, they're not aware of this and definitely should not be held accountable for the aliens' actions. I'm a half-breed myself, and I can't stand those bastards. But being immune helps and provides the humans with someone who's not affected by their tactics. If you have people among you who are immune to the green fog, it's because they are part-alien. You can help them through the process by being accepting of them."

Mike took a deep breath then slowly let it out. "I do have a few of them. I'm glad you told me about this. I'll help them privately. I don't think it's a good idea for too many to know about it."

She nodded. "True. Only a few know about me on the other end. Rick, if you and a few others would come out with us today and watch our back as we search, it would be appreciated. You'll need to have a mask on to be protected from the gas. Do you have masks?"

Rick shook his head. "No. We're not lucky enough to have such masks. We've been wearing scarfs and bandanas over our faces to protect us from the fog. Do you have any?"

Billy paused. "I think we have a few packed in the van. Carl put them there in case we needed them for any reason. We had no idea what we would see on the way. One city was turned into a giant garden with humans doing the work. We also saw humans being forced to build a temple. They have slaves and breeding camps everywhere. The humans look as if they are in some sort of trance... like they have no idea what they're doing."

Mike shook his head with disgust. "We have to find a way to win this fight and get rid of them. The human race deserves a chance to keep living. If we keep going at the rate we are now, we won't last much longer."

Charlie agreed. "So, do we have a team picked out already?"

Rick jumped up quickly. "Yes. I'll get them together so we can get going."

As the group got up, Jack looked over at Mike and said, "When we get home, I'm going to talk to Carl about sending you some of our top people to help set you up better... if that's okay, that is? Meanwhile, you figure out if you have many half-breeds. Work with them and see if they have any gifts that can benefit this war. Sort of like what Charlie does, although they're all different. When we send them down, you can build a team to come up with an efficient plan to help organize your war. I do mean your war too. We're all worlds away, and it's on each one of us to fix this situation."

After making sure the group that would be guarding them had masks, they all headed out towards the ruins. As Nick pulled into the area of the ruins, Charlie leaned forward and looked around in astonishment. "Oh, wow! I don't think I've ever seen anything so amazing. This was carved by humans using their own hands. I don't even want to know how long it took. Look at the detail in each step on that temple. I wish my camera worked." The four of them got out of the van and headed towards the ruins. "Can you imagine knowing you had something to do with building something so dynamic?"

Rick ran over to them. "Okay, I have them all watching out for the aliens. It's not hard to hear them though. It sounds like they're dragging logs. We always know when there are hovercrafts nearby too. The hum gets louder and louder." The five of them walked towards the temple.

Charlie turned on her flashlight and started searching around the temple. "They said it was around the broken temple. I'm not sure exactly what we're looking for, but I assume it doesn't fit in with the ruins." They all ran their flashlights along the walls of the temple. Each stone fell into place as if it were meant to be there.

"This looks so old," said Nick.

Charlie looked back and smiled. "Yeah, it definitely is."

Jack flipped around. "I found some ancient writing." They all turned their flashlights towards the writing as Jack ran his finger along it. "It has that symbol here, just under the picture of what looks to be a ship."

Billy took a closer look. "I've never seen anything like this."

The five looked around separately for about an hour. Thus

far the area had been quiet and free of aliens. There were a few times they thought a hovercraft was coming their way, but then the noise quickly faded. Charlie yelled for the others, "I found something!" They all ran towards her, trying not to trip over anything amidst the green fog.

Jack looked over her shoulder. "What is it?"

She continued trying to clear it off. "It looks like it's some kind of trap door or something." She tried to open it. "Can someone help me? It's really heavy."

After Jack tried and failed, Nick reached over and tried. He tugged so hard that when he let go, his finger got cut on the heavy metals of the door. "Ouch! Son of a bitch cut me!" He wiped off his finger.

Charlie grabbed it to look at it. As she examined his finger close up, her eyes widened. "Did you just self-heal?"

Nick leaned against the temple and took a deep breath. "Sure looks like it. Doesn't it? I have no idea how that happened." He looked up at her and continued, "Maybe it's like you being able to make stuff appear. Maybe I can heal stuff." They all stood, stunned at his gift.

Meanwhile, Billy reached down and gave the door a tug. It promptly flung open. "Aha!" He exclaimed. "Just needed a man with muscles to get it open."

Charlie laughed. "Well, we know who got the strength and the ego." She pointed the flashlight into the entrance of the door. "It looks pretty scary and really dark. Well, here goes nothing." She crawled down into the hole. She searched for anything that might light up the spaceship. As she walked through, she saw a board full of switches. They all looked like control panel switches, so she knew not to mess with any of them, but one stood out. It had a picture of a moon above it. "I wonder what this one does." She decided to try it and hoped to hell that it didn't blow up. The whole cabin lit up with green light from top to bottom. "Holy shit! Guys, I found light." The rest of the group piled into the ship, while one man guarded the door. They turned off the flashlights and started looking around as if they were walking into a movie set.

Nick grabbed a little black box and said, "This reminds me of a movie. Who would've ever thought any of this could be real? Not me, for sure. I was the biggest skeptic you could've ever met before all of this happened." He laid it back down. "I don't want to open this. I'm scared Pandora might be involved."

Charlie laughed as she picked up the box and popped open the lid. Inside there was a little key. "See. It's just a key. Oh my God! It's named Pandora!" Nick's eyes widened. Charlie laughed. "I'm just kidding. It's just a key." She put it in her pocket. "Keep looking, everyone."

Nick shook his head at her and gave a smirk. "You're a bad girl."

The ship was really large. Charlie looked around and said to them, "It's going to take hours to search this place. Seeing how big this is, there must have been a lot of aliens aboard!" The group split up and started searching from room to room. The

ship must have had half a dozen floors to it, Charlie thought to herself as she ran her fingers along a shelf in a very large office. *I wonder how they dug a hole to fit a ship this large. I wonder if humans dug it, or if maybe the ship crashed and caused the hole as it landed.* She came across a locked drawer. Pulling out the key, she tried to open it. The key turned, but the drawer was so heavy. It reminded her of the door. *Billy, can you hear me?* she said inside her head. *If so, I need you.*

Billy came rushing down the hall and into the room she stood in. "I'll never get used to that, but damn, it's convenient. What do you need?"

Charlie looked at the drawer. "I can't open it. Can you try?" Billy reached and it opened as if it were as light as a feather.

"This could definitely give me an ego," said Billy with a smirk on his face. Inside there was a larger box. It was dark blue, and on it was the symbol they all wore on their bodies.

Charlie gasped quietly, "Oh, wow! This has to be something." She picked it up and opened the lid. Inside was some kind of an instrument. "I don't know what this is, but I better leave it in there for the time being." She closed it and put it in her backpack, then continued looking around. She searched four separate rooms before coming across a book about what she thought was alien biology. She put it in her backpack with everything else that she found, and then looked at Billy. "I wish I knew exactly what I was looking for; it would make it easier." The two of them made their way out towards the front of the ship.

Billy took another look around the room, then yelled out, "Jack, are you guys done?" Jack, Nick and Rick came from different directions. Nick was holding a stone of different colors. "I don't know what this is for, but this rock has about ten different colors in it."

Charlie took a quick look at it. "Cool. Put it in your bag. Anything we find we can have a better look at once we get home. We should head out though. I don't think there's anything else left that will be helpful to us, and that's our sole mission." Everyone agreed and headed towards the main door of the ship. After they were all out and back in their vehicles, they all headed back to the warehouse. Charlie leaned her head against the window. "That was amazing and scary at the same time. I'm sure we found stuff that will help us—if not, at least it will show us who we're dealing with." Charlie shrugged. "Well, if we don't win, maybe we should learn to fly and steal their ship. We could move to a new planet." They all started to laugh.

Minutes later, they walked into the warehouse. Charlie wished for a moment she could blink and suddenly be home. 'I wish,' she thought to herself. She smiled at the people as she strolled by them. Mike came towards them. "Great you're back. I was just on with Carl again, and I told him where you were. We discussed how long it would be before you all would be hitting the road. They really need you back as soon as possible. I told him that my people will prepare for you to leave right away. The women are packing you some food and water."

Rick cleared his throat. "I'm going with them, Mike. I'm going to bring Carla with me. She's the only family I have left."

Mike looked concerned but shook his head. "Okay. Carl is training a few people to come down here and help us." They turned and walked towards the office. "So, how was the search?" asked Mike.

Charlie hurried to catch up to them. "It was good. I'm not sure if we found anything to stop the aliens, but once we go through it, maybe it will help us all towards putting an end to them."

When they sat down at the table, Mike pushed his glasses up onto his nose. "Let's hope that's what happens. I look forward to hearing from your people and having them come down to help us. I had one of my guys grab extra flashlights for you, in case you need them. I wish that we had met on better circumstances, but I suggest you all hit the road soon."

Rick got up. "I'm going to get my stuff and tell Carla what's happening. I'll meet you out by the van. I promise I'll be a big help, guys."

Jack stood up and reached out to shake Mike's hand. "Thank you for being so accommodating. If there's a way to put an end to all of this, I'm sure, as a team, we'll all figure it out and send these bastards back home where they belong."

They packed the van with their belongings and finds and prepared for the trip home. Jack decided he would drive first. Charlie climbed into the passenger seat. "It's such a long drive home. I've decided I'm not a fan of road trips."

Jack wrinkled up his forehead. "This is not a road trip. You need to go on a real road trip—open the windows, turn up the tunes, and make it fun every step of the way. This trip was a

straight there and straight back trip. It put us in danger. It's not like we have a choice about anything. So, this wasn't fun for any of us, and definitely not a road trip."

Charlie peered out at the moon. "It's almost full. Tomorrow night it'll fill the sky with light. It's too bad we couldn't put it on pause. I really miss the sun. This will be the most light we have in the sky for a bit. Why do you think they have no sun in this world?"

Jack shrugged. "I would assume it's because its light is from the fire of the sun. The light it lets off makes it hard for them to see well. Just like the green fog helps them see better. Didn't you notice that the light in the ship was green?"

She thought about it for a second. "Yes. It was. I never gave it much thought. I wish there was a way to switch it to benefit us. You know, turn it red. I can't imagine there's a way to do that though."

Jack shook his head slightly. "I don't think so but keep it in mind. You just never know with everything going on. I've seen so many weird things happen. I'm over being shocked."

Charlie nodded. "I agree. That ship was huge. We could live on it. There's just that much room. I really hope the stuff we found helps us fight them. I would give anything to go home."

Nick leaned forward and peered up into the front of the van. "Anyone want some water?"

Charlie looked back at him and took one for herself and for Jack. "Thanks."

Nick grinned. "No problem. Let me know when you need me to drive."

Charlie lifted the bottle up to her mouth and took a drink. "Nick healed himself today. Wouldn't it be amazing if he could heal others? It's an amazing gift to have. Billy suddenly has amazing strength. He opened the ship and, in the ship, he opened the drawer that I couldn't open. He didn't even struggle to open it. I thought that was impressive."

Jack glanced over at her. "It's really impressive. Mine are odd. I have this perfect picture of everything painted in my head. Every detail of everything is in there when I need it. I have never felt this smart. I wonder if when we go back to our world, whether we'll still have these gifts… if we get back to our world, that is."

Charlie frowned. "You can't think like that. Of course, we'll get back to our world. Maybe it's time to start looking at this situation differently instead of seeing it as an end to our world. We can start looking at it day by day and concentrate on the missions at hand. We have forty-four hours 'til we get to L.A.? Wow, it's a long drive."

Jack smiled. "Yes, it is. Nick, can you drive for a while?"

Jack pulled over to the side of the road so that he and Nick could trade spots. "I'm going to get a few hours of sleep."

They drove for a few hours, talking about what life used to be like and what they missed the most. Charlie sat with her back leaning against the window. "It sounds like we have a lot in common. How come we never ran into each other before?"

Nick shrugged. "I don't know. Maybe we just kept missing each other."

Charlie smiled. "Well, at least we know each other now, and I'm glad we do." She turned around and looked out the window. "I miss my puppy." Charlie sat up straight and asked, "What's that smell?" The air smelt burnt, like something was burning.

Just as she looked over at Nick, the van came to a stop. Nick's eyes got big. "What the hell!" He leaned forward and saw smoke as it poured out of the hood of the van. Nick slammed his hands down onto the steering wheel. "Damn it! What are we supposed to do now! Any of you know how to fix a broken-down vehicle?" Nick jumped out and opened the hood. Smoke fumed out, nearly choking them before they could get out of the way.

Jack cleared his throat. "It smells really bad, almost as if the oil has dried up… might be that the van has seized up due to lack of oil. If that's the case, we won't be able to get it going again." He looked at Charlie. "Do you think using the powers of your mind can fix this?"

She shook her head. "I don't know. I can try." She shut her eyes and hoped in her heart the van would work. It felt different this time though. She opened her eyes. "I don't think so." The six of them stood back looking at the van. "What do we do now?" Charlie asked as she leaned against the van.

Nick opened the van door and started to hand the others their bags. "We'll walk, guys, 'til we find a new way home. We are forty-one hours from L.A. A lot more by walking. We don't have time to waste though. Let's get going."

Charlie walked next to Nick. She was deep in thought as he reached down and took her hand. "You okay? You look like you're lost in thought."

She looked over at him. "Yeah, I'm good. I was just thinking it's a long way home. There has to be a better way to get there. I have no idea what my limits are when it comes to using my mind to make things happen. I've tried to wish for another red van but no such luck. It seems what I wish for has to be held by my own two hands. I definitely cannot hold a van. So, I'm not sure what would help. Any ideas?"

Nick shook his head. "No, but maybe we should find a place to camp out for the night. We've been walking for over an hour, and I would like to make sure we're heading in the right direction, at least."

They came upon an underpass. "This will work," said Charlie. "We can stay out of sight much better… not that there's much out here with us." They found a place to sit.

Rick pulled out the map and traced their steps. "We're heading in the right direction. We still have a long way to go."

Billy looked over at Charlie. "So, how about some food?" He wiggled his eyebrows at her. She started to laugh.

"Okay. Okay. Let's see what I can do about that." She closed her eyes and thought about being hungry. 'Hmmmm,' she thought, 'burgers would be wonderful right about now.' Her nose filled with the aroma of beef and melted cheese. 'That's it!' she thought as she opened her eyes slowly.

Everyone's eyes widened as they reached for something to eat, Billy grinned. "Thanks, Charlie."

After the burgers were gone, Jack looked around at the group and asked, "Any ideas on how we're getting home?"

Billy sighed. "We could get a different car."

Charlie piped up. "It has to be red and hold six of us." Carla and Rick sat closely, both wearing gas masks to protect them from the toxic gas. Charlie took a deep breath. "We have to find one soon too, so we can get these two off the streets. Carla is your sister's daughter?"

Rick nodded. "Yes. She's been with me since my sister died a few years back. Not that she needs to stay with me… she's twenty-two, but we're family, and family sticks together."

"Did your sister go missing?" Charlie asked.

Rick nodded. "Yup. One day she was just gone. I wonder if the aliens got her. I really don't know but hope she's still alive. I don't want to get my hopes up, just to have them crushed again."

Charlie leaned against Nick. "I think all we have left is hope. I don't care how many times it gets crushed, we need to set it back up and keep on going. That's the only way we're getting out of this alive. I'm going home after all this is over."

Nick leaned his head against hers. "I like your positivity." As Jack sat there looking out at the moon, a voice spoke to him through his head. It was Christie. 'Jack, are you there? Mommy wants to know you're okay.' Jack smiled to himself. He answered her in his head. 'I'm okay. We're on our way home. We have a complication though. Tell your mommy our van broke down but not to worry. It'll just take us longer to get there. Okay, Christie. Are you there?'

Seconds later, she answered, 'Okay, I'll tell Mommy what you said. Make sure you guys are safe, okay? We'll see you soon.'

Jack looked at Charlie. "I just heard from Julie."

Charlie's eyes widened. "How?"

He smiled. "Through Christie. They wanted to know if we were okay. I told her what happened, but that we were safe… that way they won't worry about us.

Billy interrupted them. "So, what's the little girl's super-power?"

Charlie responded, "She can tell if someone is part-alien. Plus, I think I remember her telling me she can detect others around by their heartbeats. I'm not sure how that works. I'll have to ask her again once we get home. I can't believe I have a niece. It's just hitting me now. Julie must've been in such shock to find out she had a child after all this time. I just can't imagine. Life is different now and I have to wonder how this will affect us all once we get our world back."

Billy leaned back against the side of the underpass. "Well, if we get home, I'm going to put my man strength to work for me and see if I can make some real money."

Charlie shook her head. "Oh, Billy, you're something else. I meant how much of our world will be there and what will people remember about all of it. I even have to wonder how many people will get to return and live life like they used to."

Jack leaned back with his arms folded behind his head. "That's a good question. I guess we'll have to see when that happens. My worry is how they will perceive half-aliens once this is over. I don't think I'll be telling anyone about it. Well, not anyone I don't trust, that is. I definitely won't ever look at the moon again the same. In fact, I'll always wonder if the

227

sun will bother to rise again in the morning."

Charlie looked up at Nick. "We need to find another van. I don't want to be out here wondering how long it'll be before we run into them."

Nick pulled her closer. "Don't worry. We'll figure out how to get home. We should start walking again, guys, and see if we can find another vehicle. At this pace, we'll never make it home." They all got up and gathered their stuff.

Charlie looked up at the moon lighting the sky. "At least it's bright tonight. Maybe it'll show us the way. If we find another van, does anyone know how to hotwire it? I've only seen it done in the movies, and I'm pretty sure they didn't really do it."

Jack looked back at her. "You're probably right. We'll figure it out then. Meanwhile, let's just walk. It's quiet out here, which gives us a chance to think. If we're lucky, one of us may come up with some really good ideas that will benefit us all." Charlie laughed and continued walking.

Chapter 14

After walking for about six hours, the group came upon a town. Charlie got excited and shouted, "Look! We actually made it somewhere. Maybe we'll find a car here or at least a bed to get some sleep. We're so far away from home right now. I really just need a little hope."

The town was small. It looked like it held about ten thousand people. It wasn't very big, so there was hope that it wasn't monitored like the bigger cities. As they walked down the sidewalk towards the center of the town, Charlie looked around frantically. "Can you hear that? I can hear the stupid hovercrafts from here. How far away do you think they are?"

Nick paused. "They sound like they're getting closer. We're wearing red though, so we should be okay. Right?"

Jack frowned as if in doubt. "Yes. That's right. I still get uncomfortable every time they come near us."

All of a sudden, Charlie got a sharp pain right behind her eye. She grabbed her face and blurted, "Oh my God, that hurt. Felt like I got jabbed in the eye." She grabbed a seat on a nearby bench and laid her face in her hands.

Nick shook his head and looked over at Jack. "I hope that isn't a migraine. Those things are nasty."

Charlie heard a buzzing in her head and then a voice. *We*

know you are there.

What the hell! Charlie thought to herself. She stood up and looked around.

The voice continued, *I can feel the half-alien in you, and I will find you. You were bred for us, not for them. You're supposed to fight for us, not against us. Now you'll die instead.*

Charlie's eyes widened as she asked, *Who are you and why can I hear you?*

A hovercraft came zooming across the sky. The hum grew louder as it approached them. The group froze in hopes that they wouldn't be spotted, but the craft started to shoot at Charlie, hitting her in the side. The bullet tore her open, and she started to bleed. Nick ran towards her and picked her up and ran towards an old garbage bin. He placed her body down behind it and held his hand over the bullet wound to try to heal it. "Come on," he said. "I know I can do this. Don't you take her from me now." His eyes filled with tears as he continued trying to close her wound.

Jack and the others flew across the parking lot and hid behind an old truck. They could see Nick from a distance trying to help Charlie. Jack whispered in his head, *Is she okay, Nick?* Nick didn't answer him. He was too busy and too upset to reply.

The hovercraft circled for a bit then continued on. The hum got further and further away from them. Nick picked Charlie up and motioned for the others to follow. "We need to find better shelter. Maybe one of these houses will be open, and we can hide out there for a bit."

Jack ran alongside Nick. "She's going to be okay?" He asked.

Nick gazed over at him. "I'm not sure yet. I tried to heal her, but I'm not sure if I can even do that or not. We'll know more once we get inside."

Jack opened the door of a big white house while the group piled in. Nick laid Charlie on the couch. "Charlie, stay with us," he uttered as he touched her wound with his hand. He closed his eyes. "Please heal her. I don't want to lose her." He opened his eyes and looked at her lifeless body as she lay there. Suddenly, she gasped for air. Nick's eyes widened as he grabbed her hand. "Charlie, are you okay?" He reached down and found that her wound was healing. "Oh, thank goodness. I thought you were a goner for a second."

Charlie pulled herself up to a sitting position. "They spoke to me."

Jack crouched down and wrinkled up his forehead. "The aliens?"

She looked at Jack and replied, "Yes. They said they knew I was half-alien, and that I was bred for them. I'm supposed to be fighting for them, and if I choose not to, then I will die like the rest of them. He found me because I answered him. That's how he was able to shoot me even though I was wearing red."

Nick paused. "But how did he know you were around to start with?" That question stumped them all.

They looked around the house. It was quite homey. Charlie stood up, and breaking the silence, said, "We should take shelter here even if it's just for the night. I think we need to know the answer to that question before we go home. I don't want to put anyone in danger." She lifted up her shirt to look at where the bullets had hit her. "Wow! It's as if I never got shot." She looked at Nick. "Thank you. I think I would be dead if you hadn't saved me."

Nick grinned. "Well, we can't have that, can we? I'm going to explore the kitchen. Why don't you see if you can find some clothes not covered in blood?"

Charlie smirked. "Good idea." She climbed up the stairs and set off towards one of the rooms. The others went in their own direction in search of some kind of comfort. Charlie entered the first room. As she looked around, she noticed paintings on the walls. They reminded her of traveling, something she had always wanted to do but hadn't had the chance as of yet. She stopped in front of one painting. The painting was of a small street in Italy. It held such detail she almost felt as if she was there. *I wish,* she thought to herself. She walked over to the closet and opened it. It was filled with women's clothes. *Jackpot!* she thought. She grabbed a shirt out of the pile. 'Oh, wait. I better grab something red.' She searched through the clothes 'til she found a red outfit then walked towards the bathroom. After getting cleaned up and putting on a new shirt, she headed back downstairs. Jack was sprawled out on the couch, Billy in the chair, and Rick and Carla were over in the corner talking. She went straight to the kitchen. "Nick, did you find anything to eat?"

Nick stood at the counter. "Not really. Everything has gone bad. That's what happens without power."

She shook her head. "Yeah. Well, at least I can get us some food."

She leaned against the counter and closed her eyes. She thought about her stomach. 'Hmm. I wish we had some pizza.' Immediately, the kitchen filled with the aroma of melted cheese. Nick grabbed onto Charlie. He pulled her over, so he could hug her. "As thankful as I am for this pizza, I am even more thankful that you are okay."

She smiled as she pulled away. "I think I'm still in shock over that." She picked up the pizza and said, "Let's go feed the crew."

They sat around eating the pizza, but none of them felt the security they felt before the shooting. Billy looked over at the window. "We all need to take turns being on the lookout. I think I had a false sense of security before; it is definitely gone now."

Jack and Rick nodded. "Good idea. We'll take shifts."

Charlie walked over to the window and looked around. "They know we're here. Maybe not exactly where we are, but they know we're in this town. We need to be really careful. Remember, don't answer them if they talk to you. How do you think they knew where we were?"

Charlie grabbed the knapsack. "We need to take a look at everything we got from their ship. Look closely to see if there's anything they can track us with." She pulled out everything from the knapsack and started sorting through it. The others did the same. She ruffled through the pages of a book and then went to open the big blue box. "I don't know what this is. I found it in the drawer." She opened the box. The device inside was odd looking. No one knew what it was, but they were certain it must be important. She picked it up to scrutinize it. Under it was a tiny blinking light. "Damn it! They had a tracer in the box." She picked it up and ran for the door. She chucked it out the door and out onto the street. The sky filled with the sound of humming as a craft came out of nowhere shooting up and down the street. She closed the door quietly. "Oh my God! Did you see that?"

Jack crouched at the window, watching quietly. Charlie continued, "If we hadn't found that, they might've found us again." She laid the device back in the box and put it back in the knapsack. She picked up the book and said, "It seemed kind of silly at the time to take a book, but I'm curious about how their system works." She put the book into the bag. "Maybe we can find a weakness that way." Charlie put her bag aside and leaned up against the door.

Jack looked over at Nick, "We need to find a way to get back to the hotel. It's not going to be easy though. We're not sitting in the lap of luxury anymore. Someone in this neighborhood must have a red van, or something big enough to carry us all home. I'm going to lie down for a bit, but afterwards, I'm going to go door to door and search for a van."

Jack got up to head towards one of the bedrooms. Nick pulled up a chair next to the window. "I'll take first watch. The rest of you get a nap and then we'll go search the neighborhood for a way home."

Nick was still sitting by the window as Charlie wandered down the stairs. "How long did I sleep?"

Nick looked up at her. "About two hours."

She walked over and sat down on his lap and leaned against the window. "Thanks for guarding while I slept. This whole situation just keeps getting crazier and crazier."

Nick smiled at her. "No problem. Want to go van searching now or do you need to wake up more?"

Charlie bounced up. "No, I'm ready. I just want to get back to the hotel. I'm not comfortable being so far away when they're in so much danger back there." Leaving the rest to sleep, the two headed out the door. Charlie looked around frantically. "I'm so nervous. I feel like they're watching me."

Nick grabbed her hand. "Well, let's not stay still, just in case." They ran from house to house peering into the garages, trying to see if there were any vans or SUVs around.

"There has to be something," said Charlie.

They came to one house where the garage had no windows. Nick went to the door. "We need to go in through the house. It's the only way we'll know what's in the garage." They tried the front door, but it was locked.

Charlie gazed up at Nick. "Maybe there's a back door. The two ran around the house in hopes of finding an unlocked door. The back door was locked too, but in the backyard stood an old yellow school bus. "Nick, look at that!" exclaimed Charlie.

They ran over to the bus and pried open the door. Nick sat down in the driver's seat. "It's bright yellow. Don't you think they'll see it?"

Charlie searched around for the keys. "Yes. They might. Why don't we paint it?"

After moving the visor, the keys fell into Nick's lap. "Well, that's pure luck. You know that idea just might work. You can imagine that there's paint. Can't you?"

Charlie shrugged. "I think so. It's small enough." She sat down in one of the seats and closed her eyes. She thought about the safety of her group. 'I wish I had red paint for this bus, so I can keep us safe.'

Nick started to laugh. "Yes! You did it." She opened her eyes and took a deep breath. "I wasn't sure if I could. I'm glad it worked."

Nick got up and put the keys in his pocket. "Let's go tell the others about this." The two ran back to the house, barely making it as a few hovercrafts decided to patrol the area. Charlie heard them inside her head: *We know you are there, and we will find you.* The two crouched down by the window and watched as they circled a few times, then flew off in the opposite direction.

Nick flopped down onto the floor, pulling her down with him. "I'm so glad we don't have that tracker in the house with us. It's bad enough they know the area we're in."

Charlie laid her head back. "I know, right. I have to wonder if we can do this and even make it home."

Jack wandered out into the living room where they sat. "Where did you two go?"

Nick looked up at him. "We went searching for the answer to get home. We actually figured it out too, 'til those bastards came patrolling again. We found a school bus in someone's backyard, just down the road. With some red paint, it'll be good as new to take us back to Richmond."

Jack looked impressed. "Good idea. So, let's get painting so we can hit the road. How long do you think it'll take to dry?"

Nick got up. "I don't know, but I guess we'll find out."

They headed over to where the bus was located. Charlie looked around. "Someone has to stay guard. Those hover-crafts could return at any time."

Jack looked over at her. "Sounds good. You want to keep an eye out while we change this beast's color?"

Charlie nodded. "I can do that." The group grabbed some paint and a brush and began painting. Charlie watched quietly. "Don't forget the very top. Don't need those damn ships spotting us from above."

Nick crawled up on top of the bus and spread the paint from one end to the other. He then jumped down. "The top is done. What else is left?"

Billy looked around at the back of the bus. I have this end almost complete."

Jack stepped back and looked the bus over. "Looks like we're almost done." After they finished up the last few spots,

Jack laid down his brush. "We'll come back in about twelve hours to see if it had a chance to dry."

They swiftly snuck back to the house. As they closed the door behind them, they could hear the hum of the craft soaring by. Charlie ran to the window. "That was close." She peered out at the tracer lying in the middle of the road. "They seem to come every time we're close to that tracer. What if it has a motion sensor in it?"

Nick pulled the curtain shut. "Don't think about it. Let's just try to relax a little before we hit the road… though once we get that bus on the road, we're not guaranteed any safety." He looked over at Jack. "If the bus passes the test, and we make it safely, then it's pure luck. When I saw Charlie get shot, that was it for me. My guard is up. It won't go down again 'til I get her home safely." Everyone agreed and headed off to get some sleep.

Nick pulled a chair over to the window. "Charlie, lie on the couch."

"You need sleep too, Nick." Charlie responded.

Nick looked over at her. "I'll sleep once I'm sure we're okay." Charlie curled up and shut her eyes. She knew it would be okay to sleep for a bit.

When she woke up a couple of hours later, she saw that Nick was still sitting at the window. She sat up and thought to herself, 'He needs sleep too. This is unfair.' Grabbing the cushions off the couch, she placed them next to the window. "If you won't leave the window to catch a nap, then the nap can come to you." Nick looked over at her as she positioned the cushions next to him. "I'm keeping watch now. You get some sleep," said Charlie firmly, motioning him to move.

Nick smirked but got off the chair and lay down on the

cushions. "You wake me if anything happens. No matter how small it is."

She nodded. "I'll do that. Don't worry." She turned and looked out the window. The moon was full that night, so the sky was bright. She wondered to herself if daytime even existed anymore or if it was actually night all the time. Time seemed to disappear for her. She couldn't even recall what day it was or if it was nighttime or daytime. Maybe time was really an allusion in her world. 'What if this is all there really ever was?' She took a deep breath. Before she had time to exhale, something caught her eye outside. She ducked down and peeked over the edge of the window. It was Zafarians on foot. It appeared that they were patrolling the area in search of them. This town was too small for it to be a coincidence. Could that be what was going on? She reached over and tapped Nick. "Hey, we have action outside. They're on foot."

Nick crawled over and peered out the window. "Oh wow! I was worried they might do that. They're keeping an eye on the tracker, seeing if we're around. When we finally get out of here, we might have to find a back way out." He lay back down and patted the cushion next to him. "Lay down with me. We really shouldn't be looking out the window right now, just in case they spot us."

Charlie curled up next to him. "I wonder how long they'll stay out there."

Nick closed his eyes. "I don't know... 'til they get tired of waiting us out, I guess. Get some sleep. I'm right here. They can't get to you without getting to me. Believe me, they walk too loudly to do that." The two shut their eyes and slowly fell asleep. The house was quiet, so it wasn't that hard to do.

About five hours later, Jack wandered into the room. He

walked over to the window. He peeked out and spotted the two patrolling the house. "Holy shit!" He reached down and patted Nick's shoulder. "Did you see what's outside the house?"

Nick frowned. "Are they still out there?"

Jack's eyes widened as he sat down next to Nick and Charlie. "Have they been there all night?"

Nick nodded. "Yeah. I think they're watching the tracker to see if anyone is around. It seems to have a motion detector attached to it somehow."

Jack looked over at the sleeping Charlie. "How are we going to get her home safely? I could sneak out and get the bus. Running them over might work."

Nick smirked as he responded, "Our luck, they'll get back up. I think when it's time to go, we go out the back way and run like the wind. If… and when we get there, if the bus isn't quite dry, we can camp out on the bus 'til it is. I'm even ready to drive the bus covered in wet paint."

Jack paused as he thought about it. "Okay. So, what do we have to do before we head out to the bus? Charlie can use her mind powers to bring us food, so we're good there. All we really need is our bags, some blankets, and maybe a few pillows, so our necks won't be so stiff when we get up." Jack peeked out the window as he got up and left to get the rest up and ready to go. "I think they're camping out there." Shaking his head, he headed up the stairs.

Nick rubbed Charlie's shoulder softly. "Hey, we're getting ready to go. You need to get up. Maybe get us some of that tasty coffee."

Charlie laughed as she opened her eyes. "Is there any other kind of coffee?"

Nick paused. "No. I guess in this case, all coffee is good, but I like the brand you get."

Rick poked his head into the room. "Everyone is pretty much ready to go."

Charlie took Nick's arm and slowly pulled herself up. "What do you say we get out of here and head home?"

They stood at the back door peering out. "I don't see anything out there. You see the trees over there behind the neighbor's house... that's where I want you all to run to," Nick said as he pointed toward the house. "I'm going to be right behind you." They quietly opened the door and then shut it gently, trying not to make a sound. Nick motioned for everyone to run as fast and as quietly as they could. They ran straight for the trees. None of them stopped to so much as look back. Nick stood behind the tree once he got there and waited to see if their movement had alerted the aliens in any way. "They don't seem to notice us gone. I think for the moment we're in the clear."

They continued towards the house that had the bus in the backyard. They stopped when they came to a giant fence blocking their access to the yard just before the one they were headed to. Charlie turned and whispered to the men. "We're going to have to go around. If we're quiet enough, they won't know we are there. I think we're far enough away from the sensor for it to detect us." They creeped up the edge, alongside the house. When the aliens turned their heads, the group booted into the backyard where the bus stood. The group piled onto the bus and flopped into the seats. "We made it," whispered Charlie out of breath. "Do you think there's any chance they will hear this bus if we drive right past them?"

Billy gasped for air. "Damn! I'm out of shape. They might

hear us, but it's red, so they'll have trouble seeing it."

Jack joined in. "I can't imagine them hearing us once we're on the move. Those damn hovercrafts are so loud; our bus will sound like it's purring next to one of those."

"I'm gonna take the first shift driving," Billy said as he got up. He looked around the bus before taking the driver's seat. "The whole back has been ripped out … turned into a camper. Not bad."

Nick handed Billy the keys. "You ever drive one of these?"

Billy shrugged. "No, but I've driven a semi-truck. It can't be much different than one of those." He turned and put the keys in the ignition. "Here goes nothing." The bus started. It was initially loud but got quieter the longer they sat. Billy pulled out and headed towards the highway. Charlie watched as they passed by the aliens. The aliens stood looking around, like they knew something was happening but at the same time didn't have a clue. As they drove away, the aliens screeched loudly and angrily.

Jack pulled out the map and checked the location. "We're still pretty far from L.A. I would guess we have somewhere between thirty-five and thirty-eight hours before we get there. I'm going to rest so I'm ready for the next driving shift. Make sure you wake me when you've had enough. Charlie, you get some rest too." Jack headed to the back of the bus, found a comfortable place to lie down and went to sleep.

Charlie and Nick sat in the front seats, right across from Rick and Carla. Charlie gazed over at Carla and asked, "What did you used to do for a living?"

Carla smiled. "I used to be a nurse. I mostly worked with older people who couldn't help themselves anymore."

Charlie looked at Rick. "And you?"

He laid his head back against the seat. "I'm a computer specialist. I can do pretty much anything on a computer and even more, but the more isn't so legal. So, I try to stay away from it, unless needed."

Charlie smiled. "Nothing wrong with that. Billy, weren't you a carpenter before all this happened?"

Billy looked in the mirror at her. "Yeah. I love working with my hands. Did a lot of work building homes for the homeless through Habitat for Humanity. It feels great when they're done, and you know someone has a home because you helped get them one."

Nick shook his head. "Yeah, that would be a great feeling. I used to be a soldier. I mostly did special missions. I liked being able to help people and keep them safe."

Charlie listened quietly before speaking. "I think when all of this is over, I'm going to write a book about it. I used to be a writer and would love to continue writing. We grabbed my bag, right?"

Nick looked over at her. "Yes, I put it in the back. If there's any way of us winning this war, it's going to entail using red in some way as a strategy. We need to plan everything around it, and our plan has to be flawless. One mistake, and we could lose our world forever and maybe even the human race." The bus got really quiet.

Billy looked back in the mirror. "That's really depressing, you know. I mean, I know it's the truth, but what a mood killer. What's that I smell?"

Charlie smiled. "I got some food for us. I figured we better keep eating good just in case it's our last."

Billy grinned. "Pass me up some of that."

Nick passed Billy a burger and a shake. "We have it so good.

Imagine what we would be eating if she couldn't get this for us."

Billy smirked. "I don't even want to give that a thought."

Charlie looked out the window. The green fog rolled across the bus windows. "What do you think that device in the blue box is? It has the same symbol on it that we have on our bodies."

Nick turned his head to look at her. "It might be a weapon. I'm not sure what kind, but they seem to want to keep track of it. Why else would they put a tracer in the box? Let's hope it can help us get rid of them, if not, at least to help. Won't it be nice when we have the sun back?" Nick looked up at the moon. "Don't get me wrong. I love the moon, but I don't think I'll ever look at it the same way again. I really miss the sun and building my days around it. It was so nice to wake up to it."

Charlie nodded. "I miss it too. I loved walking and having the sun hit my face. I hope I get to feel that again someday. I would hate to have to see only the moon for the rest of my life. Any ideas how we can change the color of this fog? I'm so sick of green. It would benefit us if it was red. I just cannot think of anything. If green allows them to see better and red keeps them from seeing, it would be in our favor for us to find a way to do that."

Charlie leaned against the window, deep in thought. Nick whispered, "You okay?" She turned and shook her head. "I guess. What do you think they meant by saying that we were born to help them win against the humans? I get it we are half-alien, but how can we be bred just for that?"

Nick bit his lip as he thought about what she said. "Maybe we were bred for that reason, but it could be the human side of us that allows us to choose our side. I think even if we were full aliens, we would somehow stand up for the humans, or at least I want to believe that. When we get out of here, and we will get out of here, I want to take you out. We can do whatever we want to do."

Charlie smiled. "I would like that. Let's hope we get out of here." She laid her head on his shoulder. A few seconds later all she could hear was: *Aunt Charlie, are you there?* Charlie's head darted up. *I'm here, but I don't know if we should use this way to speak right now. We were attacked earlier because of my talking inside my head, so we need to be super careful. Tell everyone we're okay and safe for the moment. We have a different vehicle and are headed home.* The little girl whispered, *Okay. Bye. See you soon.*

Charlie turned and looked at Nick. "Julie's daughter was speaking to me, but I don't think that it's safe to speak that way, not for the moment, at least, just in case they have a way of listening to us. I might just be paranoid."

He leaned forward and whispered, "Not at all. I think you're smart. We need to take as many precautions as we can. At least 'til we make it home safely. We don't want to take any chances. I think I'm done with road trips for a while after we get back to the hotel."

Charlie smirked. "If you ask Jack, this is not considered a road trip."

Nick smiled as he placed his head against hers. "If we're on the road and in a vehicle, then this is a road trip." The two of them giggled and continued looking out the window. They were thankful to have each other.

Chapter 15

Nick looked back at Charlie, who was leaning on the window. "We're almost home."

Charlie glanced back at him. "I know. It still seems so far away. We've been on this bus for so long. Isn't it funny we want nothing more but to get our lives back, but in reality, some of us will never be the same after all of this. When this started, I was all human, or so I thought. Now, I'm half Zafarian, related to the very monsters that want us dead. How am I supposed to feel about that?" They turned off onto the ramp that led to the hotel.

"You have to remember, Charlie, you never asked for any of this. You are who you are, and I happen to like that person. Being half-alien doesn't make us bad. What it does make us, though, is better prepared for anything to come."

Charlie smirked. "You're right. I guess I should stop feeling guilty about it. I shouldn't be sorry for who I am." Nick pulled the bus into the hotel parking lot parking right next to the hotel door. Charlie looked out the window at the hotel. "I feel different than when I left, and I'm not sure if it's a good or bad thing."

Nick got up and sat next to her. "I guess time will tell. You just remember you're not in this alone. There are a few of us in the same boat. Let's get the bags and let everyone know we made it back home."

The group stood at the door and knocked. The hotel looked really quiet. Charlie looked at Jack. "It's a good thing it looks so quiet; it means the aliens haven't detected them." Seconds later, the sky filled with a loud hum. Nick grabbed Charlie and yelled for the rest to get back on the bus. They leaned against the windows and watched as the sky above filled with hovercrafts. Charlie's eyes widened. "Damn it! Check the stuff just in case there's another tracer in with it."

Jack glanced over her way. "We already did. There's no more. I wonder if they can sense us since we're half-aliens."

Nick looked over at Charlie. "What's that little girl's name?"

Charlie looked up at him. "Christie. But, we shouldn't talk in our heads just in case they can hear."

Nick looked out at the hovercrafts. "They heard you. Not me. I'm gonna try just in case it works." Nick closed his eyes. *Christie, are you there?*

Within seconds, he heard: *Yes. Who's this?*

Nick watched the hovercrafts closely as he continued, *The hotel is surrounded by hovercrafts. We're parked outside but are not taking a chance of getting seen.*

Christie told him the aliens had been watching the area a lot the last couple of days, but never this close to the hotel. *I think they know I'm here. They can sense half-aliens, you know,* she thought to him.

Nick looked over at Charlie as he continued communicating with Christie. *We're going to send in two humans. The hotel should be emptied of anyone who is half-alien. That's the only way we can keep the humans safe. Charlie and the others will remain on the bus 'til we figure out how to keep us safe. Once you are on, we'll move the bus away from the hotel 'til we see if their hovering has anything to do with all of the half-aliens.*

Christie paused for a second. *Okay. Mommy says we'll be out in a second.*

Nick turned to everyone and said, "Okay, guys. This is how it's going to work. Rick, you and Carla are going to go into the hotel. The rest of us are going to stay on the bus. Julie and her daughter are coming out and joining us on the bus. We're going to move the bus away from the hotel and see if those bastards follow us. Christie believes they might be sensing the half-aliens and are trying to get their hands on them."

Rick and Carla went to the front of the bus. As Rick looked over at Nick, he said, "You guys be careful not to get caught. I'll look for Carl when I get in and tell him what's happening."

As they approached the hotel, they saw Julie and Christie, who stood in the doorway. Nick motioned for them to run. Once the door was shut, he pulled the bus out of the parking lot. Jack wandered to the front and sat next to Julie. "So, Nick, where are we going?"

Nick pulled up next to the bridge. "Just right here. Far enough away to watch the hotel and to see what those bastards will do."

Jack looked at Julie. She looked worried. "Hey, you don't have to worry so much. We're all here together."

Julie nodded. "I just want this to be over."

Jack looked out the window and over at the crafts. "It should be soon. This is the only way of testing them; we just need to sit and watch. They can't see the bus. We drove by so many of them, but we've had problems with them searching for us on the way back."

The hovercrafts moved away from the hotel and headed

over towards the bridge. "Damn it!" yelled Nick. "It's us. They're on the hunt for half-aliens. I bet they know we were in their ship. That thing in the blue box has to be something of importance." Nick ran down to the back of the bus and fished it out of the bag. He sat down in the seat and opened the box. The device was a shiny shade of silver. He picked it up and played with it. "It has to do something." A bright green light lit up on the device. He held it up in the air. "Look. It turns on. Now, I just have to figure out what the hell it does." As Nick was about to lay it down, he saw out of the corner of his eye a ship falling from the sky. Seconds later, two more crashed, setting the crafts aflame.

Charlie gasped. "Holy shit! What just happened?"

Nick looked down at the device. The blinking green light caught his eye. "Holy shit is right! I think we have our hands on the only thing that can stop them." Nick picked it up and ran to the front of the bus. "It doesn't make any noise or really do anything, but when that light started to flash, the hovercrafts crashed. If this is for real, then we are onto something, and that something just might get us home or at least freedom."

Julie reached over. "Let me see it, please." Julie took the device from Nick. She turned in every direction and looked at it from one end to the other. "This doesn't seem to be anything like we have on earth. Christie, have you seen this before?"

Christie looked over at it. "Yes. It makes noise that hurts the Zafarians. It won't hurt us though, only the ones who have the rods."

Julie felt puzzled. "What do you mean by the rods?"

Her daughter leaned over the seat and pointed below her ear. "The full aliens have an organ below their left ear called a rod. It is the only way they can die. This makes a really loud sound that hurts them. It won't hurt them unless you're close to them though, like maybe less than a mile away."

Julie looked over at her daughter. "How do you know this?"

Christie shrugged. "I don't know. They just talk around us like we're not there."

Julie turned to Jack and Nick. "We better leave the light on. If this does what she says it does, then they're going to be pissed that we have any idea what it is."

Jack looked out the window. "There haven't been any more around since they crashed. My worry is that if that's what happened, and this goes off, they're gonna strike at us hard."

Nick got up and walked towards the front of the bus. "I can self-heal, so I'm gonna go out there and see if it's safe."

Charlie felt sick to her stomach at the thought of this. *Be careful,* she said inside her head. Nick looked over and smiled at her, then walked off the bus. The group watched out the window, looking around to see if any new hovercrafts would come around. Nick walked over to the broken-down ship. Peering in the window, he could see the alien lying there lifeless. He looked back at the bus and gave a thumbs-up, then continued walking while observing the skies around him. Nick turned towards the bus and whispered, "Turn it off for a second and then back on when I give you the signal to." Julie reached down and switched it off. The light stopped flickering. Within minutes, the loud hum of the hovercrafts filled the sky and got louder as they got closer. Nick turned and motioned for her to switch it back on. In the distance, a bright flash filled the sky as another craft crashed. Nick ran back to the bus. "Damn it, I think we're onto something. They cannot come around as long as that's on." Nick got in

249

the driver's seat and pulled the bus over to the parking lot of the hotel. "All of us can now enter the hotel. Just whatever you do, don't turn that off. They're just waiting for us to turn it off, so they can attack."

The group got off and headed for the door. Carl ran to the door to open it. "Oh my God! I'm so glad you guys are okay. Did you see those ships crash? I have no idea what's going on, but you want to see a bunch of frightened people, just go look under the beds."

After they all piled in, Carl locked the doors. Julie pulled out the device. "This is what happened, Carl. See this flashing green light? If it's flashing, it will keep them away. We think it lets off noise that's too sharp for us to hear, but it kills the aliens if they're anywhere around us. If that's the case, we're going to be safe here in the hotel for a while, as long as they don't find a way to prevent this."

Carl looked at the device. "I've never seen anything like this. You should put it in your room, somewhere it won't get touched."

Jack looked at her. "My room might be better. I don't have pets playing or any children around."

Julie nodded and handed it to him, "Good idea."

Charlie looked at Franny as she came running down the hall. "You all are back! Carl told me what happened with the crafts. I was so worried."

Charlie smiled. "We're okay, I promise. It's been a super long trip, so we're just really glad to be back. For a minute there, I thought we would never get to see you again."

Franny looked her in the eyes. "That's not true. If you buggers would've been stuck on that bus much longer, I would have come out to join you. You guys have been like family to me for so long. Not even Carl could've stopped me."

Carl rolled his eyes at her. "That's a fact."

The group headed down the hall towards the board room. Carl looked over at Nick. "Those crafts have been hovering over this hotel since you guys left Mexico. It had to have been because they knew you found the device. But if they couldn't see you because you were all in red, how did they know?"

Nick shook his head. "We think maybe they can detect the half-alien in us. My guess is they know it was a half-alien that found the device. The ship door was too heavy for anyone else to have opened it. Billy was strong enough to open it, and the drawers it was kept in, so that's the only thing I can think of."

Carl shook his head, "Sounds about right. These gifts are a blessing and a curse at the same time." Carl paused. "Billy has supernatural strength? When did he get that?"

Charlie laughed. "A lot has happened since we left. You really need to be filled in." She nodded as they entered the board room and headed over to the table.

Nick joined Charlie and motioned for the rest of the group to go relax and maybe get some sleep. Carl watched quietly. "You're pretty good at that. You didn't even need to say a word."

Nick leaned against the table. "I spent a lot of years in training for special ops. Funny thing though, I remember being involved in some kind of combat training. It had to do with the aliens."

Charlie chimed in. "Yes. I remember something like that too. It's crazy though; it's like a really faded memory."

Carl took a deep breath. "Every time we turn around, it gets crazier with this half-alien thing. I'm so glad you're on our

251

side though. I don't think we would have a chance without you."

Nick looked at Carl with a serious look. "No. "We're all a team, and this win is a team effort. We may have gifts that help along the way, but it takes every single one of us to win this war."

Carl nodded his head in agreement. "Okay. So, start from the beginning."

Charlie leaned against Nick as she spoke. "We were on the way to Mexico, when we went through White Rock. The whole place was gone. It was one large set of crops. The aliens were guarding them as the humans tended to them. We didn't have any problems the whole way there. We did see a woman though when we hit L.A. We told her to tell everyone about using hand radios; hopefully, they listened."

Carl put his hands on the table. "Yes. I heard from a few people. One from L.A. and another from San Francisco. They told me that they saw writing on the side of a gas station telling them to use a handheld radio. I filled them both in on what's going on. Oh, and I heard from the colonel too. I forgot exactly where he's located. He's in the USA though. He followed our instructions and reported back that they've had progress. I told him we'll report anything new once you return. I see that you brought back Rick and his niece, Carla. That was a good idea. He seems to know a lot about what's going on down south. I told Mike I would send back two of ours to help get them prepared for war."

Charlie curiously asked, "Do we have anyone picked out yet?"

Carl gazed over. "Yes. Loretta has volunteered, and Chris will be joining her."

Charlie bit her lip. "The conditions down there are very poor. They don't have a lot and they're locked up in a warehouse with barely any light."

Carl leaned back. "I hate sending anyone to a place with those types of conditions, but they're desperately in need of help. Maybe we can stock up the bus with supplies before they go. So, what else happened?"

Nick reached under the table and grabbed onto Charlie's hand. He could feel she was a little tense. "We went to the ruins, and after searching for a while, came across a door in the ground beside a broken-down temple. The door was extremely heavy. We almost didn't get it open. I cut myself when I tried. Turns out, I can self-heal." Carl's eyes widened as Nick continued. "Billy gave it a shot. He opened it as if it were as light as a feather. Charlie went in first and found a light source. It lit up bright green. I think that's so they can see better ... probably why the fog is green."

Carl hurried Nick along. "Come on. What happened next?"

Nick smiled. "Hold on. I'm getting there. So, we searched the whole ship. It was really big, so it took a while. We found quite a few things, one being the key that opened the drawer for Charlie and Billy. That's where the device was. We found quite a bit, though, that has to be gone through. Anyway, moving on with the rest of the day, we hit the road and started to return home when the van broke down. I think the lack of oil seized the engine, but who knows? For all we know, they did it to stop us."

Charlie interrupted. "That's when all the problems started. We walked for what felt like forever 'til we found this town. That's where those stupid crafts found us and shot me."

Carl freaked out. "You were shot? Are you okay?"

She leaned in towards Carl. "Nick healed me. I have so much anxiety thinking about it. If he hadn't been able to heal me, I would be dead right now." Nick squeezed Charlie's hand a little. "But I did, so we don't have to worry about it, do we?"

"She's fine. I won't ever let anything happen to her again. We ran into this house across from where they shot her and took up shelter there for a while. We needed the time to stop and think about what our next move was. Those hovercrafts were camped outside the house though, so we knew something was up. Charlie found a tracer inside the blue box right under that device and threw it out onto the road."

Charlie gazed over at Nick. "Yeah, that's when they decided to guard the house on foot. It's like they sensed us, or at least the sensor. We found a bus though, painted it red, and long story short, now we're home."

Carl got up and walked over to the window. "Wow! That's one hell of a story! You guys are lucky to be back. What made you think of painting the bus?"

Nick looked at Charlie. "Charlie thought of it and then used her mind to make the paint appear for us. It took a few hours for it to dry, but it was the best idea we could come up with. Too bad we didn't know what we were carrying. Eh, Charlie?"

Charlie stood up. "I really need some sleep. You should get some too, Nick. You've been up for hours driving." Carl motioned for them to go get some sleep, then went to talk to his wife.

Charlie woke up to a tiny tongue washing her face. Opening one eye, she saw Bruno wagging his tail frantically, trying to wake her up. "Hi, boy. I'm so glad to see you too. Come here." She reached over and pulled him over to her, and scratching behind his ears, she whispered, "You make life feel so normal.

I missed you so much." Stormage jumped up onto the bed. Bruno dived at him and wrestled him. "Aww! Poor guy. He misses me too." She reached over to rub him. "You're a good boy." She looked over at Julie's bed. It was empty. 'It must still be early,' she thought to herself. She got up and threw her hair in a ponytail, then headed to the sink to splash some water on her face.

As she headed out of the bathroom, Marcy walked into the room. "Oh, hi. I was just coming to check on them. They're happy to see you, especially Bruno. He looked all over for you."

Charlie smiled. "I missed him too. I miss taking him for walks in the park or just waking up in the morning with not a care in the world."

Marcy nodded. "I know what you mean. I miss the sun so bad. Carl told us you found a device to keep the aliens away from the hotel. Is this true?"

Charlie nodded. "Yeah. So far it works. The guys still need to investigate, but we think four ships crashed because of it."

Marcy was so excited. She reached up and hugged Charlie. "Oh my God! We might make it home after all."

Charlie hugged her back but then gently pushed her away. "I don't know about home. It doesn't switch worlds; it just prevents them from getting close to us for the moment. It allows us time to find a way to get rid of them. We may eventually get rid of them, but there's no saying our home will ever be the same. That's not even a guarantee that we'll win, but we'll try."

Marcy took a deep breath. "I pray every night we'll all get home safely. Beth never got a chance, and it'll be hard to never see her again, but the rest of us must've survived for some reason. I have to believe we have a chance against them, don't you?"

Charlie thought about it for a second. "I do believe we have a shot against them. If it's not a well thought out plan, then we're screwed, but if we plan it well, maybe we can do this."

Marcy reached down and patted her leg for Bruno to come. "Hope you don't mind, I'm going to take them down to my room and entertain them for a bit."

Charlie smiled. "No. I don't mind at all." Charlie picked up the book she grabbed off the ship. "I'm going to find Julie and Christie. Have fun with Bruno and Stormage."

Charlie walked into the kitchen. Franny, Julie and Christie were all sitting at the table. "There you guys are." She pulled a chair out and sat down next to them. She laid the book on the table and pushed it next to Christie. "Can you show me where this rod is in the pictures?"

Christie nodded and opened the book. After flipping through a few pages, she pointed to a page in the book. "There it is, Aunt Charlie. See right under the left ear, like I told you."

Charlie pulled the book closer to her. "It's really small, isn't it? So that's what keeps them alive?"

Christie nodded. "Yup. It heals them."

Charlie wrinkled up her forehead. "Do you know what happens to an alien when they hear the sound of the device?"

The little girl shook her head. "I've never seen it happen before... just heard about it. It all has to do with the rod. I don't know how it works though. I heard they cannot function because of the amount of pain it causes. I don't know though."

Charlie bit her lip. "Hmm. Maybe that alien died because of the crash. I better get someone to check and make sure he's dead. He's too close to the hotel to leave him alive." Charlie got up to go look for Nick. "I'll see you in a bit. I want to check and make sure it's dead. Who knows what will happen if it's still alive?"

* * *

As they walked towards the ship, they found smoke pouring out of the engine. Nick held an axe. "It looked dead when I looked earlier. I sure hope it's dead when I look again."

Charlie placed her hand on his back. "Maybe we should hit it to make sure it's dead."

Nick gazed over at it. "You mean me, right?"

When he reached over and hit the glass window with the axe, the alien's eyes opened. Charlie screamed in shock, as Nick swung the axe at it hitting it right between the shoulder blades. The head rolled from the ship out onto the gravel. Both their eyes widened as the alien let out a screech from hell. "Oh my God! What do we do now?" yelled Charlie.

Nick looked at her. "We need fire to burn it."

Charlie reached into her pocket and pulled out a lighter. "One good thing about being a casual smoker."

After pouring the liquid all over the alien's head, she lit the head on fire. The two stood back as it screamed in horror. Nick pulled Charlie close to him. "We now know they don't die right away. We have to burn them. Go back to the hotel, will you, and send Jack and Billy out. We have three more to do."

Charlie looked down at the burning head, then turned and

ran to the hotel. It took a few minutes to round them up, but eventually they all ran out of the hotel towards Nick. Jack yelled as he approached. "I told Charlie to stay in; she doesn't need to be part of this, at the moment." The three of them spent the next hour searching for the rest of the ships, so that the aliens flying them could be killed. Each one of them was still alive. They were just unable to move because of the sound of the device.

Billy looked over at Jack. "How many of these bastards do you think are on this planet? And do you think we have to do this to all of them?" Billy shook his head in disbelief. "I'm tired just thinking about it."

Jack agreed. "This is going to be a long process; that's for sure. I wish I could get inside these guys' heads and know what they're thinking. We hear about hatred all the time, but I could never quite imagine its intensity to any degree. It shows though, with these guys. I don't think I ever imagined it being so harsh." After igniting the last one, Jack looked over at Nick. "There has to be an easier way to light them all up. What if there are millions of them?"

The three started walking back to the hotel. Nick agreed. "If there's a way, we'll think of it. Meanwhile, let's just concentrate on keeping the rest safe."

Charlie waited by the door. Julie stood next to her warning her to be careful, especially in light of the fact that she had gotten shot. Charlie phased her out, though, as she watched for the guys to return. She was worried that something might have happened to them in their attempt to keep everyone safe. "Julie, stop it, will you? I'm okay. Let's just be happy I'm alive. Just like you were when I had to worry all that time."

Julie paused and looked out the window. "There they are."

Charlie opened the door as they came running in. Nick smiled as he passed her. "All done. No more in the area either." Charlie walked off with Nick.

Julie watched, then looked at Jack. "Those two seem cozy."

Jack smiled. "Yeah, they're good for each other. He wouldn't let anything hurt her ever. He has proven that time and time again."

Julie looked at Jack. "Good. Maybe I don't have to worry so much then." The two headed down towards the kitchen. Larzo and Mark met them on the way.

"I heard you were back," said Larzo. "Nice job. So, did you get to see the ship?"

Jack nodded. "It was huge... like nothing I ever imagined. I wish the cameras worked so that we could've showed everyone. The inside was very much alien-like... nothing human about it; not to mention everything was big and heavy."

Mark reached up and ran his hand through his hair. "That must've been scary. I hear Chris and Loretta are heading to Mexico to help them. Maybe they'll get a chance to see it."

Jack thought to himself for a second before answering. "Yeah. Maybe they will." Billy asked Jack what that was all about as they walked away. "I want to try to keep these power things under wrap for a bit. Larzo knows we are immune, but if Carl wants him to know more, he'll tell him."

They entered the kitchen. Franny was standing at the counter. "I'm making soup, boys. You getting hungry?"

Billy rubbed his stomach. "When am I not hungry?"

Franny and Jack laughed. "That would be never." Franny reached over and grabbed the oven mitts. "I made cookies too. Want one... just one though? I made them for the little one.

We're running low on supplies, so I couldn't make them for

everyone."

Jack grabbed a cookie and nearly dropped it because it was hot. "Maybe Charlie can help you there. She's good at using her mind to make stuff appear. Maybe she can help with supplies... although we have it so much better than the Mexican people they saw. They were eating fruit. Not that fruit is bad, but they really needed a Charlie. Maybe when Loretta goes down there, she can help them get organized. Mike said it was the first large place they could find to gather so many people. It has to be hard living in a warehouse."

Franny smiled. "I'm sure Loretta and Chris can help them figure all of this out. Can you stir the soup for me if it needs it? I'm going to bring up the cookies."

Billy peered into the pot. "Mmmm. Smells good. Jack, we did really good today, but how are we supposed to get all of the aliens and burn them like that?"

Jack reached over and stirred the soup. "I don't now, but as long as it works, who cares how long it takes. We'll stop them, and the human race will get to live, maybe even thrive again." The two guys stood there feeling good about the situation for the first time since the whole mess began.

Chapter 16

L arzo loaded the last box of masks onto the bus. "I think that's it. Are we missing anything?"

Loretta walked to the back of the bus. After looking around, she turned and looked at Larzo. "Nope. I just need to speak to Charlie before we go. She asked me to drop by."

Charlie sat at her table in her room. Leaning back in the chair, she closed her eyes and thought about the device and how it was keeping them safe. *I wish I could help others with that. If I could only have more devices like that.* She opened her eyes. On the table was another device identical to the one in the blue box. She jumped up in disbelief. It wasn't something she was sure she could do since it was an alien device. But she was half-alien and the voice did say she was bred to fight for them, which would mean she had access to their stuff, too. Her stomach started to turn, and her knees felt weak. *Nick,* she whispered in her head. *Are you there?*

Seconds later, Nick came through the door. "You okay?"

Charlie gazed at him. "I'm having a major weak spell."

He walked over to her and squatted down next to her. "What brought it on?" He looked at the device laying on the table. "The light isn't on. What happened?"

Charlie shook her head. "That's not the device; it's a

duplicate. I found out I can copy them with my powers, but it takes a lot out of me. I don't have the strength to make more yet."

Nick reached up and ran his fingers through her hair. "Maybe you need food or something while you're doing it. You know, like gas for a car. Your body is just feeling empty."

Nick stood up. "I'm going to get you some food. Between the two of us, we'll do this. I'll take care of you, and you can try to make more devices."

She nodded as she laid her head down onto the table. "Okay."

Loretta entered the room as Nick headed down to the kitchen. "We're heading out. You said you wanted to see me before I left?"

Charlie turned her head. "Take this device with you. Turn it on while you're driving. It'll keep you safe while driving. They won't die unless you literally cut off their heads and burn them, but I advise that you just keep going. We don't want to give them any indication we're onto how to kill them. Explain the process to Mike when you get there. Tell him this device needs to remain on at all times. Carl will have to contact them on the handheld radio to fill them in on the initial attack, but this will keep them safe."

Loretta raised her eyebrows. "Wow! Okay. I'll pass this on. Thanks, Charlie. Hopefully, we'll get to talk soon." Loretta went straight to the bus.

Carl stood at the door waving as the bus drove away. He exhaled loudly then ran up the stairs and knocked as he entered Charlie's room. "That's amazing that you did that. Tell me, what do you need to be able to keep making more?"

Nick wandered into the room. "She needs sustenance. It takes a lot out of her. Maybe you can get someone cooking in the kitchen and bring her food. Her whole body shuts down without fuel in it." Nick rested the tray on the table. "I brought sandwiches and cookies. Oh, and orange juice." He smiled as he grabbed a chair. "Maybe Franny can make some soup?"

Carl slammed his hand down on the table. "I'm on it! I'll make the soup myself if she isn't up to it. We need to try to get as many of these things as we can; get them out to the others, so we can all be rid of these creatures. They may have a serious hatred for humans, but I'll tell you it's nothing compared to what I'm feeling right now."

Carl turned and darted down the hall. Nick smiled at Charlie. "Like I said, teamwork."

Charlie pulled the tray closer and started to eat. "I can do this," she said. It took about forty minutes for her to gain her strength back. "If I'm able to duplicate two every two hours, then over a three-day period I would be able to create around thirty of these devices. That's a good plan." Now feeling refreshed, she looked over at Nick and said, "I guess we best get started."

Carl stood in the kitchen with Franny and Billy. "You guys need to keep her fed. If her strength is kept up, she can keep duplicating the devices. While she's doing this, I can get on the handheld radio and make arrangements for people to come get them. This way everyone will be prepared to take down the aliens."

Billy stood stirring the soup as Franny started cutting up veggies to put in it. "Sounds good."

Carl set off for the board room to get on the handheld radio, waving at Larzo as he walked by. He plopped down in front of the radio, then turned it on. It took quite a while to get anyone on, but eventually he managed to contact the colonel. "Sorry,

Carl. We've been so busy trying to figure out everything. It's hard to have anyone monitoring full time."

Carl exhaled. "It's okay. I totally understand. I didn't mind sitting here all this time. After all, what else do I have to do other than try to save the world?"

The colonel laughed. "How long have you been trying to reach me?"

Carl paused. "For about three hours now. Hopefully, I can reach others too. Only time will tell. Anyway, the whole purpose of me contacting you is to tell you that we have a device that stuns the aliens, giving you time to kill them. After stunning them, you need to remove their heads and burn them in order for them to die. The device when on, will stun any alien within a mile, leaving them helpless. I advise leaving it on all the time. That way, your base has a safe zone. That's what we're doing."

The colonel was quiet. "That's amazing! And this works for sure?"

Carl pulled his chair up closer. "Yup. It sure does. We have a way of duplicating them, so I'm having them made and they'll be ready for you to pick up in three days. Do you have a way of having them delivered to other places, so we can get the others prepared too?"

The colonel took a deep breath and thought for a second. "I'm sure we can figure this out. As long as that device is on, whoever is near it is safe?"

Carl agreed. "Yes. They will be."

The colonel got excited, "I'll get back to you in a bit." Carl said goodbye and continued trying to contact the others. This would be a full day project, having people from different places pick up devices so that they could prepare for war.

Franny looked at Billy. "It's going to be busy the next couple of days. With Carl in there trying to plan and Charlie trying to get the devices needed to defeat the aliens, remember none of this happens overnight. We're going to have to cook up a storm to keep them going."

Billy shrugged. "Well, I guess that's what we have to do to get us all home. That's if we get home. Have you thought about the fact that even if we win, we may never get home?"

Franny stopped cutting and looked over at him. "No. I actually never gave it much thought. What do we do if we don't go home? This world is definitely not our world!"

Billy shook his head. "I really don't know. I tried to imagine what it would be like, but I couldn't even think of what life would be like after this is all over. One thing I can see is that no matter what it's like, we're all here together, and all of us are in the same boat."

Franny reached over and grabbed a green pepper. "That we are. I've been having weird dreams since our worlds switched. In my dream, I'm being stabbed. I'm lying on the ground, and when I look up, there's a tornado coming. I try to get up and run, but I can barely move. In the distance, I can see a woman holding a baby wrapped up in a pink blanket. She laughs and runs into the tornado. I then wake up in a cold sweat. I've had this dream almost every night since."

Billy reached over and popped a piece of pepper into his mouth. "Sounds crazy. I hate nightmares, though I know they're not real. We don't have a choice on whether to have them or not, and they really do interfere with our sleep."

She nodded her head. "You're right, but this feels like so much more. I don't know why, but my heart feels broken when I wake up. It gets really hard to go back to sleep and

265

having this every night makes it even harder to want to sleep."

Billy stirred the soup. "You're not the only one having nightmares. Loretta and Julie were having them too. I noticed that when we were on the road, Charlie was grunting in her sleep as if she was having nightmares. I don't know if she even knows she's having them though. I didn't mention it to her; she doesn't need anything else to worry about."

Mark walked into the kitchen holding a box of candles. "Hey, guys. I'm just doing rounds. I want to make sure no one is sitting in the dark. How are your flashlights?"

Billy reached down into his pocket and grabbed his flashlight. He flickered the button. "Mine's working great... might leave a spare in the kitchen though in case someone's dies. How have you been doing, Mark?"

Mark placed the candles on the table. "I haven't been too bad. Trying to keep busy so I don't have to think about all of this. Before you even ask how that's going, just don't. I just can't find enough to do. I have a permanent migraine just thinking about it."

Billy laid down the spoon. "Well, if you want something to do, check with me. I'll find you something to do. We have some broken hovercrafts out there. I want to go through them and see what's in them. I just have to finish up in the kitchen first, then we can go."

Franny looked over at him. "Go. I have this covered. There's always so much to do, and this is not one them." Franny moved the cutting board closer to the pot of soup. "See. I can reach both."

Billy glanced over at Mark. "You up for checking them out?"

Mark grabbed the box. "Okay. Just let me finish my rounds first, and I'll meet you out front."

Franny pulled her chair closer and continued chopping veggies. "While you're waiting, can you do me a favor? Can you find Julie for me?"

Billy laid down his apron. "I can do that. I think she's up in her room with Christie." Billy headed out to find her.

Julie sat on the edge of the bed. "Are you sure you want me to read the same story to you again?"

Christie giggled. "Yes, Mommy. I love that story so much."

Julie looked up when she heard a knock at the door. "Come in."

Billy popped his head in. "Franny's looking for you. I think she wants you to come to the kitchen... maybe to help cook. I don't know."

Julie looked over at Christie. "Can the story wait?"

The little girl squealed, "Yes! I get to cook with Aunt Franny." The two got up and headed down towards the kitchen. Billy took off to search the ships.

Franny sat humming to herself as Julie entered the kitchen. "Aww, there you are."

Down the hall, she could hear Christie giggling. "Bruno, let go of my pants. Mommy, he has my pants leg again." Christie wrestled with the puppy. "You silly little guy." Bruno jumped up, gave a little growl and booted down the hall after the cat. Christie got up and ran into the kitchen. "I tried to get here faster, but the puppy wouldn't let me." She grabbed a chair and pulled it over to the counter. "What are you making?"

Franny laughed and shook her head. "I made you a treat earlier."

Christie's eyes widened. "What is it?"

Franny reached over and grabbed a Popsicle from the freezer. "It's frozen juice. You don't bite it; you suck on it.

Have you had one before?"

Christie shook her head. "No. I never did." She grabbed onto the Popsicle and slurped. "It's so cold."

Julie looked at Franny. "You want some help?"

Franny smiled. "I washed the big bowl. If you want to make some bread, that would be great."

Billy and Mark walked across the parking lot towards the broken craft. Billy ran his hand across its shiny side. "Think that's actually metal?"

Mark got closer to have a good look. "Nope. It has a shimmer of purple in it. I don't know what this is, but it isn't metal. I wonder what the purple is."

Billy peered into the broken window. "I need to get this body out." Billy reached in and pulled the giant body out. "Man, these guys are big." He threw the body off to the side and crawled into the craft. The ship shimmered as if it were built with crystals. "We need to have this moved to the basement of the hotel."

Mark frowned. "Yeah, that's great for business. A giant hovercraft in the basement."

Billy sneered. "Yeah, look around at all your customers. Do they look like they would have a problem?"

Mark's frown got deeper as he picked up on Billy's sarcasm. "Fine. Maybe we can chain it up and leave it in the supply entrance."

Billy agreed. "Okay. Well, can you set that up with Larzo and have it done right away? We need to have a better look at this metal; plus, I want to know what's up with the crystal."

Mark sighed. "Okay. I'll do it right away."

Billy headed back into the hotel. As he headed down the hall, he glanced into the board room. Carl sat tapping his fingers on the table. "What's up Carl? You okay?"

Carl looked over at him. "Yes. I'm fine. Just a little frustrated. I've been trying to contact the others all day. I got a hold of the colonel and the contacts in Mexico, but it seems like no one else is out there. How are we going to beat them if we can't communicate with others around the world?"

Billy walked over to Carl. "Don't give up, man. If they're out there and they can answer, they will. We just need to keep trying. Maybe we have to actually go there and search for people. We might not get them all in one go. I believe as long as we get some, we can keep going 'til we get them all."

Carl looked over at Billy. "What if it's never ending?"

He shrugged. "I don't have the answers, but if we're going to fight, let's do it right. Maybe this is what we were born for, and maybe it's the last thing we'll see in life."

Billy patted Carl's shoulder. "Try to get a hold of them. If we can't we do it without them, then after we win, we move on and help the next. There isn't anything more we can do, other than that. Oh, by the way, we're pulling the ships into the hotel basement. They contain metals and crystals, and I want to study them more."

As Billy laughed and walked out of the room, he said to Carl, "Who would've guessed we'd be some kind of superheroes?"

Carl laughed under his breath and shook his head softly. "Only you, Billy."

Two days passed. The group had been running steady with very little sleep in between. Charlie leaned against the back of the chair as she finished the soup Franny made. "That woman can definitely cook," she said to Nick. Setting her bowl on the table, she looked over at Nick. "The more I do this, the more it weakens me. The more it weakens me, the more memories come flooding back. This feels so weird; things I just never knew about myself. I remember some kind of combat training I had when I was younger, and I remember building something. I just don't know what it was, but we were building something pretty important."

Nick nodded as he shared his memories. "I remember training too. I never did anything like building, but I worked with soldiers... lots of them. I remember seeing weapons that we've never seen on earth. Compared to the soldiers here, we would be considered deadly weapons."

Charlie sighed. "It's a little messed up having such mixed-up memories. If we get our lives back, I'm not telling anyone about all of this. I'm just going to live a normal human life, although I won't give up a chance to kick a little alien ass." She laughed.

Nick laughed with her. "So, are you seriously going to write about this later?"

She nodded. "Yup. I'll tell the world about how it was won back. I might have to make it science fiction though, so they don't think I'm a quack. How many of these did Carl say we needed?"

Nick paused for a minute then responded, "Twenty-five in total. We're almost there. We'll be done by tomorrow. I guess the Army has been busy painting choppers and jets red. They're flying here in choppers, then sending jets overseas to deliver these devices. The pilots are planning to wear gas masks and run these devices the whole way there. They're taking a few troops to search for groups like ours and filling them in on the procedures. Carl doesn't know it, but he has saved so many lives just by sitting on the handheld for so many hours. The more people we can reach, the more aliens get killed, and the chances get better that we get to live life as we choose, not as prisoners locked up in a hotel. Imagine though, not having the luxury we have right now, here with comfortable rooms and food. There are so many people out there stuck in warehouses or starving. We really need to help them. I think people here get to pretend it isn't as serious as it really is, but as long as everything that needs to be done is done, and everyone is safe, then that's their right, if it gets them through the day."

Charlie smiled. "I like the way you think. Let's get this finished so I can find something new to do for a bit. Doing the same thing over and over is very tiresome."

The skies around the hotel filled with a loud whooping noise. Carl ran towards the front door. "They're here." He unlocked the hotel and waited.

A man ran up to him. "Carl, I'm Captain Timmonds. I believe you have a few packages for me to pick up."

Larzo and Mark came running out with some boxes. "They have the destinations marked right on the boxes. This one is for you guys though. Make sure this button is turned on at all times.

It's the only thing that will distance you and the aliens, and it will keep them stunned and helpless. Make sure you wear a gas mask. Though this doesn't remove the gas, it will keep you from being affected by the fumes." The soldier nodded and saluted, then turned and ran back to the chopper. Carl turned and looked at Larzo. "We have someone else coming in about four hours. Have the parcels ready for them to go. Are the instructions written out clearly?"

Larzo nodded. "Yes. I wrote them out myself."

Carl smiled. "Okay. Then I'm going to see if I can contact

271

Mexico and see if our people arrived yet."

Larzo wandered down the hall. He grabbed Mark, and the two began to set up the next delivery. Carl sat at the radio. "Mike, this is Carl. Are you there?"

Carl did this for about an hour, until he heard, "This is Mike."

Carl smiled to himself. "I'm so glad to hear your voice, buddy. Did they make it there?"

Mike paused for a moment, then he heard Loretta's voice. "Carl, we made it just fine. We've been busy setting them up and teaching them what to do. Since we turned on the machine, we've killed seven aliens around the warehouse. We've been super busy, but I promise we're okay. Charlie sent a second machine down with us, and I tell you, it's a godsend. We take it out on the supply hunt; it gives us more time to gather the food that's necessary to feed the people. Things have picked up here in the warehouse a hundred percent, and the people here are super happy."

Carl smiled. "Oh, that makes me feel good. I'm so glad we made a difference. Charlie told me to ask when we spoke for Mike to find out if there were any folks immune there?"

The radio was quiet for a few minutes. "Mike says he has four that are immune and to tell Charlie he took her advice."

Carl took a deep breath. "Good, good. I'm pleased to hear that. Okay, Loretta. I'll fill everyone in on your situation. Keep in contact with us." Carl hung up the receiver and took a second to think about the situation. *What is left?* He asked himself.

Day three came, and the group started winding down. Carl walked up to Larzo. "Now that the deliveries are out and gone, you need to get some rest. Tomorrow is going to be an extremely long day, the kind of day that doesn't end 'til the task at hand is done. Some may never see the end of the day.

Meditate, sleep, eat, do whatever it takes; just be ready." Carl saw Charlie wandering down the hall. "You should be resting. You've done a magnificent thing, but your body needs to heal now. You should be proud of yourself. The human race has more of a chance because you were able to make more of those machines. The whole group worked as a team, and now we're prepared—as prepared as we will ever be, that is."

Charlie nodded. "I'm going to bed now. Nick and I just took the dishes down to the kitchen."

Nick came racing out from the kitchen. "Hey, Carl. We were just cleaning up. Gonna get this woman up to bed. She has done an amazing job, don't you think?"

Carl smiled. "I was just telling her that." The two headed down the hall. Charlie smiled as they walked away.

Carl walked into the kitchen where his lovely wife sat. "You did great. Do you know you are the glue that holds us all together?" he said as he looked at his wife.

She smiled. "I know. What would you do without me?" She laughed then got him a bowl of soup. "You need to eat. You've been a very busy man." She laid the soup down in front of him and wrapped her arms around him. "No matter what happens tomorrow, you need to know how much I love you and am very proud of you."

He smiled. "I know."

Jack wandered into the kitchen. "I know I'm supposed to be guarding the device. I needed to get some more coffee. I'm near done, though, for now. Might get some sleep soon, but 'til then, I could use another cup of coffee. Everything is going so smoothly. I'm a little worried about what may go wrong.

Have you given any backup plans any thought? How do we know if everyone is okay and whether the job is done or not?"

Carl frowned. "You've made a good point. How about we see if Charlie will make some air horns appear so that if someone is need of help, they can blow it 'til we find them. Best hurry though; she's off to sleep."

Jack agreed. As he set off to find Charlie, he replied, "Hopefully, this will work."

Franny got up and walked over to the sink to wash her hands. "I'm so nervous about tomorrow. I hope I can get some sleep tonight. I would like to be rested for tomorrow."

Carl put his feet up on one of the chairs. "Maybe you just need to talk about what's on your mind. Is it those damn nightmares? Are you worried you'll have them tonight?"

Franny's frown disappeared. "That might be part of it. I hate these nightmares so much. It's so unfair the way I have to relive it over and over, and what's up with the child? It's like rubbing salt in the wound that we never could have a child. Now we may not even have the chance to keep trying. Carl, all I ever wanted was a family. Don't get me wrong, if it's only you and me for the rest of our lives, I'm okay with that. You're the love of my life. I just wanted to make our love as big as the world around us."

Carl smiled. "I know how much you love me. We'll get the chance to keep trying, and if we never make a bigger family, then I know you're okay with that. Don't worry, baby. You'll get to be a mom someday."

Franny smiled. "Let's try to get some sleep." She pulled her husband off the chair and down the hall towards their room.

Jack headed back to his room after speaking to Charlie. He was glad he had caught her on time and that she agreed to the idea of bringing them some air horns. As he was walking down the hall, he spotted Marcy. "You better get some sleep. Tomorrow is going to be a big day."

She smiled as she approached him. "I'm going there in a few minutes. I was just stretching my legs before heading to bed. I'm a little scared about tomorrow. After losing Beth, it seemed like she died for nothing. This feels almost doable now, so I kinda feel maybe she died to show us the way. I miss her, Jack. We were in love and supposed to have a chance at life together."

Jack nodded. "Yeah. I know you did. She didn't die for nothing. She showed us the power behind those creatures, so that we could be safe. This whole situation makes everything so much more real for us all. It points out what's important in life and who you can't live without. We'll be okay. You'll see, Marcy."

She smiled. "Night, Jack."

Jack continued to his room. As he entered, he thought to himself that tomorrow could end it all. After tomorrow, none of them could be alive. Maybe he was wrong. Maybe all of them would survive, and life would continue, and when they woke up, the sun would shine through the window, brightness making them squint their eyes, reminding them they were alive.' Oh, how much he wanted for that to happen. He sat on the edge of the bed and looked out the window at the moon. He used to love the moon, but never imagined such a dark side to something so beautiful. He would have given anything to just know all of this long before it even started. He lay on the bed as his thoughts continued. If he survived tomorrow, he wouldn't waste another day without telling her how he felt. He picked up a picture from the side table beside his bed. It was of Julie. He smiled as he looked at it. He didn't n want her to know yet. They didn't need to be distracted at this point, but he and Julie were just beginning. He didn't plan on wasting a single moment of his life after this.' He set the picture down and took a deep breath.

Just as he turned to switch off the light, he heard Billy's voice. *Jack, can you hear me?*

Jack leaned back. *Yeah. What's up?*

Billy took a second then continued, *I need to tell you something. I didn't tell the others yet. When I was in the ship earlier, I saw something. There was something lodged onto the dashboard of the vessel. I don't think it has anything to do with tomorrow. I just wanted you to know, I put the ship in the basement. That way you and I can study it further when all of this is over, if it's ever over.'*

Jack took a deep breath. *Okay. Once this is over, you and I will do more research and see if we can figure it out together. Don't worry, Billy, this will be over, one way or another.*

Jack lay down and closed his eyes. Just as he was close to dozing off, he whispered to himself, "One way or another, this will be over."

Chapter 17

The hotel was unusually quiet the next morning. Carl slowly gathered them and sent them towards the board room. He intended to review the plan with them, to make sure everyone was on the same page. Charlie was awake. She sat on the edge of the bed putting her socks on. She glanced over at the window at the green fog. "There has to be something I can do about that," She murmured under her breath. She got up and headed towards the window. She closed her eyes and leaned her forehead against the window. "I'm so sick of the fog." She said. "Please make it go away."

As she opened her eyes, she wondered why she thought she would be able to change the weather.? She laughed as she turned to walk away, heading down towards the board room. The room was full. People sat wall to wall waiting for Carl, who had just walked into the room. Larzo followed him closely, waving his hands in the air. Charlie leaned over and whispered in Jack's ear, "Larzo looks a little frazzled. Is he okay?"

Jack glanced over at her. "He does, doesn't he? Let's hope he gets it together before we head out. We have to keep it together to do this right." Jack looked Charlie in the eyes and asked, "How are you doing?"

She smiled faintly. "I'm ok. I just want this to be over, but since it isn't going to be that easy, then I'm ready to kick some alien ass. Damn fog! I'm sick of it. Just wish it would go away. My eyes are constantly strained trying to look through it."

Jack looked over at it as it rolled across the window. "Well, I don't think it's going anywhere, so you may as well get used to it."

Carl stood up in front of the group. "Listen up everyone." After getting their full attention, he continued, "In a few hours, our lives are going to change, hopefully for the better. It's going to get bad, and it's going to be dangerous. Those of you who think you can't handle it need to get that thought out of your head; there isn't a choice anymore. Everyone has a job to do today, and that job will continue 'til we win. Every car will have a person who stays with the device, someone who will chop the head off, and someone ready to light it on fire. Never leave any of them alive. If they get away, we may have to go through this again, and I know we don't want that.

"Those of you who need to wear masks, keep them on tight. We don't need any accidents. So, with that said, I wish you all luck, and I pray that afterwards, I will have the pleasure of seeing each and every one of your faces sitting here with us once again." Carl walked off to the side and started to talk to one of the men.

Charlie looked around. "Time to put our plan to action. You ready for this, Jack?"

Jack nodded. "Yeah. If this device does its job right, then all we have to do is get a system going. One chops then one burns, and we keep going 'til we have them all. I know that almost sounds too simple. Let's hope that's all that is needed."

Charlie frowned. "What if we run into our father?"

Jack turned and looked her in the eyes as he said, "Then we kill him. He's one of them, and I'm sure he won't hesitate to try to kill us. For all we know, he could be the one who shot you. Do you know different?"

She shook her head no. "You're right. With no hesitation, we just kill him."

Nick walked up to them. "Oh, my God. I smell sausages. Is someone cooking them?" Charlie smiled.

"I think Julie is in the kitchen cooking something for everyone to eat before we head out. Funny, just before you mentioned it, I was thinking about how I smelled them too." Charlie laughed.

The three headed towards the kitchen. Julie stood at the counter putting sausages into hotdog buns. "Hi, guys," she said, when she looked up. "Help yourself. I'm putting them out for everyone to eat before we go. Christie and I are going to be riding with Franny and Carl. That way we can keep an eye on the device. Who's going with you, Charlie?"

Charlie looked over at Julie. She tried to empty her mouth before answering but felt compelled to speak to her with her mouth full. "I'm with Nick. I think Billy and Carla are coming with us. The two guys will cut off their heads, I'll light them on fire, while Carla stays in the car with the device. I think Jack is going with you guys to help Carl with the cutting. These creatures are so strong. I don't know where we would be if we didn't have these devices. I want us in the same area though, even if we are in separate groups. This way, if anyone needs help, we're not too far away."

Julie frowned. "I don't think I could handle it if anything ever happened to you or Jack. You make sure you're careful today."

279

The groups piled into their vehicles and headed towards their allotted destinations. Each group had a device in the vehicle, and the plan was simple and direct. One would stay in the car to protect the device and two would chop, while the last would light the head on fire. Charlie whispered to Nick, "I know we have a plan, and it seems like a great plan, but have we given it any thought how the aliens on foot may react to the device? I mean the ones in the ship fell out of the sky and crashed; they didn't have much choice other than to lie there. They were stuck in the broken-down craft."

Nick thought about what she said. "Maybe they won't be as easy, but as long as we are careful, we should be able to handle the situation. I need you to be extra careful. If anything happens to you, I won't be able to handle it."

Charlie laid her head on his shoulder. "I promise I'll be really careful."

The groups stopped multiple times to deal with a few crafts that crashed due to the device. Having fallen out of the sky, they were not that hard to deal with. After reaching their destination, Charlie and the rest of her crew jumped out of the car. The men grabbed their axes and headed towards the bodies of the aliens. In the distance, they could see Carl and Jack doing the same. The bodies of the aliens lay everywhere. They weren't like the ones in the hovercrafts. Their bodies swung around fiercely, filled with anger, their tails swinging and beating against the pavement with deep thumps when they hit the ground. Charlie yelled out to the guys, "Be careful! Watch out for the tails!"

Nick swung, hitting the first one right between the shoulder blades. Charlie poured lighter fluid all over it and lit it on fire. The screams coming from it were unbearable. Within moments, there were screams coming from all over. The men continued killing alien after alien. Jack jumped, after nearly being hit by a tail. "Damn it! That was too close."

Carl's eyes were wide open. "You think that's bad! I'm scared I'm going to lose a foot due to these claws."

Franny quickly lit the head on fire, watching it closely as the head slowly burned. "Oh, this is gross!" she grumbled.

Carl looked over quickly. "Concentrate, Franny."

Across the way, Larzo, Mark and Marcy stood listening to the screams around them. Marcy's eyes filled with tears. "They're so loud. I don't like this at all."

Mark turned and looked at her. "Really? Do you think any of us like it?"

An alien lay on the ground in front of them, his tail swinging and breaking up pavement each time it landed. Larzo ran over and swung his axe but missed, barely making it out of the way as the tail came at him. He turned and looked at Mark. "Holy shit! That was close."

Mark ran over to help his friend. As he approached, the alien swung up and took a chunk out of Larzo's neck. Mark stopped dead in his tracks. Frozen in fear, he watched as Larzo fell to the ground. The alien ran his claws across Larzo's body, ripping him open. Mark watched as his insides hit the ground. Mark took a deep breath and ran to the alien, keeping an eye on the tail as he swung his axe, hitting the alien right across the neck. The alien started to screech. As its head rolled off, it knocked Mark off balance. His mask came loose and fell to the ground. Mark panicked and reached for his mask, but before he could get it, the gas took hold of him. He fell to his knees and looked around, his eyes filled with tears. He started to scream, "I just want to go home. I'm never getting home."

Mark grabbed his chest tightly as he cried even louder.

Franny looked over and saw Mark as he hit the ground. "Oh my God, Carl!" she screamed. "I think Mark is having a heart attack."

Carl glanced at Mark. "He lost his mask. We can't do anything for him now. Keep lighting them on fire, Franny. If we don't keep going, that could be us next."

Marcy became hysterical when she saw Mark hit the ground. She started to scream after she realized that she was the only one left in their little group. She ran towards Mark, grabbed his axe and then headed towards another alien. She thought she could kill it by herself. She swung the axe hard, coming down on the alien's head, cracking open the skull but not removing the head from the neck. "Damn it!" She exclaimed.

The tail swung at her, but luckily, she jumped out of the way. As she moved, she tripped over Larzo's body causing her mask to fall to the ground. She looked at his lifeless body, and her thoughts turned to Beth. "Oh my God," she whispered as Beth's death ran through her mind over and over again. The effects of the gas had gotten to Marcy. She never thought to pick up her mask, which was lying on the ground. She got up and ran as if she were running towards someone or something. She was angry. Her eyes filled with tears.

Carl stopped what he was doing and chased after her. "Marcy! Stop! It's just the gas affecting you." Marcy turned, her face filled with anger and fear at the same time. Carl watched as her body tore open right before his eyes. He looked around. "It has to be the gas," he said aloud, as he didn't see any aliens attacking her. She fell to the ground. Blood poured from her body. Carl hurried back. "Sorry, Franny. There wasn't any chance of saving her. Just concentrate, baby. We need to be focused, or that could be us."

Franny took a breath and lit the match, then threw it on the alien's head. From that time onward, she looked at her group and only her group. "Don't worry about me, Carl. I'm here to do my job."

Charlie ran towards the men as they made their way towards the next alien. This one was different. She recognized this one. It was her father. She walked up to him and crouched, but not close enough to get hurt. "Father, is that you?"

The alien looked up at her. They hated speaking English, but in such a case, he made an exception. "Charlie, it's you? Save me. I'm not part of this. Anything I've done, I was forced to."

Charlie's eyes widened. Her heart felt soft. "Really?" She asked, hoping there was a chance.

Nick reached over and pulled her up. "It's a trick, Charlie. Don't fall for it. Step back and let us deal with him."

Charlie took a breath then stepped back. "Wait," she said. She looked at her father. "You need to know something. Jack and I are stronger than you. You may have bred us to fight for you, but we have a choice. I will fight 'til there are none of you left, and then I will go home as a human." She got up and turned her back. "Go ahead, guys." She got her lighter fluid ready and lit the match, and when the guys were done, she lit her father on fire.

Nick pulled Charlie aside. "Are you okay?"

Charlie took a breath. "I will be when this is all over."

Nick waved for Carl and his team to come over. As the group approached, he said. "Just touching base. I think it's important for a breather once in a while, even if it's to get in touch with reality for a second. The aliens don't seem to be getting up and running. So as long as we are careful, we can take our time."

Carl let out a huge sigh. "We lost a few—Larzo, Mark and Marcy. It was gruesome. Two out of the three deaths were gas related."

Jack grabbed Charlie's arm. "You okay?"

She looked up at her brother. "We killed our father. He tried to play on my human emotions, but Nick didn't let that happen. I told him we were stronger than he was, and then I turned my back as it happened."

Jack reached over and hugged her. "I'm sorry you had to do that. We'll talk more about it later, when all of this is done." Jack turned and looked around, then took a deep breath. "I don't know about you, but I want to do this and get it over with. I want to find a way home." He smiled at Julie, who was peering out the car window.

The two groups got back to work, killing more and more aliens as the day dragged on. Sometimes they would stop and listen to a human scream they heard in the background and would bow their heads in sorrow. Quickly turning and continuing her job, Charlie looked around and asked, "Have you noticed the fog has lightened? You can actually see a bit further. Do you think it had anything to do with my wish?"

Nick glanced over. "I don't think so. If you wished for it, wouldn't it all be gone?" He swung the axe down on the alien's neck as he spoke. The head rolled towards Charlie. She started to squeal. As she jumped back, she poured the lighter fluid over the alien's head and lit it on fire. She took a deep breath then looked at Nick and Billy.

"That was gross."

Nick smirked. "I bet it was."

Carl swung the axe, hitting the alien as it tried to come at him. Its head flew off and rolled past him. Jack tried to jump out of the way as the body of the alien fell back, landing right on top of Jack. "Holy shit! He's heavy!"

Jack struggled to breathe as Carl tried to pull it off him. "Billy, hurry! We need you."

Billy ran over to them both and pulled the body off of Jack. Carl's eyes widened. "Wow! They weren't kidding when they said you were strong. You okay, Jack? Anything broken?"

Jack got up. "No. I may not feel great in the morning though. Thanks, Billy. That bugger was heavy. He had to have weighed about five hundred pounds."

Billy shook his head. "Felt more than that."

The groups got back to work. Carl said to himself as he continued to chop off the alien's heads, "My God, if we're having this much trouble on our end, I don't want to know what's happening out there around the world."

Hours passed. The two groups stepped aside to catch their breath. Franny looked around at the alien bodies that lay everywhere. "How many more can there be? So many of them all over the place."

Carl wrapped his arm around her. "I don't know, but we must keep going 'til we're confident that we've won. I don't know about you guys, but that won't be 'til we see none with a head, or we see that our world is back." He kissed his wife on the forehead and motioned for everyone to get back to work.

As they continued killing the aliens, Julie and her daughter watched closely. Her daughter looked at her and said, "Mommy, I don't see the head guy anywhere."

Julie looked over at her daughter. "You know what he looks like? How can you tell the difference? They all kind of look the same, don't you think?"

Christie nodded. "But he has a different shaped head, and his neck is longer."

Julie pulled her closer. "You have a great sense of observation, my child. He is the one who made this world, so I know he's still alive." Julie looked out the window. "I'm not sure I understand how that makes a difference."

Christie looked up at her mother. "If he was dead, your world would be here; not his."

Julie's eyes widened. "Oh, I never thought of that. So, we'll know when we see our world reappear." Reaching over, she kissed her daughter on the forehead. "You're such a big help. I've been trying to figure out how they built this world to start with. So, once the main guy's dead, we are home." Across the way, she could see Jack swinging the axe and coming down on the alien hard. "I sure hope they're all safe when this is done."

Jack motioned for Franny to burn the head. Carl and Jack moved onto the next one. Carl swung his axe, but as he did, the alien moved. Franny came up to them ready to burn the head, but instead, the alien grabbed her, digging his claws deep into her stomach, and then again across her chest. Carl yelled and fell to the ground next to her. Jack swung his axe, hitting the alien right across the neck. "Nick, come here! We need you!" He yelled.

Jack sat next to Franny and held her hand. Nick came running. "Move!" he yelled. "Out of my way!" Jack stood up and backed away. Nick lay his hand on Franny's wounds. He closed his eyes and prayed they would close. He never knew what it was that did the healing; he just continued to try every way he could to save her life. Blood gushed out between his fingers as he held her wounds. *Please let her heal,* he thought. *Don't let her die.*

Minutes later, he heard her gasp. Franny's eyes were open, and tears were flowing down Carl's face as he looked over at Nick. "Thank you for saving her. I don't know what I would've done if I lost her." He looked down at his wife as she put her hand on his face. Nick took a deep breath, still unsure of how the whole thing worked but thankful it did.

Franny sat up and reached down to touch her shirt. Her shirt was shredded. Carl reached up and pulled his shirt off. "Here, put this on."

He helped her up, but not before she noticed the tears in her husband's eyes. "Don't worry. I'm okay now. I'll be more careful from now on." He nodded as they all continued working. Franny now worried that her husband's attention would not be on his job.

They fought for hours, bringing the aliens down. Their heads pounded from the screams the aliens let out, and with so many dying, it seemed to be constant throughout the day. Charlie crouched close to the ground. Nick walked over and crouched next to her. "All okay?"

She looked over at him. "I'm glad you're okay. I don't know what I would've done if I'd lost you today."

He grabbed her chin and looked into her eyes. "I'm okay. I need you to remember that." He ran his hand across her face.

"You keep me going. I'm pretty sure I was put on this earth just for you; therefore, I better survive this, don't you think?"

She gave a slight grin. "Yeah, I think you'd better."

He stood up and looked over at the rest of the group. "This has been such a long day. Does this ever end?"

Charlie stood up and looked around too. "What if we kill them all and we still have to live here in their world?"

Nick continued to look around. "Then we make the best of it. You and I will walk Bruno through the nasty green fog through an alien-built park and remember that we kicked their asses."

She giggled. "Only you can make me laugh in such a grotesque situation."

Christie started to scream, "Mommy! It's him!"

Julie looked around and spotted an alien crawling away. "No way, you bastard!" She jumped into the front seat of the car. "Hold on, baby." She turned the car on and stepped on the gas. The group stood in awe as she rammed the alien with the car.

Jack ran over and gasped at the front end of the car as he looked in. "Are you okay?"

She nodded. "That's the head guy. He was trying to crawl away." Jack motioned for her to back up. Julie put the car into reverse and pulled away.

The group looked at the alien as he swung his tail trying to hit them. "Stupid humans!" he screamed.

Jack was surprised. "Oh, you can speak? We don't look so stupid now, do we? You're the one lying on the ground about to die."

The alien squinted his eyes. "This will never be over, not 'til every last one of you is dead."

Carl looked around at all the dead aliens and asked him, "Have you not looked around? It's you guys lying dead, and now we're standing over you. Any last words, asshole, before we kill you?"

The alien turned his head and looked at Charlie. "You will never be human. Go ahead and kill me. You will never own this earth. We will take you down no matter what. You will always wonder what is next, and if you will ever sleep peacefully again."

Jack swung his axe and came down across his neck. "Enough of that! I don't want to hear any more bullshit out of that mouth."

His head rolled across the way. Charlie walked over to it. Before she lit it on fire, she squatted down next to him. "What do you mean I'll never be human?"

The alien laughed. "Kill me, you stupid human."

Charlie stood back and looked at him. Then she poured the fluid over his head and lit him on fire. She looked at Billy, who stood next to her. "What do you think he meant by I'll never be human?"

Billy shook his head. "I don't know, but don't let him get to you. Look at him. He'll be dead in a few minutes, and you and I will have one less alien to deal with."

Charlie smiled. "You're right." She glanced over at Franny and repeated, "One less alien."

Franny smiled. "Let's get this finished, guys. Do you see any more that need to be killed?"

The group stood looking around. In the distance, they could see a few. "Over there!" yelled Carl. The group ran over towards them.

Before joining them, Charlie looked down at the burning head. He wasn't quite dead yet. His eyeball twitched as he stared back at her. She got up and ran towards the group. Her steps felt light-footed every time they hit the ground. She said to herself, "What the hell?"

She stopped and looked around as the air around her felt strange. "Nick, what's going on?"

Nick ran towards Charlie. The rest of the group followed

him also. Charlie stood there in a daze. Soon everyone felt what she had felt. "What the hell is that?" Asked Nick.

Franny grabbed onto Carl. "What's happening?"

Nick took Charlie's hand. "I'm not sure what's happening. Let's get out of here. We can continue this tomorrow."

Each group jumped back into their cars. As they drove away, they opened the windows and let the air horns go off several times so the others knew to meet them back at the hotel. Carl turned to Franny. "I sure hope they heard that."

Franny shook her head. "Keep doing it just in case they didn't hear you."

Carl continued blowing the air horn out the window, hoping others would hear it. Charlie held Nick's hand tightly as Julie drove. "So, you all felt that too, right?"

Billy turned around and looked into the back seat. "I did. It was like there was a vibration coming from the ground. Maybe we're getting an earthquake or something."

Charlie shook her head. "Maybe, but I felt it in the air too."

Nick stared out the window. He could feel the change in the air, but he didn't know what it was either. "Let's just get back in one piece, and we'll worry about this tomorrow. As long as the devices are on, we're safe for the night. Tomorrow, we'll take down the rest of them."

The group drove for about thirty minutes before pulling up to the hotel. As they pulled in, they leaned forward. Charlie asked, "Are the hotel lights on?"

Billy looked closely. "No. Just the porch light. Damn it. I got excited for a second."

Julie parked the car and got out. "But why just the porch light?"

Jack and the others got out of their car too. "Is that the

porch light, guys? Do we have power?"

Julie glanced at the hotel. "No. It's just the one light on. It's probably a glitch." They headed into the hotel and sat down in the lobby. They talked about what had occurred that day for the next half hour. Meanwhile, the hotel flooded with others that were returning from the battle with the aliens.

Carl stood up, "I was so worried none of you would hear the horn." The men and women agreed that blowing the horn was a smart thing to do. Carl stood up on a chair and looked over at the crowd. "This war isn't over yet. We had some safety measures we were worried about, and thought it was best to continue this tomorrow. Maybe tomorrow will be easier, since we have experience." The crowd agreed.

Carl continued, "I'm sorry for any losses we've had today, and I know there have been a few. We knew going into this that none of it was going to be easy. Once again, tomorrow we'll face this situation head on. Get some sleep tonight. Tomorrow morning we'll meet in the lobby and head out there again. Maybe this time we will be successful."

A tiny voice yelled from the crowd, "Any dead alien is a sign of success!"

Carl nodded. "You're right."

Everyone began to head off to their rooms. Finally, the hotel became quiet once again. Concerned about her daughter,

Julie said, "I need to go tuck Christie in." She headed up the stairs with Jack shortly behind her.

Charlie looked at Carl. "I wasn't sure we would make it back to the hotel tonight. I'm glad you guys made it." She smiled at Franny as she took Nick's hand and went up the stairs.

Billy nodded and headed off to bed too. "See you tomorrow."

Carl looked at his wife and took a deep breath. "Man, you

scared me today."

Franny nodded. "I scared myself too."

He looked at her. "I'm serious. I thought I lost you. I don't ever want to experience that again. Tomorrow, you can stay here. I'm not willing to take that chance."

Franny looked at him crossly. "Don't you tell me what to do. I'm out there with you, or you're not out there."

Carl growled under his breath. "Damn it, woman." He grabbed her hand and headed up the stairs. "I just don't want to lose you."

She smiled at him. "I don't want to lose you either. That's why I'm going with you. We'll keep each other safe." Just as they entered their room, a bright flash of light came through their window. The hotel lit up like a light bulb. Carl pushed Franny down next to the bed and covered her head. "What is it, Carl? What's happening?"

Carl whispered to her, "I don't know what's going on." The bright light slowly disappeared. Carl peered over the bed. He got up and headed towards the window. Nothing else appeared to be affected by the light. He turned to Franny. "I don't know what that was, but it seems to be gone now." He walked over to the door and looked out into the hall. Jack was peering out his door too.

Jack yelled, "I don't know what that was, but it seems to be gone now."

Carl nodded. "Yeah. I don't see anything either." He shut his door and headed back into the room. He sat down in the chair and sighed. "Franny, I'm so tired. Let this be the end for the night. We need to get some sleep and be fresh in the morning, so we can finish kicking the rest of the aliens' asses back to where they came from."

Franny smiled. "Sounds good."

Chapter 18

Bruno jumped up on the bed and started to lick Charlie's face. She laughed as his tongue tickled her. She opened her eyes slowly, then quickly squinted her eyes. 'What the hell?' she thought as she sat up and looked over at the window. The green fog was gone. Her eyes widened as she looked at the light rolling in across her floor and onto her bed. "Julie, wake up," urged Charlie as she jumped onto Julie's bed. Julie's eyes opened and so did Christie's.

Julie was just about to scold Charlie for waking her up that way until her eyes were drawn towards the window. Julie jumped up and ran towards it. "Charlie, do you know what this means?" Charlie and Christie both ran over to the window. Julie continued. "We're home. We have sunshine, and the fog is gone. That ugly green fog is history." Julie turned around and grabbed her socks. She started to put them on.

Christie peered out the window in amazement and remarked, "I've never seen sunshine before."

Charlie smiled at the little girl. "Bruno loves it. He loves to go for walks through the park, and have the sun beat down on him." The three girls got ready and headed out into the hall.

They could hear the rise of chatter fill the hall. Charlie ran down the stairs with Bruno on her heels. She looked out the front doors of the hotel. "Is this for real?"

Nick ran up behind her. "I don't know what's going on, but this is definitely a good sign. Don't you think?" He swung open the door and walked outside to look around. "We need someone to test and see if the gas is gone too."

Franny came out after them. She looked around and breathed in the air. "We're home," she said. "The air is fine. I feel great."

People started to pour out of the hotel and out into the parking lot. They cheered, "The war is over!"

Carl walked behind them and looked around in disbelief. He peered over at Billy, "This was too easy."

Billy nodded in agreement and added, "Though it does look as if we have our world back."

Julie grabbed the cat and Christie. "Do you want me to take Bruno back to the house with me? That way you can look around and see if everything is okay?"

Charlie passed Bruno over to her. "Yeah. I'm sure it is, but I wouldn't mind looking around and making sure." Julie smiled as she walked away. Christie was laughing and playing with Bruno all the way to the car. Charlie looked at Nick. "If this is home, what happened to all the alien bodies, and where are all the slaves?" They walked down the sidewalk for a bit and looked around. The buildings were all there as if their world had never disappeared. People peered out their windows as if nothing had ever happened, smiling as they tucked their heads back in. Charlie looked at Nick. "It's like nothing happened to them."

Jack pulled up in a car. "Get in, you two." They jumped into the car and drove down the road. Jack drove slowly as they passed large groups of people.

"They look confused," said Charlie. Jack pulled over. Charlie got out for a second. "Are you okay?" she asked.

A lady walked over to her and inquired, "What happened? How did I get out here?"

Charlie looked at the woman. "You don't remember?" She shook her head no. Charlie took a deep breath. "What's the last thing you remember?"

She looked at Charlie. "I was watching my favorite television show, but I don't remember leaving my house."

Charlie smiled at the woman. "I'm sure everything will be okay. Why don't you go home and finish your show?" Charlie turned and got back in the car. "They have no idea what has happened. It's like they never left. Maybe they've been affected by some sort of memory wipe." They sat for a moment and looked around. Hundreds of people wandered aimlessly, looking confused.

Jack finally drove off. "We'll know more in a bit." He drove until they got to where they fought the aliens the night before. "Let's look around."

The group got out and started to look around. People were everywhere, milling round in confusion. Groups of Army soldiers men flew through the crowd. They tried to calm the people and directed them to their homes. "Go home. Someone will come check on you later this evening."

A man in an Army uniform approached Jack. "Do you know what happened here?"

Jack looked at Charlie, then back at the man. "Not really, but I'm fairly sure it was something bad. Do you guys know what it was?"

The man shook his head. "No, I wish. This has been very confusing. No one knows what happened."

Jack looked at the man and said, "tell me what you saw."

The man looked around, then back at Jack and whispered, "All of North America and Mexico were gone. Not a soul was here ... then, poof! You all showed up again. One week not a word from anyone. Now, suddenly I am surrounded by everyone. Where did you all go?"

Jack whispered back. "You wouldn't believe me if I told you." He reached into his pocket and found a card with his number on it. "Take this. When you find out more, let me know, and I'll do the same for you."

The man patted Jack on the back. "Sure thing." The guy walked away and continued leading people back to their homes.

Charlie looked over. "Jess, is that you?"

A young man, around thirteen years of age, ran over towards her. "Where's Julie!" he yelled.

Charlie reached over and grabbed a hold of him. "Are you okay?"

He nodded. "I'm really confused though. I was camping one day and then all of a sudden, I found myself here. How did I get here?"

Charlie pointed to the car. "You go sit in the car. I'll take you home in a bit to Julie and Stormage." Jesse walked to the car smiling to himself. Nick stood there staring. Charlie looked over to see what he was staring at. A crowd of women walked by, each one either pregnant or holding a child. "Holy shit!" said Charlie. "I've never seen so many pregnant women before in my whole life." She glanced to see what was behind the women. Children ran everywhere. She ran over towards them and asked, "Are you guys okay?" The children danced and twirled in the street. Charlie smiled. She knew they were reacting to the sun. "Hi, I'm Charlie."

Some of the kids stopped and looked at her. "You're like us," said one of the girls.

Charlie smiled. "Yes. I'm like you. Where are your mothers?"

The little girl looked over at her. "My mom isn't here right now; I'm looking for her."

Charlie looked at her. "Do you want me to help you find her?"

The little girl smiled at her. "Yes, please."

Charlie knew the kids were all half-aliens. How could she keep them safe? She asked herself. A group of men wearing Army gear started to gather up the children. Charlie asked them, "Where are you taking the children?"

One man looked over at her and responded, "Back to the base 'til someone comes to claim them. This whole situation is crazy. These poor kids out here without their parents. It's our job to keep them safe, or at least try to."

He smiled as he continued, Charlie looked down at the little girl. "Can you let them all know that they should not to tell those men they are half-aliens?" The little girl nodded. Charlie continued, "Tell them someone will come to claim them and find them a home." Charlie walked over to Nick. "We need to get a hold of the group and find someone to claim these kids." Nick agreed. They got back into the car and headed next to Charlie's house.

They pulled into the driveway. Charlie sat, frozen. "I never thought I'd see this house again." She leaned back in the car seat. "What if all of this is a dream?"

Nick looked over at her. "There's no way we're all having the same dream. The one thing that worries me, though, is that somehow, they have created our world to trick us. I'd like to believe that's not the case, but I can't help but feel it's not over."

Charlie glanced over at him. "I feel that way too. I don't want to tell everyone else, though, and ruin this for them."

She looked over at him as if waiting for his consent. He nodded. "Okay, as long as we're paying attention to everything around us, we don't have to say anything yet." The two smiled and got out of the car.

Julie, who was standing at the front door, motioned for them to hurry. Charlie rushed up the steps and into the house. Stormage was running across the floor playing with a tiny kitten.

"Where did he come from?" Charlie asked as she looked up at Julie.

"I don't know," she replied. "He was just here when I got home, and the three of them have been playing ever since." Charlie ran up the stairs and into the living room. She flopped down onto the couch. "Julie, has anyone called?"

Julie peeked around the corner from the kitchen. "Actually, yes. Franny did."

Charlie motioned for her to come here. Julie looked over at the young girl as she sat with Jesse playing with the animals. "She's just one of many half-alien children. None of them have a home. I told her to let them know not to say they were half-alien, but all of them are sitting on the base waiting for someone to claim them. I promised her I would help her find her mom. I don't even know how I'll do that."

Jack sat on the couch. He pulled out his phone. "I'm so glad this works again. The only problem is what do I say to everyone. 'Hey, there. How was your alien experience?'

299

How do we know who remembers what? I don't want to send anyone to the hospital with a heart attack over all of this."

Billy came out of the kitchen eating a sandwich. Charlie laughed. "Save us some too."

Billy looked at the group as he found a place to sit. "So, where did all the bodies go?" Even Larzo's, Marcy's and Mark's bodies are gone. There's no evidence of any of them dying. That doesn't make any sense, does it?"

Jack sneered at the thought. "I don't know. Who knows if any of this will make sense, ever. I'm exhausted at the thought of it not being over."

Charlie got up and walked out to the patio. Nick followed her out. They sat and watched the main street. "The Army has no clue what's going on, do they? What did that guy mean by one week? We were gone a lot longer than that, weren't we?"

Nick looked around at the city. "For sure, a lot longer than a week. The guy said North America and Mexico were missing, so if they were not affected by this, then what happened to the jets they sent over to make sure they had devices? We haven't heard back from anyone since we last spoke before the war. Shouldn't we contact them and find out what's going on?"

Charlie pulled her phone out of her pocket. "Needs to be charged… but after we can get a hold of people and find out more."

Julie screamed for the others to come into the living room. "Look! On TV, they're talking about what happened."

The lady on the news continued to speak, "Good afternoon, folks. We're here with more information on the silence of North America and Mexico. This morning, the countries woke up. Where were you all? What's with all the secrets?

300

There are rumors that no one really knows what happened, that people from these countries are in the dark about what really happened. Then there are other people who believe aliens stole them and then sent them back. Where would we be without the old alien tales?" The lady laughed and continued on with the news.

Julie turned down the sound. "They have no clue what happened, do they? If we even talk about it, we'll be the crazy ones." Julie stormed off into the kitchen.

Jack sighed. "She's right." He got up and headed to the kitchen.

Billy plugged his phone in next to Charlie's. "If I get this up and running, I can do some checking to see how everyone is. It doesn't feel right us being all apart, like just 'cause the sun is shining we all separate."

Nick agreed. "Just keep your eyes open, Billy. We can't interfere with others going home. They're entitled to live their lives, just as we are. I think the problem is it felt too easy, and it all feels just a little too strange. The humans will adjust a whole lot easier. Now that we know we are half-aliens, our lives will never be the same. That might be our problem. Maybe it's because we know now that our lives were a lie."

"Jack seems okay, though," said Charlie.

Nick looked over at her and smiled. "That's good that he does, but he might just be in denial that life won't be the same."

Charlie's phone started to ring. "Must be charged enough to receive calls." She pressed the speaker phone. "Hello?"

"Charlie. It's Carl. I wanted to check on you guys. Are you all okay?"

She smiled when she heard his voice. "I was thinking the same. I was so worried about you and Franny. How is she?"

He was quiet for a second, but then continued. "She's sound asleep on the couch. Do you have any idea what's going on with the Army surrounding the city?"

Charlie took a deep breath. "Yup. Apparently, both North America and Mexico disappeared. I mean… all the people, of course. But the guy told us it was only a week we were all gone."

Carl laughed. "A week? I don't think so. Do they know what happened to us?"

She leaned back in the chair and got comfortable. "Nope. They have no clue. Does everyone in the group remember?"

Carl got quiet. "Now that I think about it, just the ones wearing masks. Anyone that wasn't wearing one seemed confused. I sent them home."

Nick jumped into the conversation. "They have many half-alien kids at the Army base. They said they'll hold them there 'til someone claims them. Someone needs to claim them right away. We can't leave them there—homeless and without a family."

Carl raised his voice, "But they're aliens!"

Nick quieted him quickly. "We're half-aliens too. Does that make us bad?"

Carl paused. "No, you guys are my family. You're right; they're just kids. This situation is just so hard. Now we all have to deal with huge changes. Okay, so I'm on my way over after I make some phone calls, and we'll get those kids claimed right away."

Charlie turned the phone off. 'It's going to be hard to be accepted after all of this happening. I don't think we should tell anyone about us being half-alien. If it took Carl a second to grasp his thoughts about half-aliens, imagine what people unfamiliar with us will do."

About an hour later, Carl and Franny showed up at the house. Behind them were a dozen cars. Franny ran into the house. "Carl is waiting on anyone going to the base." Franny took her shoes off and headed up to the kitchen.

Nick and Billy ran past Charlie. "Be back later." Charlie gave a nod of approval. She was proud that Nick was going to go save some children.

Sophie walked up to Charlie and said, "That was her."

Charlie crouched next to the little girl a feeling puzzled, "Who do you mean?"

She grabbed Charlie's hand and peered into the kitchen. "That's my mommy."

Charlie felt taken aback. "That can't be your mommy. That's Franny. She doesn't have any children, but you can talk

to her if you like." They walked into the kitchen. Franny turned and smiled at the child. She paused, and her mouth fell open.

The little girl looked up at Charlie. "See. I told you that was my mommy."

Franny started to cry. "You're real?"

The little girl ran up to her and wrapped her arms around her. "I thought I'd never see you again."

Franny looked at her. "When did I last see you?"

She looked up at her. "When you had me."

Franny sat down at the table. "I thought I imagined you." She looked the little girl in the face. "You're my daughter." She looked over at Charlie. "I have a daughter."

The little girl looked at her and said, "My name is Sophie. I'm going to go play with Bruno. Thanks, Charlie, for helping me find my mommy."

Franny looked over at Charlie. "Am I dreaming?"

Charlie shook her head. "Nope. But I wasn't expecting that one. Both of you have children. What the hell?"

Jesse yelled out, "Julie! I think the cats are hungry. Can you feed them?" Julie grabbed the cat food. "Yup." She poured the food into the bowls and then fed Bruno too. Stormage and Bruno scooted across the floor and out to the kitchen. The kitten followed behind them. Charlie reached out to touch the kitten but ended up frightening him by accident. The kitten spazzed out. He lay squirming on the floor with four extra legs suddenly grabbing at her foot. Charlie laughed as she picked him up. "Well, well, well, we're not the only half-aliens around here. I think I'll call you Squidward." She looked over at Julie. "Did you know he was like us?"

Julie shook her head. "No. I thought he was just an ordinary kitten."

When Charlie put the kitten down, he ran over to the food bowl and started to munch. "It was like it was meant to be."

Julie laughed. "I run a household for half-aliens."

Charlie laughed then looked over at Franny who sat there watching the little girl. "My memories are all coming back," she said, as she looked over at Charlie.

Jack wandered into the kitchen. "That guy texted me. You know, the soldier. He says that the Army has been watching this city all week. They've gone door to door doing searches, trying to figure out where all the people disappeared to. They're going to blame it on a gas leak, so that the rest of the world will move on. I told him I would tell him what I know if he keeps us in the loop, but not today though."

Charlie picked up her phone to make a call but continued talking to Jack. "Has anyone tried to get a hold of the colonel

or the guys in Mexico? We need to know what happened…
where did they actually fly to when they took the devices
to Europe? Are any of them alive? Even more, do they
remember?" Charlie continued, "I'll speak to Carl about that.
He and I can find them this week sometime. Make sure they're
safe and see what they remember, if anything." Charlie placed
her phone back down. "Okay, good. We have to remember
Loretta and Chris are down there. I want to know they
survived. I also want to know every detail about the war
and what happened. I want to write a book about it."

A couple of hours passed. A few vehicles pulled into the
driveway. A few others honked as they drove away. Carl,
Billy and Nick got out. Four young children got out of the car
with them. Charlie's eyes widened. 'Hmm. I wonder what's
going on,' she thought to herself. The men walked in the door.
"We're back."

Charlie walked to the top of the stairs and smiled. Nick
smiled as he motioned for the children to go upstairs and play.
The two walked up the stairs and stopped in front of her. Nick
looked at her. "We couldn't expect others to take in orphans
if we're not willing to do the same."

She looked over at the children. "We're adopting kids?" He
pointed at one of them. "Just the little girl. The other one is
Carl's and Franny's. He wanted to surprise her."

Charlie's eyes widened as she turned and headed to the
kitchen. "She's about to surprise him too."

Charlie watched Carl's face turn to shock as he glanced over
at the little girl. "For real?"

She nodded, "Yes, for real."

He smiled at his loving wife. "Well, now we have two
children."

He laughed. "You thought we would never have any." He got up and leaned against the table. "Nick brought Charlie home one too."

Franny looked over at her and smiled. "Do they have names?"

Carl glanced at Nick. "What did they say they were called?"

Nick paused. "Laura and Fredrick."

Franny grinned. "Those seem like reasonable names."

Charlie motioned over to the other two kids. "Who are the two sitting with Billy?"

Nick smiled. Billy took both home. "That's Thomas and Ellie. They're twins. He figured why stop at one. Guess his house is feeling a little empty." The kitten ran across the floor and grabbed Nick's ankle. He looked down. "Who do we have here?" The kitten spazzed out and grabbed him with all eight legs. Nick gently put him down then glanced at Charlie. "A little souvenir?" Charlie laughed, "Yeah. He found us. Couldn't have found a more perfect home for him. He fits in with the rest of us half-aliens."

A few hours later, Carl and Franny gathered their kids. "Come on, guys. Let's head home. We have tons to do. We have to get your rooms ready, so you'll have a place to sleep." The kids got up and headed out the door with them. Franny smiled as she headed out to the car. Charlie went to shut the door.

Billy headed down the stairs with the twins. "We need to get going too. I have to get them set up too. I might need to find a bigger place now." He laughed as he headed out the door and motioned for Carl to wait up. Charlie shut the door and headed up to the living room. She looked at Nick. "So, umm... we have a moment and now we have kids."

Nick quieted her by kissing her. She smiled as she pulled away. "Okay. Fair enough." She laughed as she turned and motioned for the kids to come eat.

Nick looked at Jack. "What do you make of all of this?"

Jack sat down on the couch with Nick alongside him. "I worry that it's not over, but I don't want to upset the girls."

Nick shook his head. "Don't worry about Charlie; she already suspects that it isn't over."

Jack looked at Nick. "I look around, and we have our home back. Who is to say they're not out there? How do we know we killed them all?" He sat back and shook his head.

Nick leaned back too. "I don't think we did. I would be naive to think that. I'm so happy to have our home back. It's nice to not be in the dark anymore. But, until I get used to it, I'll worry every time the sun leaves the sky. I'm sure Charlie will feel the same way."

Jack sighed. "Yeah. It's almost scarier this way. We know what they can do. If they're out there, they'll hide better, and it'll be harder to find them."

Nick got up, but not before looking at Jack. "They may hide, but I plan on hunting each and every one of them down 'til they're all dead. I won't stop 'til that day comes. Charlie said the same thing too. Being home is superficial if it means we have to walk on eggshells wondering when or if they'll come at us."

Nick went to the kitchen to see if they needed help with the kids. Jack took a deep breath. He said to himself, "Nick is right. This isn't over 'til there's not a single alien left in this world." He got up and went to the kitchen. He watched as the kids sat at the table eating the food Julie prepared for them. "You're right, Nick," he said. "I think we need to keep the group together as much as possible and keep an eye on the situation at hand. It was us that recognized them to start with. That leads me to believe it'll be us that will know if and when it will start up again."

Julie looked over at Jack. "You don't think it's over?"

Jack shook his head. "Not fully. I know we're home, and that's great. Now we can find some normality to life., but that was too easy. Plus, where are all the bodies? It's like when our world came back, they all disappeared. The humans who were slaves are here though, and so are the women they used as breeders."

Julie walked over towards Jack. "Shhhh. Not so loud. We don't know what they know, and we have to remember they're still children."

Jack peeked over her shoulder at them as they sat munching the sandwiches. "They sure do love those sandwiches, don't they?"

Julie smiled. "Yes. They do." She smiled as she turned and looked at them. "Hard to believe they were mixed up in all of this." Jack reached down and took Julie's hand. She smiled and squeezed his hand lightly. "So, what's next, Jack? What do we do next if this isn't over?" She turned and looked him in the eye. He took a deep breath.

"You leave it up to me. I'll keep an eye on things and fill you in if we see anything strange happening. Don't you worry about any of it." He reached over and kissed her, pulling her closer.

A moment later, she looked up at him and grinned. "Took you long enough." She smiled as she walked over to the fridge and got a drink. "Want anything?" He smiled and shook his head no.

A few hours later, Charlie tucked Laura into bed. "I'm glad you're with us," she said to the little girl.

The little girl smiled at her. "Can I stay forever?"

Charlie smiled. "Of course, you can. We're going to be a family now—you, me and Nick."

The little girl smiled. "I like Nick; he's funny."

Charlie reached over and kissed the child on her forehead. "Yes. He is."

Nick walked by and peeked his head in the door. "Night, Laura. I'll see you in the morning."

Charlie walked out of the room and grinned at him. "She loves you. She thinks you're so funny, almost as much as you think you are." She laughed and walked down the hall.

"Very funny," Nick said. He followed her up the hall. She flopped down on the couch and patted the seat next to her for him to sit, too.

"So, what do we do next? Do we move on with life and try to forget or do we investigate and see what happened after the flash of light?" Charlie hesitated before continuing. "Speaking of that … what was that?"

Nick leaned back against the couch. "I'm not sure what it was. It was weird though. What if it was the sun breaking free?"

Charlie looked puzzled. "Maybe. I guess it could be. It's not like I ever experienced the sun breaking free before. Do you think that's all it was?"

Nick shrugged. "Yeah. I guess. I don't see any damage from it, and the sun is finally shining again."

She shook her head in agreement. "That's probably what it was, then." She laid her head on his lap and looked up at the ceiling, then at him. "I wonder if I'll ever feel the same about the moon."

Nick started to laugh. "I doubt it. We'll always be paranoid of the moon after what we've been through, but I don't want you to worry any more about it. Whatever happens from this day forward, we'll face it as a team."

Charlie smiled as she answered her phone on the second ring. She put it on speaker phone and listened. A voice spoke in a gruff tone. "You really think you won? You seriously cannot be that naive. You and your race will pay for what you've done." Then the phone went dead.

Charlie sat up straight and looked Nick in the eye. "You still think we're safe? What do we do now?"

Nick wrapped his arms around her and pulled her closer. "Like I said, don't worry about it today. Let's make that tomorrow's worry."

She smiled and rested her head on his chest. "You're right. Let's just live for today. We'll deal with them tomorrow."

About the Author

Tayler Macneill is a talented and imaginative writer. She is a published poet with the American poet society under the name Cole Vaughan. Her music is posted in the Nashville music catalog under the name Haven Macintyre. She is family oriented and loves to travel with her loving family and her four-legged best friends. She is a true animal lover!

You can connect with me on:
- https://twitter.com/AuthorTMacneill
- https://www.facebook.com/AuthorTaylerMacneill/
- https://www.amazon.com/Tayler-Macneill/e/B07C7H1SMG/

CPSIA information can be obtained
at www.ICGtesting.com
Printed in the USA
LVHW040911210719
624764LV00001B/13